Cover Girls

Cover Girls

A Novel

T.D. JAKES

WARNER
Faith

A Division of AOL Time Warner Book Group

I would like to dedicate this novel to those ladies who have made the very difficult choice to become better rather than bitter. It is my prayer that *Cover Girls* will do far more than entertain you: It is written in the hope that it will inspire you.

Acknowledgments

Special thanks go to Rolf Zettersten, my publisher; Leslie Peterson, my editor; and all the others at Warner Faith who have worked so hard to make sure this book is the best it can be. Thank you to Sharon Ewell Foster for her invaluable help in the writing process. Thank you to my assistant, Beverly, for keeping things on track. And thank you to my own Leading Lady—my lovely wife, Serita—for her constant strength and guidance.

Introduction

Just as there are seasons in nature, there are seasons in our lives. Nowhere can the beauty of seasons be seen more clearly than in the gentleness and femininity of woman.

Spring is the first season of life. It is the time of new birth, seedlings, and tender and fragile young plants. It is a time of new buds and beautiful blooms. Spring parallels this beauty in the feminine life. At birth and through childhood our daughters appear like tiny tender leaves. They rely on our care, protection, and nurturing to grow into the lovely flower of youth and young womanhood.

By summer, the plants are strong and hardy. They are usually, in shape and substance, what they will be for the rest of their lives. So it is in the life of a woman. The seeds that have been planted when her youth began show forth fully bloomed in the summer. In adulthood, women emblazon all that has been cultivated in them.

Fall is harvest time and resting time. That which is not productive begins to wither, while that which is good remains strong.

In a woman's life, this is a season where the possibility exists for great peace, a kind of settling into and comfort with who she is and who she has become.

Finally, there is winter. It is probably the most elusive season. Things appear dead and cold in the winter. It seems like a useless time for growing. However, many times, just beneath the surface things are waiting. New life is waiting to spring forth. The same is true of the winter woman. Many people are fooled by the frost they see in her hair. They believe that she is done, finished, that her life is over. But not so! If you peek just beneath the surface, you might be surprised at what you find.

In *Cover Girls,* come with me as we meet four women in different seasons of their lives. First to grace the stage is Michelle. Michelle sweeps onto the Cover Girls stage in the summer of her life. She is beauty and she is sensuality, but if you peer beneath her mask you might find the childhood secret that keeps her from being a leading lady.

Tonya enters the stage next as a woman of autumn. She has been a loving wife and doting mother, a woman on the Lord's side. If you observe closely, you will begin to see the slightest crack in her armor. Even church girls have struggles beneath the smiles they wear.

Michelle and Tonya are joined by Delores Judson, a woman of winter. Mrs. Judson is a no-nonsense executive, a successful entrepreneur, and a respected citizen who after years of hard work is seemingly at the pinnacle of success. It appears that she has it all, but you and I know that appearances are often deceiving.

Finally, Miz Ida takes center stage. She has survived many years with little to show for it—no high-priced home, no fancy cars. Miz Ida is at an age where most people don't have any use for her; like a tree in winter, her beauty and vigor seem to have faded. The winter season has covered her hair with frost, dimmed her eyes, and slowed her stride. But don't be fooled—sometimes what looks like winter is just a frosty spring. It might be a little too soon to count Miz Ida out!

These four women entertain us and invite us to join in their lives. As they welcome us, they also introduce us to the men in their lives. The men play supporting roles, adding color and zest to the lives of our Cover Girls.

Welcome, my daughters, into the lives of the Cover Girls— women who conceal what God wants to heal. Come, find your place on stage and in the changing seasons. Whatever your season, be assured that God is still blessing you and He wants to see you loosed!

Bishop T. D. Jakes

Part One

Summer–Michelle

Chapter One

inderella was a lie!"

Michelle made sure that the emphasis she put on the words didn't shake her hair out of place. She patted her elaborate coiffure to make sure that it was still high and tight, and to make sure that the sides were still smoothed tight to the sides of her head. With one subtle move of a well-manicured, fire-engine-red baby fingernail, Michelle checked to make sure that the hot-iron-flattened piece of hair—the piece that really made her hairdo a 'do—still draped from the top of her coif to hang just to the side of her right eye. When she was sure she was together, she stared into her supervisor's eyes. Well, really her team leader's eyes. "I mean, if you keep cleaning up other people's messes, if you keep inviting other people to dinner and letting them eat first, you are not going to get a prince."

Michelle tugged at the bottom of her form-fitting yellow suit jacket. "What you're going to get, sister girl, is leftovers."

Tonya, Michelle's team leader, was smart, but common sense avoided home girl like the plague. She held the key to Michelle getting the promotion that was due her, but at this moment, Michelle didn't care. She was going to say what was on her mind. She put her hands on her hips.

"No disrespect to Dr. Phil, but I'm telling you what I learned at the school of hard knocks. You have to tell people, 'No thank you.' You keep inviting yourself to leftovers and toilet scrubbing, that's what you'll get. And it won't be anybody's fault but yours."

She stared at Tonya. Really, she hadn't said half of what she wanted to say. Michelle really wanted to tell Tonya that she was sick of her. She was tired of the woman walking back and forth in front of her desk to check up on her like she was the work police. She was tired of Tonya acting like she knew it all, especially like she had a personal hotline to Jesus. She was sick of Tonya acting like she lived on her own personal cross with a halo on her head. And if she heard Tonya say, "Praise the Lord!" one more time, Michelle wasn't sure she would be able to keep herself from jumping the desk and going crazy on her hair-always-pulled-back, cross-wearing, plain-suit-with-no-jewelry-wearing, flat-shoe-wearing, boring, whining, pseudo-boss!

Tonya shook her head. She was always shaking her head. "Well, Michelle, I'm sure that there's some truth to what you're saying."

Michelle watched her but blocked out her words. It was kind of like the teacher on the Charlie Brown cartoons. Just a lot of noise, like wah, wah, wah-wah-wah-wah. She didn't even know why she bothered talking to Tonya. It just ticked her off anyway. Besides, Tonya was in her forties—probably breathing down fifty's neck—and it wasn't like she was going to change or anything. It really didn't matter anyway . . . just as long as Tonya didn't say, "Praise the Lord!" Michelle would be able to hold it together as long as Tonya just didn't say, "Praise the Lord!"

Please, please, Michelle thought. *Just don't let me lose it up in here, up in here!*

Tonya kept shaking her head and droned on. "It's so much easier for you, Michelle. You're young, still in your twenties. No responsibilities. Trouble hasn't even put a wrinkle on your face." Tonya laid her hand on her chest. "I mean, I've got a son and I know he's almost grown, but I just can't kick him out. I can't just get what I need first then give him what's left over. He's my baby, I'm his mother, I have to look out for him first."

Everything about Tonya irritated Michelle. She was too much like a chocolate-covered June Cleaver, recently escaped from the old *Leave It to Beaver* television show. Even Tonya's desk got on her nerves. It was so predictable. There was a light-yellow-ceramic framed picture of the woman's two sons. Next to it was a yellow vase and yellow tissue holder. There was an assortment of pens and pencils in a yellow cup.

It made Michelle shudder.

She shrugged her shoulders. "What is it that he's doing to you? You can't count on any man. Not even your son. That's why I work—so I will never be under any man's thumb. I'll say it again: Cinderella is a lie. Prince Charming will just eat your food, then leave you to go sit at someone else's table."

Tonya shook her head again. "You just don't understand. But—"

Michelle held her breath. *Don't let her say it. Please don't let her say it—not PTL. I will lose it up in here.*

"But that's not even why I stopped by to talk to you. I just wanted to remind you to watch the personal phone calls. You know personal phone calls really irritate Mrs. Judson. We want to make sure that everything is in order so you can get your promotion. But don't worry, Michelle."

Michelle squinted her eyes. Just what she needed, another visit from the telephone police. And if she was going to be the telephone police, Tonya needed a new uniform. How could anyone be so plain, so gray, so lackluster? She relaxed her shoulders—maybe Tonya wasn't going to say it.

"No, I wouldn't worry, Michelle. Because, Praise the Lord—"

Michelle wasn't sure how she got to the other side of her desk. But faster than a speeding bullet and swifter than a thousand midnights, she leaped—no, dove (or could it more aptly be described as scrambled?) forward—her eyes red and her nostrils flared. Whatever the case, there she was clutching Tonya by the throat. "I am sick of this and I am sick of you!" She couldn't take any more—it felt like a million years of her nerves being worked. It was too many years of working in positions where people thought she was their personal flunky. It was too many years of being passed over for promotion just to now have her chance at a new life blocked by an uptight holy roller—especially one that was probably a hypocrite, just like all the rest. Just like her own mother.

Michelle shouted and drew back her hand to slap Tonya, but with all the agility of a martial arts expert, Tonya slipped away. Then, just like in the cartoons, they ran around the desk, papers flying everywhere. If Michelle wasn't so angry, she would have laughed hysterically. They had to look like Tom and Jerry scurrying about. Instead of laughter, though, all she could think were acrid thoughts of shutting down Tonya's endlessly nagging voice. When Michelle got her hands on Tonya, she was going to slap her back to reality!

Tonya turned and hauled bootie. Michelle had never seen a bun bob up and down like that. First they ran around the office area several times, knocking books off of desks. They even sent a computer monitor crashing to the floor, where the screen disintegrated into tiny shining silver shards of glass. Each time Michelle reached for Tonya, the woman somehow managed to elude her grasp. Then the circle broadened and they ran around the outer ring of the office. Michelle would never have expected Tonya was in good enough shape to keep running so long—but fear had been known to transform people.

By their last lap around the outer circle, all the executives were standing in the doorways of their offices, including the business owner, Mrs. Judson. The CEO stood with arms folded, an eyebrow lifted and frozen into place. She wore the cool scowl that was her trademark—along with an ultra conservative suit that looked like it was a designer original—but she didn't speak or lift a finger as she watched Michelle chase Tonya out of the office and into the lobby. When they passed by the bank of elevators, Michelle noticed Shadrach, a brother—an upright, single brother—and a contract worker in the building, was standing just in front of a set of doors. He waved, as best he could with an arm full of packages, while they ran past, like he was waving at a parade.

Just beyond the elevators, Tonya bolted down the stairs. Michelle kept grabbing, but couldn't get Tonya as she flew down the stairs behind her. The Bible-thumping fuddy-duddy was in great shape!

All the running and pounding down the stairs—Michelle's heels *clack, clacking*, while Tonya's *thud, thudded*—was putting some wear on the heels of Michelle's new pumps, but she didn't care. It was going to be worth it to rid the world of Tonya.

Soon they were out on the street. Tonya was almost kicking herself in the behind, she was running so fast, but Michelle was keeping up. It just seemed no matter how she turned on the steam, Tonya stayed out of her grasp.

They passed by a policeman on a corner who tipped his hat and laughed. They crossed the street and out of the corner of her eye Michelle noticed Trench, her hot and steaming bad-boy-toy, riding by on a bus. He was looking fine as always—his skin chocolate-y smooth and his wavy hair short and well-groomed. If she had had the time, she would have crooked her finger and called him from the bus, but—she looked ahead of her at Tonya's feet kicking up dirt and trash on the city sidewalk—right now she had her hands full!

A few blocks down the street, Tonya saw her husband—well, her soon to be *ex-husband*—Todd, with roses in his hand, sitting at a table in a restaurant. He looked as though he were about to stand, looked as though he was about to start asking questions, asking her if what she was doing was the right thing to do, but Michelle didn't have time to explain or chitchat with him, because. She was so close! So close to Tonya. Michelle pumped her arms and legs, gaining on the woman.

She had her! Michelle leapt and grabbed—

Beep-beep-beep-beep!

Michelle bolted up right in the bed. Her hand was drawn back in the air. Dreaming. She'd been dreaming!

No job was worth this, not even one with a promotion!

Hitting the button that turned off the clock alarm, she turned so that her feet landed on the floor, then held her head. She was still a little foggy. "This is crazy," she mumbled to herself. "Absolutely crazy!" Now she was dreaming about personal phone calls. Work was taking over her home time.

Besides, she was getting her work done. What was the issue? It was just Todd and sweet old Miz. Ida—Miz Ida who was always her backbone, who had practically raised her, who usually kept her from going postal on Tonya and the rest of the pit crew—and Trench, sometimes.

But obviously, what was making Michelle really crazy wasn't Tonya monitoring the calls. Michelle tilted her head to the right and then to the left; she could hear the muscles and tendons in her neck and back popping and cracking. All this was too much! It was Tonya—Miss Praise the Lord herself! Mrs. Judson and the phone calls were bad enough, but Tonya just wore her out.

If it weren't for that stupid promotion and the power it held over her, dangling wildly over her head like the proverbial carrot . . . If it weren't for the job, there wouldn't be any pressure. Michelle couldn't deny it; she wanted the chance at a promotion. Sure she did. It was her breakthrough.

She pushed back the covers of her sleep-tossed bed and prepared herself to get up and get going.

Was it really worth it all? Sure, the job was an upwardly mobile position, which made it easier to get promoted. She needed the job.

What she didn't need was Tonya, her very own self-appointed, do-good-all-the-time missionary.

Belief in God wasn't the issue. Michelle didn't need anyone treating her like she didn't know God. He knew her heart. It just wasn't necessary to be a holy roller twenty-four hours a day seven days a week. It was like having Todd at work and that—too much Jesus stuff—was exactly why the two of them were separated. She was tired of people like him in her life telling her how she should do things, telling her that she always had to be good. Bump Todd, bump Tonya, bump them all!

Michelle got up from the bed and stomped to the bathroom as though there was someone to hear her. As she stepped from her warm bedroom rug onto the cold tile of her bathroom floor, the big checkerboard pattern of black-and-white tiles offered no comfort to her feet. She winced and stepped gingerly forward. Her feet clapped against the floor, sounding almost like Miz Ida's hands had sounded years ago clapping in the church Michelle had been forced to go to with her from time to time—after her momma got religion. That was a joke, too. Her momma was just another hypocrite—after years of doing wrong, suddenly everyone expected her to forgive her mama. They wanted Michelle to play along and act like her momma was suddenly qualified for the big-hat-church-sister club. Well, there was a time when she herself had wanted to go, when she got religion herself. But she could never get passed her momma. It was too much to swallow. Her momma sitting in church made it hard for Michelle to find her own way to God—but that was a story for another morning.

Michelle opened the patterned-glass shower door and turned the water on hard and hot. She didn't need someone telling her how to live her life—enough of her young years had been spent with people doing that, with people eating from the table at her expense. A job with a future that would bring in more cash was good, but at what price? She stepped into the steam and under the water. It ran down her soft, supple skin and rushed to the floor, forming warm puddles beneath her feet.

Michelle mused over her life—where she was and where she was going. There was one thing about which there was no doubt. No one was going to control her or hurt her again. That, she was certain of; it was definitely not negotiable. She had been hurt and misused as a child when she couldn't fight for herself. But no one was ever going to control her or hurt her again.

Michelle took a rough loofah from the plastic loop just to the right of the showerhead. She had promised herself she would not get used again, and it was a promise she was going to keep.

She pulled the cracked shower door closed. Nothing was worth being used. Not marriage. Not her family. Not even a job. No one was going to use her. No one.

That was Michelle's last thought before the hot water completely enveloped her and translocated her into an imaginary spa, and for the briefest of moments she was insulated from the toil of thought and worry by the comfort of the steamy water's tender caress. She sighed and drifted into a moment of tranquility beneath the cascade of water that washed her worries off and sent them swirling down into the drain.

Chapter Two

wenty-four stories up from the concrete sidewalks and streets below, there were windows all around the floor on which Michelle worked. Of course, none of the *real* workers could see them. That is, unless one of the office doors—the offices that faced the outside and formed a cage around the large, wide open inner office—were left ajar. The workers were like inmates in a prison. Unless some light, some hint of the outside, escaped into the pit when a door was left accidentally opened or closed, there was no evidence of an outside world.

The outer offices with windows belonged to the bigwigs, the big shots, to those that had arrived. The outer offices belonged to those who had earned the right to daylight and to a view of the city because they had climbed the ladder and jumped the hoops to get there.

The people in the pit—in the inner office jammed with rows of desks, computer monitors, copy machines, and chairs—were all wannabes. They all wanted to be something, to be somebody. The temps wanted to be permanent. The secretaries wanted to be administrative assistants. The administrative assistants wanted to be executive assistants or even make the career jump to become investigators, analysts, team leaders, or project leaders. All the wannabes wanted to be managers and executives who worked long hours. Executives who dressed like strangers and pretended to be someone they were not so they could hide who they really were behind the doors of the offices that ringed the inner office—the offices that kept the wannabes in the pit.

Michelle scanned the room. She wasn't sure if she wanted to play the game. She didn't want to be a wannabe. She was sure she wanted the money, but she didn't want to be someone's assistant, or support staff forever. She just wasn't sure if the price was too high.

What she was sure of was elevators. She looked at the bank of them—the doors painted a salmon color—that were just beyond the invisible line that separated her office from the hall. Thank heaven for elevators, because she was definitely not a stairs girl. There was no way she was hiking stairs, especially not twenty-four flights of them. If the elevators ever went, no doubt Miss Michelle would be gone too.

Just then, one of the elevators opened. Shadrach emerged and waved as though he knew she would be looking for him. His arms were full of express mail envelopes but he waved them at her in some kind of crazy mailroom sign language, some kind of weird secret postal Morse code. She had no clue what he was saying, but she nodded and smiled anyway.

Shadrach was cool. Not fine, but nice enough looking. Not pushy, but he had a good head on his shoulders. If she were really smart, she would just relax with some older man like Shad . . .

Michelle pushed the thought aside. The last thing she needed to think about was another man. She had Todd calling to nag her every day and Trench running in and out of her life and her apartment like she and it belonged to him. Her plate was full, and she wasn't sure that everything on her plate was a good choice.

Shad kept waving and mouthing something. He knew she couldn't hear him! Her phone rang. She pointed to it, waved him away, and mouthed, "I'll talk to you later." Shad nodded and then moved on as she lifted the receiver.

It was Todd. What was new?

While he nagged at her over the phone—*"Are you going to church, Michelle? I love you, Michelle. When can I see you, Michelle?"*— she nodded and scribbled on a pad as if she were taking notes. Of course, no one in the office who watched her believed she was taking notes. No one believed she was on a business call, but the charade was enough to create a reasonable doubt. The scribbling was enough to create a sustainable defense, should she need one. Like, say, should the telephone police make an unexpected visit.

Todd was droning on and on. Michelle turned on her radio. Hip-hop queen Mary J. Blige was singing her hit "No More Drama." Mary was right on time. That's exactly what Michelle wanted: no more drama. She cleared her throat. "Todd?"

He kept right on talking. "Michelle, I'm not trying to pressure you."

That was pretty silly. In fact, it was a lie. How could Todd not be trying to pressure her when he was calling every day, sometimes two and three times a day? "Michelle, I miss you," he said. He said it every day, and it made her sick.

Well, not really sick, but she wasn't going to be responsible for how he felt. He was on his own if he wanted to call, if he wanted to hang on and wait or send flowers or anything else. She wasn't promising him anything.

Sure, it felt good to know someone thought the sun rose and set in her. And it felt good to know if she called, he always came running. Yeah, it felt good. But that didn't have to mean anything. Anybody would be a fool not to accept the attention he gave, and one thing she was not was a fool.

"I love you, Michelle. And I'm willing to wait until you're ready, until you feel the time is right."

But accepting his attention didn't mean she loved him. For sure, it didn't mean she was in love with him. When it came to love, he was on his own. "Look, Todd, that's on you." Michelle could hear her voice raising and feel her chest beginning to tighten. "If you want to call and say all this stuff, it's on you. The way things are right now, we may never get back together. You know that, right?"

She scanned the office as she spoke and saw Tonya looking in her direction. Tonya looked at her, then appeared to be looking around the office as though to see if other people were watching.

What was her malfunction? Forget Tonya. Michelle sat forward. She had to get this straight with Todd. She could feel her heart rate beginning to increase; the strain and tension felt like a band around her head and chest. "Look, I know you're saying you aren't putting pressure on me, but that's exactly what you're doing." She mocked his voice. " 'Michelle, I'll wait for you.' How is that supposed to make me feel, Todd?" She made her voice sound more assertive. "You know my situation, right?" There was no answer. Why did he always have to make her bring it up? Why couldn't he just leave well enough alone?

But he'd started it, so she was going to finish it. If Todd was going to talk to her, he was going to do it on her terms. "I said, you *do* know my situation, right?" He was not going to box her in.

His voice was just above a whisper. "You're seeing someone."

If he was going to call every day and send gifts she didn't ask for, he was not going to be able to rub it in her face later. She was telling him the real deal. Let *him* feel stressed. Let *his* neck and shoulders tighten. She was getting the drama out of her life.

"That's a nice way of putting it, Todd." Sarcasm dripped from the side of her mouth. "I'm doing more than seeing him. *Him* has a name, remember? And you do remember that you and I are legally separated."

"You don't have to be nasty, Michelle." Todd's voice sounded steady and serious—very serious. "I know what you've said, Michelle, but I still love you." His voice rose, forceful and masculine. "I know what you're saying and I know what you've said. But you're my woman. You're my wife."

It was that sound in his voice that always made Michelle reconsider walking away. She stopped scribbling on the pad. Who was she kidding anyway? What did she care about what the wannabes thought? She had to take care of this with Todd once and for all—to get this monkey off of her back! Her coworkers shouldn't be minding her business anyway. If it offended them to hear a real woman handling her business, too bad for them! Michelle swiveled in her chair so her back was to the telephone police and to most of the others in the pit.

Todd kept talking. "You don't expect me to just walk away, do you? You don't expect me to not fight for the one true love of my life, do you?"

Michelle imagined Todd's face as he spoke. When he was passionate like this, the muscles near his temple rippled. It still surprised her that a man so gentle could be so full of fire and strength.

"You can pretend all you want to, Michelle, but I know who you really are and what's in your heart. Don't mistake my patience and my faith for foolishness."

It was a strength she still did not understand. It was a kind of love she still did not understand, that she still did not trust.

His voice lowered. "Remember, baby, I'm not the one who hurt you years ago. I'm not that man. You're a gift from God to me, Michelle. And if I have to fight my way in and out of hell to get you back, that's what I'm prepared to do." He cleared his throat. "If I have to endure your hurting my feelings, playing mind games, and testing my love to see if it's real—then okay, that's what I'm prepared to do. I'm in this for life."

Michelle's face was hot. She unbuttoned her jacket. When she swiveled back around in her seat, it seemed that at least half the people in the pit—including Tonya—were staring at her and hanging on her every word. She took a deep breath. "Look, Todd, I can't talk about this, now. We'll have to talk about this later." She nodded as though he could see her. "Call me later."

For an hour, without interruption, Michelle worked her way through the stack of papers and requests in her inbox. She worked Todd out of her mind. Besides, she wasn't a slacker. She got her work done. It just didn't take her all day like it did *some* people.

What was the big deal anyway? The work didn't require her to use her mind. She didn't have to be creative. It was just the same old routine over and over again. While she was doing the work, plenty of ideas came to her about how to do it easier, better, and faster. But no one asked her, and Michelle had found that people's noses got out of joint and they seemed to feel threatened when she made suggestions. So, okay, she would serve their plates the way they wanted it. No reason for her to sweat up her suit or break a nail. They didn't pay her to think. They didn't want her commitment or her enthusiasm. So she gave them what they wanted—in abundance.

When the in box was empty, Michelle went back to what made the day pass, what kept her from falling out of her seat with boredom. She lifted the telephone receiver and used the other manicured hand to press seven buttons.

Chapter Three

sweet, elderly voice answered the phone. At least it sounded sweet to Michelle. She didn't hear the raspiness or the quivering. She didn't hear the heaviness. She didn't hear any of the things she had heard others describe, just the voice of the woman who had been her angel. "This is the day that the Lord has made! And this is Miz Ida. What can I do for you, baby?"

Michelle was always happy to hear Miz Ida's voice, even when she said stuff that was hard to swallow. If there was a woman full of God in the world, Michelle knew that Miz Ida was that woman. She could always count on Miz Ida. Miz Ida was her deliverer.

"How did you know it was me, Miz Ida?" Michelle could hear the innocent, little-girl excitement in her voice. It didn't sound like she talked to Miz Ida regularly. But she did.

"Oh, it's my baby, Michelle! How are you sugar?" No matter how many times she called, Miz Ida always sounded just as pleased to hear from her.

"How did you know it was me, Miz Ida?"

"I didn't, baby." Miz Ida chuckled.

"But you said 'baby.' Did you get caller I.D. or something?"

"Old as I am, everybody's a baby to me. And no, chile, you know I don't have no caller I.D., or whatever it is." Miz Ida laughed, again. "For goodness sakes, Michelle, I'm still using the same old telephone I've had for years. I don't have no pennies to waste, so it's good enough for me."

Michelle could just imagine the bright pink rotary-dial telephone—affectionately known as "the Princess"—that Miz Ida kept on the lamp table in her living room. It was a phone the older woman had found at some thrift shop a couple of years back. True enough, Miz Ida was one of those people that the answering service recordings referred to when they said, "If you have a rotary dial, please remain on the line . . ." Miz Ida always stayed on the line.

Her ice-age phone sat on the table right next to the ceramic praying hands and right in front her big, ancient family Bible—not the tattered and frayed one she used every day—but, the decorative one she kept on display.

Miz Ida was what church folks call a prayer warrior. Between praying and visiting Jose, her border baby, Miz Ida's hands were full. "How's your little friend, Miz Ida?"

"Oh, he's coming along. Jose is coming along. He's a sweet baby and I'm going to love him as long as he's around to be loved. But I tell you who's not coming along. That young man that's always hanging around outside the door of this building. People keep telling me to leave him alone. Michelle, somebody's got to do something about our children that have been thrown away. People keep telling me I'm too old—I better leave that young man alone, that he's probably on crack. But I tell you one day I'm gone get hold to the boy, or my name ain't Ida. You mark my word."

"Miz Ida, you better leave that hop head alone."

"Somebody's got to do something, baby. That's one of my sons lying at the front door. I may not have birthed him, but he's still my son. Everybody can't keep walking by people that need help. All the women can't keep walking by. I might as well be the one."

"Miz Ida, you can't save the whole world."

"But I can sure try to help that what's in front of me."

Michelle thought back to the times before Miz Ida even had a phone, to the times when she came to use Michelle's mother's phone, to the time when they had first met. She was much younger, her hair still in little girl's braids.

Miz Ida lived in an apartment in the same building in which Michelle grew up. Miz Ida still lived in that very same apartment. Michelle had heard stories about Miz Ida— stories that she had overheard when her mother Cassie talked to her best friend, Twana. Miz Ida had just been gossip, until the old woman appeared at Michelle's mother's apartment door.

Without thinking, Michelle had opened the door wide, even wider when she saw the peculiar-looking old lady.

∾

"Hey."

Recalling her mother's warnings, Michelle closed the door to a crack. "Oh, I forgot. My mama always told me to ask who is it. I can't talk to strangers."

The old woman nodded. "You know, your mother's right to some degree. But you know the Bible says, 'Be careful how you entertain strangers, for you may be entertaining an angel unaware.' "

"Huh?"

The funny-looking woman kept smiling and she kept talking. "You'll understand soon enough."

The old woman was strange. Michelle closed the door even more. "Momma said I can't talk to strangers. I'm sorry."

"Child, everybody know me. I'm Miz Ida."

Michelle spoke before she thought. "Miz Ida? Oh, I heard Momma talking about you. She says you're crazy."

Miz Ida's smile was rich and deep. It was not broad, but it

made Michelle feel something. "You think I'm crazy?" She stared into Michelle's eyes.

"No. But you dress kind of funny with all them different patterns." She waved her hands at Miz Ida's clothes.

Miz Ida chuckled and looked down at the clothes she was wearing. "If you want to know real answers, just ask a child." She laughed again. "You think your mother would mind if I use the phone?"

Michelle shrugged and opened the door to let Miz Ida enter. Something about the woman's presence made her feel safe. "I guess not since you live next door. It's right over there." She pointed toward the phone.

Miz Ida kept talking to her as she walked toward the phone. She looked at her as though she cared. As though she was concerned. "What is your name, child?"

"Michelle."

"Michelle? Such a pretty name for such a pretty little girl."

"Pretty? You think I'm pretty? My mama doesn't think so. She tells me all the time, 'You so ugly. You look just like your no-good daddy.' "

Miz Ida reached out her hand and touched Michelle's face. "See, when your mother looks at you, she looks at the sin that made you and not the beauty that came out of it."

Michelle shook her head and moved her face away from Miz Ida's hand. She quickly changed the subject. "Do you have any children?"

Miz Ida held the receiver in her hand and smiled. "All my children are older than your mother."

"Oh, that's too bad. I was hoping you had kids my age so that I would have someone to play with."

Miz Ida beamed at Michelle and slapped one old knee. "Child, I'll play with you."

"Really?"

Something about Miz Ida stopped looking like an old woman

and began to look like a little girl. "I play jacks, I play Uno, and I play Scrabble."

"Well, what about video games?"

Miz Ida frowned, then lifted her thick eyeglasses. "Now what you say? Who do— Child, you speaking in tongues."

"Speaking in what?"

The old woman shook her head and smiled. "Never mind."

"Well, maybe I could show you how to play it sometime."

"I'd like that."

"Great."

Just then Michelle's mother yelled from the back bedroom. Momma sounded tired and irritated. She was fussing as she came up the hallway. "Who is that in my house?" Michelle's heart pounded when she saw the anger on her mother's face. She didn't want to hear the yelling. "Michelle, what are you doing letting somebody up in my house this time of night? Have you lost your last mind?"

Miz Ida spoke right up. "No harm done, Miss Cassie." Michelle was surprised that Miz Ida knew her mother's name. Miz Ida spoke to her mother with respect, but she was firm. "I think you need to change your tone of voice talking to your child." She wasn't afraid. Michelle wasn't sure how to feel—no one had ever defended her.

Momma's voice softened, though she kept frowning at Michelle. "Nothing personal, Miz Ida." She nodded in the old woman's direction. "But she does this all the time. I'm just trying to teach her a lesson."

Miz Ida stood her ground. "Some lessons have too high of a price for a child to pay."

⊖

Michelle smiled at the memory. Miz Ida had become her friend that day long ago. She was still her friend; more than a friend, she was a mother to her. Miz Ida's voice still had the ability to settle and protect her. She was more of a mother to Michelle than her own mother had ever been.

"So, Michelle, have you talked to your mother?" Miz Ida was obviously still reading minds.

"It's been a while since the last time I've seen or heard from her—Momma—I mean, *Cassie*." Michelle began to hit the stapler she was using with the flat of her hand. It seemed like she was having a harder time than normal getting the staples to go through the four page groupings. She cleared her throat. "Miz Ida, you know how I feel. I don't hate my mother. I love her, but I can't forget what happened to me. I tried . . . I even thought I had. But the memories keep coming back." Michelle lowered her voice. "What she let happen to me . . . that man putting his hands all over me . . . I can't forget that."

"You mean can't, or won't?"

"Miz Ida, I don't mean any disrespect, but I really don't want to talk about this, okay?" She hadn't called for this. If she wanted a headache, she could have kept talking to Todd. "Please, not now. You know what I've been through. How it messed up my whole life."

Michelle's voice dropped to a whisper. "Because of my mother and her loser, dopefiend boyfriend I went to jail when I finally stood up for myself. And she let it happen when she knew what he was doing to me. He was raping me, Miz Ida. Over and over again. She saw the bloody sheets! She was my momma and I was a child, Miz Ida! She knew what he was doing and she didn't do anything about it. She chose him over me. Over her own daughter! I was a child—I couldn't make any choices. The two of them were making choices for me."

"Michelle, baby, your mother made bad choices, but that doesn't mean she doesn't love you. That she didn't love you back then. It's no excuse, but sometimes there are no good choices for a single woman with a child."

"Choices? My mother chose to look out for her own needs. She may be saved, and she may have made it up with Jesus. But it makes me sick to think of her sitting up in church somewhere like Sweet Polly Purebread when she knows good and well what she let that man . . . that dog . . . do to me. She let me sit and rot in jail to protect that scum's reputation—to protect her reputation. What about me, Miz Ida? I've tried to let it go—I thought it was over—but, I can't."

Michelle could feel Miz Ida's presence on the phone, but there was silence for a while. Then she spoke. "I know it's hard, Michelle. You've still got little girl scars that you are carrying around. Little girl scars are hard to heal."

"Well, I'm grown now and I'm doing just like my momma taught me. I'm looking out for Number One. I'm going for myself. I've got a right to be angry after all that was done to me. She didn't talk to me when I needed someone to talk to, so I'm not talking to her now. I'm not going along with the little fake show like everything's okay. I love you, Miz Ida, but . . ." She continued to pound the stapler even though the palm of her hand was now bright red.

"Michelle. Michelle. You're right. You've been through more than any child should have to suffer. You had your childhood ripped away from you. I wouldn't be telling the truth if I told you that I know just how you feel. But I know that every child needs to feel safe in her own home.

"No, your mother didn't do what she should have. I'll grant you that. And by the time she got around to doing something right, it was a little late in the day . . . a lot late in the day."

Michelle could hear his voice. It was almost as though she were a child again. She was sitting in the office, but inside she was a child and Gary, her mother's boyfriend, was so close his hot breath burned her ear. She could almost taste the smell of stale alcohol on his breath. She felt his hand in her hair and the other around her waist, forcing her closer. She could feel him pushing against her. Michelle could still feel the pain, then the dirty, confused feelings that followed. And she could hear him whispering, insisting that she better not tell . . .

Tears burned her eyes, and she shook her head. She reminded herself that Gary was gone . . . finally. It was worth the price she had had to pay. Never again. Never again. Neither one of them would ever get the chance to hurt her again.

"Miz Ida, when I see her, when I hear her voice, when I think of her, I think of him—and I can feel it all over again." She forced herself to whisper and fought to keep anger from choking off her words. "His dirty hands on me. His funky breath. His . . . voice . . . What am I supposed to do with that?"

"Michelle, no child should ever be used the way you were used. That man raped you. It's bad enough to rape a woman, but a child . . ." Miz Ida's sigh was full of weariness. "When we've been through hard things, the worst part is facing up to the pain, finding the courage to walk back through the door where we were hurt and overcome the hurt that we find there. We just want to cover it up and pretend it never happened, but that's not the answer. We want to walk around and fool people, make them think that we're perfect and that we've never been hurt. It's like we believe that being hurt and having feelings makes us weak. Michelle, baby, I know it's hard. But you know nothing's ever going to go right until you make some peace with who you are and where you come from."

"Miz Ida, I know you mean well, and I don't mean any disrespect, but that's the past. When I look back, all I can see is hurt. All I can see is the same people, people who were supposed to love me, but who used me instead."

"Michelle, no doubt about it. They were both wrong. Dead wrong. And you got every human right to be hurt and angry. And you got every right to take all the time you need. I'm not going to pressure you."

There was that word, again—*pressure*. Of course, Miz Ida was pressuring her. Todd was pressuring her. Tonya was pressuring her. They were all pressuring her.

"I just want you to consider one thing. Don't answer me now, just think on it. All right?"

Michelle nodded as though Miz Ida could see her over the phone.

"Michelle, do you want anger to be the end of your story? Is that where you want it to end?"

She stopped stapling and lifted her hand to cover her eyes. "I have to go, Miz Ida." She laid the receiver in the cradle as though it were as fragile as she was feeling. She reached into her desk drawer for a tissue and quickly wiped away the tears. Swiveling in her chair, she turned her back to the office and reached for her purse. Looking in her compact mirror, she powdered her face to cover the tracks the tears had made in her foundation. She reapplied her lipstick.

Do you want anger to be the end of your story?

That was Miz Ida's question. But the question that nagged Michelle every waking moment, even in her dreams, was "How?" How was it that her mother chose a man who yelled at her, cursed at her, beat on her, over her own daughter?

Michelle put her things away, then turned back to face the pit. Wasn't blood supposed to be thicker than water? Didn't people say that no one loved you like your own momma? Well, if that was true—she laughed a short, hard laugh—a laugh that was more like a cackle. There was no way anyone was ever going to be able to convince her to trust love.

No, if you didn't want tears, you couldn't trust love.

Chapter Four

he day seemed like it was never going to end.

Michelle looked around the office and things were just like she thought they would be. Tonya's eyes were boring a hole in her. Forget Tonya. If she signed up her whole life to be on the Jesus plan and to work this stupid job, then goody for her. But Miss Telephone Police shouldn't try to get other people to sign up for the same stupid long distance service.

Bringgg! Bringgg!

Michelle looked at the caller I.D. and kidded herself, for an instant, that she was not going to answer. Before the third ring could end she answered, though she tried not to sound excited. It was him.

"Hey, baby."

It was Trench. Arthur Trench, but no one called him *Arthur.*

"How's my girl?" Even over the phone, he had a way of wrapping himself around her like dark, sweet, strong molasses.

"Your girl?" He was an M-A-N, but she was a W-O-M-A-N, and she was time enough for him. "You must have confused me with whoever you've been with for the past three days."

"Meow!" Trench laughed as though what she said was rolling off of him like water off of a duck's back. "Oh, baby. You know I got work to do." He said it as though that should be adequate explanation for why she hadn't seen or heard from him, for why he felt he could come in and out of her life and her apartment like a revolving door. He sighed into the phone like he was wrapping his arms around her and nibbling on her ear. "A man's got to handle his business." Trench knew his business, all right, and he knew how to play the game. "Besides, baby, you know it's not like that between us. You my girl. Nobody makes Trench feel like you do." His laugh was low and gravelly. Then he spoke, again, even more softly. "But you said it yourself, right? No papers, no pressure. We just take each other to the moon." He breathed into her ear. "You know Trench takes his baby to the moon, right?"

Michelle slid forward in her seat and put one hand over her face to shield her eyes, as though Trench were standing in front of her and she didn't want him to see how she was feeling, to see the effect he was having on her. He was good. He was like some kind of funky drug. A small taste, the smell, even the memory of him made you forget why you had ever sworn off, why you had ever said that you were never going to do it again.

"Whatever, Trench." It was the best she could do. This sister was going to have to regroup.

"Come on, baby. Don't be that way." He sounded so earnest; he was such a good liar. "Trench got a little something for you. Something I know you're going to like. Don't you want it, baby?" He almost purred into the phone.

Michelle could feel herself giving in. She could feel herself getting ready to be played. And there was no way she was going out like that—no matter what bells Trench was trying to ring. "Look, *Arthur.*" That ought to bite him. He hated being called Arthur. "I am not some hoochie that you can dial up when the mood hits you. I know the words *Holiday Inn* are not stamped on my forehead or on my back."

Trench whistled. "Wow! It sounds like I called just in time, like you need a little trip to the wild side."

She was on a roll and she was not going to let Trench sidetrack her. "And I sure ain't your momma. You can't keep coming to me when you need a place to sleep, or when you've got no place else to go." Trench was quiet, so she might as well sink the knife to the hilt and twist it. "And you're right. We both know the deal. And my deal is that I'm a married woman. So, you're right—you and I are casual. Way too casual for you to think I'm open twenty-four hours, or that you can come in and out like I'm a swinging door."

Trench laughed out loud. "Married?" He laughed again. "This is Michelle, right? Married?"

Michelle's face stung and she sat straight up in her seat.

"Look, baby, tell that married stuff to somebody else."

Michelle could imagine the smirk on his face as he talked. She had seen it before when his voice had this kind of mean edge.

"Married . . . Todd must have called you today with his dull self. But don't play yourself, sugar. I know how you like your bread buttered, where, and how often." It sounded as though he was sneering into the phone. "Married? Were you married last Saturday?" He paused. "Bump all this. You know what? I'm not going through all this. I don't have to explain to you where I've been or what I've been doing. And I sure don't have to play any little school-yard games with you. I tell you what, baby girl." It sounded like Trench was licking his lips. "I'll talk back at you when you're grown enough to talk with your head on straight. When you're ready to talk like a woman."

Click. The phone went dead. Michelle's cheeks burned. She felt uncovered and naked. She hung up the phone and then looked around the office—it felt like each person was staring at her, as though all of them had heard how he spoke to her. Of course they didn't know. But, reality didn't matter; it was how *she* felt.

Ashamed.

Trench could read right through her. He could get past all the makeup, past the suit, the hair, and punch her right in the gut. That was part of the thing with Trench. Why that was attractive to her, Michelle wasn't sure, but something about it felt genuine and familiar. For all of the turmoil he took her through, she knew Trench was real.

Michelle smoothed her hair, then reached into her purse for a mirror and lipstick. She touched up her lips, then restored the items to her purse and adjusted her jacket.

There was something exciting about the way Trench could embarrass her and make her feel like a young girl, like a child. Michelle turned to her computer screen and watched the minutes clicking by on the digital clock on the tool bar at the bottom of her computer screen.

Maybe he would call back. Maybe he wouldn't. But what was sure was that she was not going to spend the rest of her forty-five minutes at work worrying about him. She leafed through some papers next to her hand. She sighed. Might as well do some work for the man.

Chapter Five

he walked with her shoes in her hand. Good thing no one was in the hall; Michelle was prepared to beat the snot out of the first person who said something to her about walking barefoot. It was hot outside, she was sweating, her dogs were barking—and it was too far to walk even the twenty feet from the elevator to her apartment door with her shoes on and her dogs hurting.

What she needed more than anything was a shower. She needed to wash it all away—nine boring hours at a job that took more out of her than it gave Tonya, Mrs. Judson, Todd, Trench, and even Miz Ida. Michelle imagined herself walking straight to her bedroom, peeling out of her clothes, and padding directly to the shower. The hot water always soothed her. She would just stand under the water until she felt clean again. Mary J. was right: what Michelle needed in her life was no more drama.

The minute she opened the front door, she knew he was inside.

She continued to her bedroom, to her bathroom and shower, anyway. When she had finished, she wrapped her thick, green, terry-cloth robe around herself and tied the belt.

What was on his mind? He didn't pay rent here. She didn't ask him to; it was less complicated—fewer questions and much less attitude—that way. He had way too much nerve as it was. Way too much nerve.

He was lying on his back on the couch. His mouth was open and his chest moved up and down. There was no slobber. That was one thing she liked about him—no slobber.

Something about the position of his body reminded her of a rag doll. One of his knees was bent, his bare foot flat on floor. The other leg pointed east, the foot hanging over the back of the sofa—the brocade sofa she had worked hard to pay for. She had spent a lot of weeks sitting on boxes before she was able to get it out of layaway. Michelle put down the house slippers she held in her hand, moved closer, and sat on the coffee table across from him.

Trench might be lying like a rag doll, but he didn't smell like one. Rag dolls didn't smoke reefer. Rag dolls didn't have tight, defined muscles. Trench did, though, because with no job he had lots of time to work out.

She stared at his face. It looked peaceful. His jaw was soft and relaxed. His long eyelashes looked like those they painted on babies in advertisements. This was the Trench you only got to see when his guard was down—and that might as well be never. It might be cool to be tender with this Trench—this babylike, sweet-looking Trench. But to deal with the real Trench, she had to give him back what he dished out.

"Trench . . . Trench . . ." She made her voice stern. *"Trench."*

He bolted upright. His eyes and the expression on his face said he was trying to remember where he was, trying to get himself together. First frightened, then off-balance, then cool and cruel when he came back to himself.

"Trench, what are you doing here?"

"I thought we needed to finish our conversation." He reached his hand forward and touched the damp hair at the nape of her neck. "Enjoy your shower?" He used his index finger to wipe beads of water off of her forearm.

"Trench, I didn't give you permission to come in here."

He smiled that I-know-this-will-work-when-nothing-else-does smile of his. "Do I need permission to come in, Michelle?" He stroked her cheek. "I hope it's not like that between us." He turned on his innocent, wide-eyed, little-boy smile. He rubbed his fore-finger over her chin. "Have I messed up that bad that I'm back to square one? I got to give up my key and ask permission before I come." He pouted almost like a little cherub in one of those church pictures.

Michelle was going to hold her ground no matter how he was making her feel. "Trench, we didn't end our conversation on a note where you could just come over here and make yourself at home."

"I'm sorry, baby." He pushed his lips into even more of a pout as he ran his finger over the ridge of her ear. He leaned forward to kiss the tip of her nose. His eyes, focused on hers, were doe-like and gentle. "I'm sorry, okay?" He nodded as though he were trying to get her to agree. "It was my fault. You mentioned your ex—and I just lost it, baby. You know how I feel about you." He turned to face her. "You know that you push my buttons. You know that, right? I shouldn't let you get to me." He edged himself closer to her. "But you know you do, Michelle." He tilted his head. "You know you do." He moved to kiss her.

"Trench." Michelle turned her head so that he could not kiss her lips. But she knew better. It was going to be the same old thing. He would be nice tonight, maybe for another day or two. Then he would be gone, again. No explanation. Just gone. And no matter what she told anyone else—no matter what she even tried to tell her-self—when he left, there would be a hole where he had been.

"Look, baby, we're real with each other. You know who I am, what I am. And I know you—who you are and where you come from. I know the time you spent turned out on the street . . . your old man . . . I know it all. We don't have no games with between us. Another man might not accept you—not many men strong enough to deal with what you been through. But you know I'm here for you. You my girl. You my baby. You my boo."

She knew better. "Trench, you can't keep going and coming."

He kissed her then, and she didn't resist. He put his arms around her, gently at first, and then tighter. "Let's not talk about it, now. Okay?" He looked into her eyes. "We've got plenty of time to talk."

She knew better. He kissed her neck. Michelle shivered. She knew better. But what difference did it make? She was no schoolgirl; she was no pure flower. It had been a long day. *A long day.* And maybe what Trench had was just the medicine she needed.

It was the last thought Michelle had before she closed her eyes and surrendered to the relief Trench offered.

Chapter Six

ichelle walked toward her desk humming a song she had heard on the radio—someone named Yolanda Adams singing a song she thought was called "Speak to My Heart." She was definitely exhaling this morning—a walk on the wild side was just what she had needed. Trench's medicine was just what the doctor ordered. There were a lot of issues and mess that came along with the prescription, but sometimes a girl had to do what a girl had to do!

It wasn't a permanent solution, but sometimes a temporary fix was enough—and she was looking fine. Red was her color. Bright red. Men's heads had been turning the whole way in to work. The suit was loud, no doubt about it. There was also no doubt that the dull, drab office she worked in needed all the color it could get. And she was just the one to bring it.

The people in the office were pale and dead. Someone might as well dig a six-foot hole and shovel them all in. Green might be the color of new life in the Emerald City, but gray was the color in the pit.

Michelle was almost skipping. She nodded at her fellow pit-dwellers as she walked past them to her desk. She even spoke to some of those who didn't work her nerves too badly.

Still, she wasn't up for any foolishness. It had been a tough few weeks. Todd was, as usual, still putting on the pressure. Trench was in and out, acting like he was doing her a favor to stop by—though his stopping by did loosen the valve just a little bit. Miz Ida was acting like she had just forgotten all the years of pain Michelle's mother had put her through. Or at least Miz Ida was acting like Michelle should just order up a plate full of joy and forgiveness or pretend that she didn't remember what her mother—Cassie—had done. Sometimes it was easier to think of her as a woman named Cassie than as *Momma*. Anyway, how did Miz Ida figure that was going to happen? There was no way Michelle was going to forgive—and try all she wanted, she couldn't forget. Drugs didn't do it, alcohol didn't do it, running away didn't do it.

But that was enough of that. Right now she was feeling good and she was looking good. No doubt. Sister had it going on!

When she turned the corner, Shadrach was in the middle of the aisle with a cart. He didn't have to deliver packages anymore; he was over the group of men that delivered. But Shad said he liked mixing with the people, keeping his ear open to what was going on. Of course, it could have been that he was trying to keep his eyes on her. Michelle laughed to herself. In fact, that was much more likely.

"Hey, baby girl."

Something about Shadrach always made her smile. "What's up, Shad?"

"Just a brotha man trying to stay warm and alive in a cold, cruel, and lonely world." His arms were full of boxes and large envelopes. "How about you?"

"You know what, Shad? If I told you everything, we'd be standing in this aisle until Kingdom Come." She sighed, then shook her head. "But I'm not going to let it get me down. Michelle is going to survive." She adjusted her jacket and touched her hair. "And I'm going to survive with style!" *Snap!* She popped her fingers.

Shadrach laughed out loud. "I know that's right." He admired her from head to toe as she approached. "And you got it together, baby girl, from the hairdo to the shoes."

Michelle laughed, too. Shad was good medicine. He was good-looking enough; his body was heavy and solid in that way men's bodies settle into after years of football. Shad was older than the men she normally dealt with, but someday she was going to be smart enough to let someone like Shad into her life . . .

She caught her mind before it wandered too far and got it back on track. "Like I said, I'm going to take care of Michelle." She stopped talking when she could see Tonya out of the corner of her eye. It seemed that the telephone police never missed work. Her team leader was talking and smiling with some of the other pit dwellers.

"I'm not going to let the man get me down—" Michelle looked in Tonya's direction. "—even if he does look like a sister."

Shadrach threw back his head and his laugh boomed through the office. It was one of the things Michelle liked about Shad. He didn't care what anyone thought about him being happy and he let it show. "Aw, man, you sure give your boss lady a hard time."

"She's not my boss. And more than that, I'm tired of her thinking she's better than me." Michelle wasn't speaking too loudly, but she also really didn't care who overheard. They could like it or choke on it.

"You give Tonya a hard time." It was funny to hear Shadrach say her name. Michelle hadn't even known he knew Tonya existed. "She's not so bad. A little settled for my taste, maybe. But she's got a good heart. She's good people as far as I can see."

"That's cause you *don't* see her. You don't have to work with her—she's not policing your telephone calls. And all that holier-than-thou stuff, Shad? Every day she comes in here with her *'Jesus, Jesus, Jesus.'* She don't know how close she is to a beat-down. And this morning, I'm telling you, I'm about two seconds from going postal on her. I'm not about to let her ruin my inner glow today."

Shadrach pretended to be shocked. "Take it easy, Miss Lady. You wound a little tight this morning, aren't you?"

"Not until I saw her. I'm just tired of her Goody Two-shoes self trying to keep me in line."

"Wow. You know that's something about you females. You all don't cut each other any slack."

"What slack?" No. Shad *wasn't* trying to defend Tonya?

"Wait a minute. Don't start rolling your neck at me, baby girl." Shadrach smiled. "Peace, okay?" He looked up at the clock. "I've got to run anyway." He started to walk away and then turned. "You got lunch plans? We could pick this up later."

Shad, you old dog. Michelle didn't answer right away. Was he trying to hit on her? She smiled. What difference did it make? It would be good conversation. He would make her laugh. She wasn't trying to marry him. "Sure, Shad. How about the cafeteria restaurant on the lower level?"

He winked. "You got it, baby girl."

Michelle watched Shadrach walk away. Maybe the day was going to turn out all right after all . . . if she could just get through the day without going off on Tonya.

She walked further into the pit and turned her head so she wouldn't have to look at Tonya, so she wouldn't have to speak to her. The last thing she needed was for her dream to come true. Michelle could still remember the image of herself running around the office chasing after Tonya. She had only a few weeks to go until the review for her promotion; she was pretty sure that chasing Tonya around the office and pulling at the bun the woman wore on the back of her head would not be viewed as a good thing. She made herself smile. Snatching that bun out might feel good, but Michelle was pretty sure Mrs. Judson would not see it as a career-enhancing move.

When Michelle got close enough to see her desk, she smiled. There was a small bouquet there—pink, yellow, and white carnations; daisies; and some mums that were almost purple—arranged in a brightly colored vase. A card leaned against the vase.

She dropped her purse and slid into her seat. She pulled the vase toward her, pushed her nose against the flowers, closed her eyes and inhaled. It was just what she needed. The flowers didn't match her red suit, but color was color.

She rotated the vase. It was too thoughtful a gift from Trench. The flowers had to be from Todd. It was funny, but he always seemed to know exactly when she needed cheering. Michelle breathed the scent in, again, even more deeply.

"Good morning, Michelle." It was Tonya. She was sitting at her desk with a goofy smile on her face. Michelle nodded her head and then closed her eyes again. She was not going to let Tonya ruin this moment. She let the petals of the flowers tickle her nose.

Todd really was a good man, always thinking of her and doing nice things for her. Sometimes it was too much. He was too kind, too forgiving. It confused her. Michelle couldn't tell if it was just something he did—something he would do for anyone—or if it was special just for her. She didn't know if he was so strong he didn't care what people thought, or if he just didn't have sense enough to know that people would use him.

She hadn't been good to him. She thought of all the things she had said to Todd . . . and she thought about Trench. Her relationship with Trench had to make Todd feel like less of a man. It had to make him doubt himself. She had thought it was the one thing that was sure to make Todd leave, but he still held on.

Michelle opened her eyes. Tonya waved at her. What was *wrong* with her? Why didn't she get a life? But even Tonya's goofiness wasn't enough to ruin the moment.

Michelle could hear Todd's voice. *"I'm fighting for you. You're my wife, my gift from God."*

Yes, Todd was fighting. She just wasn't sure why. Was it because he didn't have enough sense to know better, or because he loved her that much? It bothered her.

No one could love another person that much. That kind of love was only in fairy tales. That kind of love couldn't really exist . . . could it? That kind of love wasn't even human.

There were times when Todd reached in and touched her heart, or something even more elemental than her heart—something that fluttered inside of her, something with wings like a tiny bird. There was something delicate and alive in her that only Todd seemed to see, believe in, and touch. When he was able to climb over her insecurities, crest the height of her anger, and ford the rivers of her disappointments and fears—when he arrived at the shores of that delicate fluttering place, it renewed her. It was like drinking from some eternal, crystal fountain that nourishes, refreshes, and cleanses.

When Todd held Michelle, her past washed away—the drugs, the prostitution, the molestation . . . But the place he took her to also frightened her. It gave him too much power, too easy access to her heart. What Todd did, what he made her feel, was too good to surrender to. It was too good to trust.

At least for now.

Michelle smelled the flowers again. Maybe . . . some day.

She filled her lungs with the sweet perfume then set the vase down and, avoiding eye contact with Tonya, opened the card.

There were flowers on the front of the card that looked like the bouquet on her desk, only they were tied with pink ribbon.

This is the day that the Lord has made, the front of the card read. *Rejoice and be glad!*

Definitely Todd. He couldn't resist putting in a good one for the Lord, even when he was trying to sweet talk her. Michelle could feel a big, cheesy smile spreading across her face. She looked up to see that Tonya's smile had gotten even bigger. So what? What difference did it make anyway? Maybe Shad was right. Maybe Tonya wasn't so bad after all.

She smiled briefly at her team leader, then opened the card. The inscription was handwritten. It had been a while since she had seen Todd's handwriting.

Michelle, I know the past few months have been hard for you.

Todd was always thinking of her, always sensitive to what was going on in her life. He always felt her. Maybe the R&B singer Ralph Tresvant was right; maybe she did need a man with sensitivity. And wasn't it just like Todd to be thinking of her even when he was in a hurry. His handwriting looked familiar, but unfamiliar. He must have been rushed.

Don't give up, Michelle. The Lord loves you and He is always with you. For, as the Bible says, even when your father and your mother abandon you the Lord will receive you.[1]

He was always putting himself out for her. He made her feel warm and protected. Why was she ever stupid enough to leave him?

Michelle, things will get better. Trust the Lord. He will not fail you.

She didn't deserve such a sweet, loving man.

Know that you are always in my prayers.

Todd must have definitely been in a hurry. His handwriting was so strange. But that was Todd, always praying. He was a good man, a very good man.

Michelle read the salutation. *Blessings to you, Michelle . . . Tonya.*

Todd was the sweetest man. How many women wouldn't kill for a husband who sent them flowers, who prayed for them day and night, who was a passionate and powerful lover—

Michelle's head snapped up at the same instance she snapped back to reality. She reread the salutation.

Blessings to you . . . Tonya.

Tonya?

Tonya!

Tonya?

Another name came to Michelle's mind and to her lips—a word that was sure, once she said it, to get her fired.

---

[1]See Psalm 27:10

Chapter Seven

t was ridiculous. There was no space in the office that seemed to be hers. There was no space that was free of Tonya's influence. Michelle was sick of her.

Let them fire her if they wanted to—Michelle was not going to be driven crazy by people at a job. She stared daggers at her team leader. Tonya still had that goofy smile on her face. What was it going to take for her to get it?

She didn't care what happened, she was going to give Tonya a piece of her mind. Michelle jerked her desk drawers open. How could she have been so stupid? How could she have gotten sucked in? Of course it wasn't Todd's handwriting. Of course it was Tonya. It was Tonya, who had taken Michelle on as her personal missionary task. It was Tonya, who kept giving her unwanted gifts—unwanted because Michelle knew there was really a price to be paid for everything.

She looked in her lower right-hand drawer at all the little books of *inspiration* Tonya had left on her desk in the past few months. Of course it was Tonya. Who else was so very *holy?* Who else was out to make her life so miserable? The books were irritating and Tonya was irritating.

Michelle looked across the room. Tonya was still sitting there—looking tired, dried up, and stupid. Where did she get off doing this kind of stuff? Michelle used her hand to knock the little books around her drawer. They were all colors—blue, red, yellow, purple, orange, and white. There were booklets authored by people with names unfamiliar to her. Michelle had read about one page of each of them before she dropped them into the black hole at the bottom of her desk drawer. The drawer was filled with them, all little gifts from Tonya. And underneath all the books that were scattered like confetti was a Bible—a *Woman Thou Art Loosed* Bible. It was still in its original packaging, still unopened.

This was it. *This was it!* Michelle shoved the flowers toward the edge of her desk and almost knocked them over. This was it. Why couldn't she just have some peace? This was the last straw.

What is Tonya's malfunction anyway? Is she stalking me? Michelle slammed the drawer shut. She was sick of all of them—Trench, Todd, and Tonya.

Actually, Michelle knew what the malfunction was. She didn't need advice from Ann Landers, and she didn't need to ask Abby or even Erma Bombeck. It was the same thing that had been going on, probably since time began. It was the story of someone who viewed himself as more powerful trying to lord it over the little guy. It was Goliath against David. It was corporations against small business. It was bosses against employees. It was men against women. It was superpowers against third world countries.

It was Tonya against her.

Let's get ready to rumble!

It was all the same thing—someone more powerful, someone with more authority, forcing his or her will on someone weaker. The issue might change but it was all the same thing. It was the basis for time clocks at work. It was all about power. Power made her mother's boyfriend feel that he could abuse her. Power made her mother force Michelle to be silent about it. Power made Todd think after he married her that he could control her. Power made Tonya think she could keep Michelle off the phone and that she could make her *find religion*.

She grabbed the used tissues off her desk. Not today, not anymore—she was not the one. It was time to get rid of the clutter in her life. She was going to get stuff out of her life that was confusing her and causing her pain—and she was going to start right here and right now.

This was where the throw-down was going to go down. Michelle threw the tissue into the trash, then popped and stretched her neck. She got up from behind her desk. She'd started with the tissue and right now she was going to move on to Miss Tonya. Her can was going to be next for the can.

Michelle began to laugh to herself as she walked toward Tonya's desk, shaking tension out of her muscles so she would be ready to pounce on Tonya like a cat on a mouse. This was it. Whatever happened, it was going to be worth it. Sometimes a sister just had to take a stand. As Michelle walked, she looked back at the floral arrangement on her desk. They were going to be planting those flowers on girlfriend's grave. Job or no job—Tonya was not going to make her lose her mind up in here. As she walked toward Tonya's desk, Michelle felt as though she was walking in slow motion, wading through water in cement boots.

Time was winding up for the busybody, the Jesus lover, Miss Holier-than-thou!

Chapter Eight

ichelle sat at a table in the cafeteria-style restaurant on the lower floor of the building. Shadrach sat across from her, shaking his head.

"I swear, a man will never be able to understand the mind of a woman. I don't understand how two women going through the same thing—two women who have so much in common—refuse to help each other and end up fighting instead. I don't understand it." Shad used his fork to pick at the boneless spareribs on his plate. "I just don't get it."

Michelle almost gagged on a French fry. "Shad, what are you *talking* about? Me and Tonya are as different as night and day. *Look* at her." Michelle picked up another fry and gestured in the air. "You know I'm not like her, with her dried up, boring, dull self. And she so caught up in this job—and Mrs. Judson, like Mrs. Judson is the be-all, end-all. Me and Tonya alike? I don't know where you get that from, Shad. I really don't."

Shadrach scooted his chair back from the table and crossed his legs, as though he was preparing to sit for a while. "You go right ahead, baby girl. I don't want to interrupt you while you're on a roll." He lay down his fork and pushed his plate forward. "You got it. You got it all figured out. Go for it. Let it flow."

"Look, Shad, I am just tired of taking stuff off of her. What for? For a job? Other people can take that stuff if they want to, but I'm not the one."

Shadrach whistled. He leaned forward and stared Michelle in the eye. "Girl, you gonna lose your job. And I don't know whether you know it or not, but the rent man don't take *pride* for payment, and you can't deposit *I know I'm right* in the bank."

"Shad. Come on, give me a break." Michelle would not let the tears that popped into her eyes—tears that surprised her—fall. "Shad, this is not the time to be difficult. I could get fired here."

Shadrach scooted his chair forward and lowered his voice. "That's exactly what I'm trying to get across to you. That's what I'm talking about. What did you think was going to happen?"

"I didn't think. I just saw red. I'm sick of her, Shad, with all the stupid books, cards . . . and the Bible. This is a job, and she's my team leader, not my momma or my supervisor. I'm sick of her telling me what to do and when to do it. I'm sick of her signifying, looking down her nose at me and trying to throw off on me with all her religious stuff."

Shadrach's expression softened. "Do you think that's really what Tonya's trying to do?"

"What else? She doesn't know me. Why would she do something for me—just out of the goodness of her heart? Tonya makes me sick. She thinks she's so holy."

"Maybe Tonya is trying to do what she thinks will help."

Michelle tapped the perfectly manicured, acrylic-tipped nail of one index finger on the table. "I don't need her help, or anybody else's for that matter."

"That may be. You may be the one person alive who doesn't

need anybody. May be, but I doubt it. But, seriously, Tonya might be trying to be a friend to you in the only way she knows how."

"Why? What for? Look, this is just a *job*. I didn't come here looking for friends, or for a new momma—I already had one and that was enough."

"That may be, too, but life is funny like that. We're always finding things where we least expect them. Maybe she's just trying to be good—"

"I don't *need* anybody to be good to me! When people are good to you, it always has a price. I've already given; I'm not paying anymore!"

Shadrach closed one eye and cocked his head. "Whew! Where did that come from?" He looked straight at Michelle. "What I was about to say is that I think she is trying to be good people. You know what I mean?"

Michelle frowned.

Shad continued talking. "You know how it is. Most people go through life and they don't give a good kitty for other people. You on your own—it's every man for himself. They may not try to hurt you, but they sure as living are not going to go out of their way to help you. I think Tonya tries to be good people. Maybe she's trying too hard, but I think her heart is in the right place."

Michelle narrowed her eyes. "What do you know about Tonya's heart?"

Shadrach placed one of his ankles on the opposite knee. "I keep my eyes open." He shrugged. "I've just seen and heard of her doing things for people. You know, I'm old school. I watch a long time, taking notes and names. I'm pretty sure that Tonya is not doing stuff for show—I've heard of her giving people a little change or car rides, showing up at people's family member's funerals. Just stuff like that. It's not a big deal, but these are folks that can't do nothing for her. I've never heard of her running back and telling what she's done. If the other people don't tell it, the story never gets told." He shrugged. "That says something to me."

Michelle pursed her lips. "Well, if you're so impressed, why aren't you eating lunch with *her?*"

"Because I asked you, that's why."

Michelle rolled her eyes. "Mm-hmm." She wasn't so sure she believed him.

"I just think she's good people."

Michelle picked up another fry. "You keep saying that, but she's dull and dried up." She dipped the fry in a little pool of ketchup. "No spice and no flavor."

Shadrach uncrossed his legs. "Well, I just think Tonya's all right. You're right, though. She could use a little help with the wardrobe—a little something to make her look like there is still some life in her. I'll grant you that. But it seems like to me that what's not working on the outside don't cancel out the inside. That's something funny to me about women, anyway." Shadrach looked puzzled. "Its hard to find a woman with both things working together. So many sisters look good on the outside, but they're full of junk on the inside. Or else, they're good on the inside and tore down on the outside."

He dusted invisible lint off of his pants. "I just haven't been able, in my lifetime, to decide which is better." Shadrach smiled. "Maybe that's why I'm not married."

Michelle waved a French fry at him and laughed. "Shad, you're full of it."

"For real. I keep thinking, if a brother could get you two together—that would be something for the mind, the body, and the soul!"

Michelle trailed the fry back and forth through the ketchup. She wet her lips and winked. "Yeah, right, Shad. Whatever."

"Really, Michelle, maybe Tonya is just trying to be nice to you."

"I've been trying not to say this, but the truth is the truth. What the problem really is is that Tonya is jealous. You just admitted yourself that she is tired and dried up looking." Michelle wiped her hands on her napkin. "I try to keep myself up." She straightened her jacket and touched her hair. "And she sure doesn't have a life outside of this job. You know how it is—she hears me on the phone, or some man asks me out to lunch." Michelle winked at Shadrach again. "It makes her mad and she tries to make my life as miserable as hers. You know how people are. There is nothing I can do about how she feels, but I'm sure not going to let her ruin my life because she has issues."

"You think that's what it is, huh?"

"I know it is."

Shadrach cracked his knuckles. "So, exactly what did happen?"

"Shad, you would not believe this, but it was just like a dream I had. In the dream, I was fed up with her and I went after her—chasing her and stuff. Only Tonya didn't run in real life, like she ran in my dream. I was surprised. I tore into her. I called her everything I could think of. I told Miss Lady all about herself. I was all up in her face. Tonya wouldn't fight back . . . but she didn't run."

Shadrach cleared his throat and straightened his sleeves. "Look, Michelle, you and Tonya are gonna have to talk and work this thing out. *Together.* Because what I hear and know about Mrs. Judson is that she can and *will* fire you, Tonya, or both of you all. She doesn't play that 'being emotional' stuff at work. I guess since she is the boss, she got her stuff all together—so she doesn't want anybody else's issues infecting her office. You are going to have to get it together, Michelle."

She pouted. "So I guess you're saying that everything that happened was my fault. Tonya was all goodness and light, and I'm just too hotheaded to work in an office."

"What I'm saying, Michelle, is that you two—you and Tonya—need to have lunch, or something, and figure out how to get this together before both of you all end up going down." He smiled. "I'm even willing to sacrifice myself and referee."

"Shad, you're not fooling anybody. You're just looking to see a cat fight."

Shad put on an innocent expression and opened his palms wide. "Baby, I'm being for real. But you can't blame a brother, can you?" His expression changed. "Really, though, I just want to help. Maybe if you all get together . . . You could eat lunch like this and talk—you know, try to talk things over."

Michelle smirked. "You've got to be kidding. Me and Tonya at lunch . . . out in public? I'm too real for her. We can't even get it together in an office full of people where we're under the gun to follow the rules."

"I told you I would meet with the two of you."

"Like a referee."

Shad leaned back in his chair and smiled. "Yeah, like a referee, or like a coach."

"So who is going to invite her?"

Shad laughed out loud. "You!" He stretched the word out for a few measures.

"Me? It was your big idea. How am I supposed to— What is going to make her say *yes*?"

Shad folded his arms across his chest. "Well, I'm willing to meet you here. You're going to have to figure out the *how* all by yourself."

Chapter Nine

think I need a vacation!"

Michelle needed a break from everything. She needed to go to a land where people looked out for one another, where they had the other person's best interest at heart. When Miz Ida answered the door, Michelle held out the flowers—the ones she had gotten from Tonya—to her. There was no point in letting them go to waste.

"Oh, baby! Come on in."

It was good, Michelle thought, that there was one person in her life who always did what was expected, and what was expected was always good. "I wasn't thinking to see you so soon." Miz Ida's eyes looked a question that her mouth did not ask.

"I just thought I would drop by." Michelle held back what was on her mind for as long as she could. She drank the sweet red Kool-Aid Miz Ida gave her—so sweet that Michelle always wanted a glass of water when she finished. Michelle talked about the old neighborhood, how it had gone down, and she asked Miz Ida when she was going to move.

"You know I ain't moving, baby."

Michelle talked about nothing until she just couldn't hold it anymore. Then she let it all out, like helium from a balloon, about work, about Tonya, and about Shadrach's suggestion. It was good to have someone—at least one someone that she could tell all the details, all the shameful pieces she would have held back from anyone else. And then, since she was telling, she told Miz Ida about Todd and about the drama with Trench.

"By the time I got through fooling with Tonya in the office, she had blown all the good feeling I got from Trench."

"Oh, baby, why you got to be with somebody like that—somebody that talks bad to you? Why is it so hard to let Todd love you?"

Michelle just shrugged. There was no point in hiding anything. Miz Ida knew everything anyway. She knew about the molestation, the prostitution, the drugs and jail, and about her mother. Miz Ida knew everything. Michelle could stand naked in front of Miz Ida. The old woman knew who she was and loved her anyway.

Michelle laid her head on Miz Ida's shoulder. *Thank God for her.*

Miz Ida shook her head, her chin brushing the top of Michelle's hair. "You acted all crazy in the office, like that? So, you think this woman at work is trying to hurt you?" Michelle could feel Miz Ida's chest rising and falling as she spoke.

"Well, maybe not hurt me, Miz Ida. More like she's trying to control me and trying to make me be like her. She keeps watching me and trying to tell me what to do, like she's some kind of preacher or like she's my momma."

"And we all know how you feel about that."

Michelle lifted her head from Miz Ida's shoulder. "What do you mean? Why did you say it that way?"

Miz Ida looked Michelle square in the eye. "Because that issue—*the momma thing*—just hangs around your neck like a rope waiting to choke you. Things in your life are always going to be off-kilter until you make some peace with who you are and where you come from and about who you belong to."

"Miz Ida, we keep having this conversation about my momma, about God and everything. What is it you want me to do?"

She put her arm around Michelle's shoulders. "What I want is for you to get yourself together on this thing. Look, Michelle, your momma wasn't perfect. But she did what she knew to do. She fed you and she kept a roof over your head. She didn't have to bear you into this world. Don't forget that."

Michelle wanted to pull away. She would have pulled away from anyone else . . . but then, she wouldn't have let any one else touch her in the first place. "You're right, Miz Ida. My momma kept me clothed and fed, but where was she when I just needed someone to be there—someone to play with me, talk to me, or to hold me? Where was she when I was crying out?"

"Someday, Michelle, I just pray that the Lord will help you understand."

"Oh, I understand, Miz Ida. She put that man first. She just didn't care—she let that man treat her any kind of way. She let him use her. Then she let him use me."

Miz Ida nodded. "You're right, you know. Cassandra wasn't strong. But, you need to know that your momma did everything she knew to do. What's wrong in her life didn't start with her. It probably started way before she was born."

"Miz Ida, you sound like all those people on television. It's not her fault? Well, you know what, Miz Ida? When does it get to be her fault? *She* left me out there open and unprotected. *She* let a man in her life—in my life—who used me and made me feel like nothing. I would never do that to a child."

Miz Ida shook her gray head. "No, you doing it to yourself."

Michelle pulled away from Miz Ida's embrace at that.

"I know you don't like what I'm saying, but a true friend tells the truth. Now, your momma's not in your life bringing men to hurt you. You took over that job yourself."

The old woman reached to touch one of Michelle's hands. "Like I been trying to tell you, Michelle, you don't want to deal with the past, so you just keep repeating it over and over again. Like some kind of pattern. But you can stop it. You got to see it clear and then you got to pray about it. Something bad probably happened to your mother, and she did the same thing to you without knowing it. She couldn't see it. You *can* see what went wrong, that means you *can* change it. You don't have to let that history repeat. You don't have to let another child be hurt, and you don't have to let yourself be hurt. The good man in your life, you can't hardly stand. The bad man, you just let him right on in." She shook her head. "You have to ask yourself what that means."

Michelle rolled her neck to release the tension and frustration. "I don't really know what you're talking about, Miz Ida."

"No, I believe you do. You may not *want* to know, but I believe you do."

"So I guess this same conversation we have is always going to come back to the same old place—my momma, God, and church."

"Well, if you say so."

Michelle gritted her teeth. "Miz Ida, it's going to be a cold day in . . . before I see my momma. Now that's just that. As for God, He made me. He knows my heart and I don't have to go to church and pay my money to some man in order for God to see me. He knows every hair on my head—you taught me that."

"He does know every hair. You were listening when I was talking to you, weren't you, baby?" Miz Ida pinched Michelle's cheek with one hand and put the other arm back around Michelle's shoulders, but Michelle resisted. "Don't you try to pull away from me." Miz Ida held on until Michelle surrendered. "If you're going to change your life, don't just change it on the outside. Make the change through and through. The only one that I know of that can do a heart change is the Lord. If I knew somebody else, I would recommend him, but in all my time, it's only the Lord I been able to see do it. If we could really sit at home and do what we need to do to find Him and learn about Him, I wouldn't bug you so much." She squeezed her. "I know you don't like it. But tell the truth—you know the Lord by yourself, but when was the last time you opened a Bible to read anything about Him? All you know the Lord to be is what you've heard people say. All they say ain't all He wants to be to you."

"It's not the Lord, Miz Ida. I would go to church, but I just hate all those people asking for money."

Miz Ida laughed out loud. "Girl, now you know better than to pull my leg. You know you got to give me a better excuse than that." She let go of Michelle, rose from the couch, and walked into the kitchen. Miz Ida opened the door to her refrigerator and started moving things around. "Let me see if I can fix you something to eat." She pulled a pot from the refrigerator and set it on the stove.

She started laughing again, and laid her hand on her chest. "I don't mean to laugh." She doubled over. "Yes, I do. You know why I'm laughing? If that ain't the biggest bunch of nothing. *I ain't paying no man my money.* The people who say that are the same people that will pay all kinds of money for lottery tickets that got a million-to-one chance to win. They will pay twenty dollars a day for cigarettes and other stuff. When you pay for them, who you paying if not some man?

"When you go to church, you got the choice to pray and never give—you give cause your heart say so. Them other things—drinking, gambling, drugs, candy, whatever your poison is, just like me and all the sugar I put in my drinks—you know you got to pay to play. You gone pay for somebody to give you something that's gone take life away or leave you worse off, but you don't want to give back to something that's giving hope."

Miz Ida shook her head and laughed again, then waved Michelle into the kitchen area. "Now, enough of this. Come on in here and help me get this food on." Michelle chopped lettuce, and then began to slice tomato and cucumbers. Miz Ida began to laugh again.

"*I ain't gone give no man my money.* People gone have to come up with a new excuse."

Part Two

Fall—Tonya

Chapter Ten

onya made a left turn onto Wabash Avenue on her way home. In her soul and spirit, she kept the running prayer going—the prayer she prayed every day as she drove home. A prayer that God would just let her make it home safely, that the car she was driving—her mid-sized, I'm-only-five-years-old-but-if-you-don't-keep-an-eye-on-me-I'm-going-to-break-down-right-in-the-middle-of-this-traffic car would just keep going a little bit longer. She prayed that her car would keep going until her change came, until things got better, or until she walked into her season.

The radio announcer said it was five-fifteen. In fact, he said it like everybody ought to shout *Hallelujah!* Then, just before the digital clock on her dashboard could register five-sixteen, he said, "Hallelujah! Everybody say *hallelujah!*"

Obediently, because she was nothing if not obedient, Tonya said, "Hallelujah." Only if there was a praise meter in heaven, her accolade or jubilation probably registered less like *Hallelujah* and more like *So what?*

Tonya had started off her day with the praise song "This Is the Day That the Lord Has Made" in her heart and in her mind. By the afternoon, her joy was gone. What remained was a kind of pained weariness that she felt on her face and in her chest. It was the tiredness that can be seen on some church folks' faces when they don't know anyone is looking. Tiredness that says they love the Lord, that they are committed to Him come rain or come shine, but that they have been through a season that has been mostly wind and rain.

It is a tired expression that goes away when they are serving or helping others. It disappears when singing their favorite gospel song along with the radio or a choir, or when they hear the Word being preached on Sunday morning. But sometimes, Tonya knew, when they are alone and thinking—when there is no one around that they need to uplift or encourage—they sink. It is the sinking of people who are waiting for a change that looks like it will never come.

The same sinking Tonya felt so often.

She understood. It wasn't that they didn't have faith that change would come. But it was hard not to grow weary of waiting. Tonya had seen the same look on the faces of women who had been loving, submissive, and celibate only to see the men they loved marry women that gave them what they wanted when they wanted it—whether those "giving" women were the right women, the beloved women, or not. It was the weariness of saints who dutifully paid their tithes while their ends hardly ever met, while crooks—both thugs and corporate hoods—drove fancy cars and lived in houses with pools and Jacuzzis.

Tonya thought this must be like the exhaustion of salmon that swim upstream hoping against hope to spawn. It must be the almost hopeless hope of players who sit on the bench wanting to throw in the towel, but who want even more to get into the game.

Tonya had stopped looking in the mirror so she wouldn't see that there were faint, dark circles under her eyes. Stray hairs had come undone from her bun—the perennial bun or ponytail she wore because they were the fastest hairdos (or hair-don'ts) she could comb without having to look at her reflection. The gray tiredness in her face spoke volumes. It was the drained, glassy-eyed look of the *for-God-I-live-or-for-God-I-will-die* saints when it looks like the Grim Reaper is sharpening his blade. She wore the look of people whose hope is almost gone—all wrapped up in an overstretch, oversized navy-blue sweater. The sister was just tired.

She was tired of doing the same thing every day with the same results. She was lonely, too. She was godly, and she did her best to be holy. She wasn't slobbering for a man, but she was still lonely. Yes, she had the look of women who think, *Jesus is enough, but it would be nice to have a man.* She didn't *need* a man; so she wasn't asking, grooming, or looking. She didn't need a house or a new car to make her complete, so she wasn't asking God for it.

But she was waiting for something.

What really bothered her, though, was that while Tonya was waiting, it seemed as though life had moved on for everyone else she knew. While she was waiting to exhale, as Ms. MacMillan might say, Stella had already gotten her groove back—five or six times. It would have been easier for Tonya if she could have given up or just thrown in the towel. But Tonya had a promise. She was waiting on her season, waiting for her change to come, waiting for her time to shine. If she didn't have to believe that things were going to get better—if she could have just packed it up, put it away, or iced it down—things would have been tidier and so much easier.

But underneath all Tonya's affected dowdiness was a passionate woman with her eye open for a more abundant life. She couldn't explain it; it was sort of a prickling desire. It just wasn't nice, tidy, and neat. It wasn't a Vaseline-on-your-patent-leather-shoes kind of desire. It wasn't an overstuff-your-plate-at-Sunday-dinner desire. Tonya wrestled with her promise like the saints of old wrestled as they waited for Emmanuel.

What had her bunched up now, on her way home from work, was mostly Michelle.

"Lord," she talked with her eyes open, monitoring the obstacles and the traffic. She talked to God without moving her lips so that people in the car next to her wouldn't think she was crazy and report her to the police over their cell phones. "Lord, what are You trying to do to me?" She slowed so that the car to her right could change lanes in front of her. "I have done everything You told me. I've bought her books and cards using money You know I don't have. And today I even took her the flowers You told me to take her." Humiliation brought tears to her eyes. "And I told you before I did it that I thought it was a bad idea. I told you!"

The air conditioning in the car was going full blast, but Tonya could feel heat creeping up her neck to her face and ears. "You saw her, God. She acted like I had smacked her in the face and insulted her. There she was in the middle of the office yelling at me . . . calling me everything but a child of God." An audible sob—not too loud, but just like a baby before it drifted off to sleep—came from Tonya's throat. "And all those people were looking at me, Lord. Looking at both of us like we were crazy. I just don't understand it, Lord. I don't understand it."

The Lord said nothing.

"She hates me. Michelle hates me for no reason. I try to be nice to her. I pray for her. I tried to smooth things over for her with Mrs. Judson—not to mention that I'm going to need someone to smooth things over for *me* with Mrs. Judson after this." Tonya sighed as she checked her rearview mirror. "I'm tired, Lord. I can't keep doing this and all the while Michelle just keeps kicking me in my face."

In her heart, Tonya heard the Lord speak. *Keep doing what you've been doing, daughter.*

"Lord?" Tears slipped from the corners of Tonya's eyes and burned her face. "Lord, she hates me. You know she hates me. Michelle acts like I'm trying to hurt her. Like I'm trying to kill her. And, Lord, You know that I've been praying for her. You know that

I've stuck up for her when Mrs. Judson has wanted me to let her go—even to the point where now Mrs. Judson is threatening both of us.

"Lord, I just need peace. I just need peace somewhere—at home, at work, anywhere. Some place where there is peace. I'm so tired, God. I'm just tired."

It's hard, my daughter, to kick against the pricks.

Her tears dried quickly. Tonya took three deep breaths. The Lord never said a lot when He spoke to her heart. He was thrifty with words; He was efficient. But what He said always got the point across.

Kicking against the pricks. Tonya knew what it meant. It was what the Lord had said to Saul when he was having his Damascus Road experience. She knew the King James passage by heart.

Kicking against the pricks. It was those times when God was giving His people—a son or a daughter—information, or requiring one of His children to behave in a way that went against common sense, against experience, against book learning, even against home training. Tonya remembered when she had first read the passage. In the account, something unseen had caused Saul to fall from his horse. There was a great light around him, and he heard a voice.

"Saul, Saul, why persecutest thou me?" Saul had answered, "Who art thou, Lord?" and the Lord had said, "I am Jesus whom thou persecutest: it is hard for thee to kick against the pricks." Saul, trembling and astonished, had answered, "Lord, what wilt thou have me to do?" And the Lord had said to him, "Arise, and go into the city, and it shall be told thee what thou must do."[2]

Paul, who had been Saul, had known the same struggle that educated men and women face when they wrestle in their minds with notions of God as superstition, while even in their hearts, minds, and spirits they witness that there is something greater, something infinite, that they cannot explain. *Kicking against the pricks.* It was those

[2]See Acts 9:4–6

times when, like Paul, God was saying something that went against the teachings of friends, of family, even against one's own mind.

It was those times when God was leading in one direction and one of his stubborn children—like an ox in a yoke—tried to go in another. Tonya knew that the Lord was telling her that the pain she was feeling was the spiritual equivalent of the pain that oxen experience when they pull against the direction of the person leading them and are wounded by a yoke or collar of thorns—by the pricks. The Lord was telling her to stop causing her own pain, to surrender and stop fighting, to trust Him. He had a good plan, a plan to bless her and Michelle, not to cause them harm.

Right now, though, it didn't feel like it. It hurt. *Kicking against the pricks.* Tonya definitely felt like she was being knocked from her horse, or at least from her desk, by something she knew, and her name was Michelle. She felt like she was in an unwanted spotlight at work. But she just wasn't so sure that God was speaking with her like he did to Saul, or that she knew the plan.

"God, I spent money I don't have, for nothing." Tonya took a deep breath. "It hurt my feelings, God, and it embarrassed me."

Finally, there it was—the truth. It wasn't about the money. Tonya was hurt and humiliated.

Then she felt the Lord draw near. It was the closeness of a loving father taking his child on his knee. The tenderness of a father consoling a child when she is heartbroken or injured. It was the kindness of a father who is infinitely, faithfully, and unequivocally concerned about the welfare and happiness of his children.

Tonya pulled into her parking space in front of her and her son's building in the apartment complex. She sat in her car for a few minutes, just until one of her favorite gospel songs ended—just until Tonya could get herself together.

Then she slipped from the car and went inside.

"Hey, Malik. I'm home," she called to her son when she stepped through the front door.

"Hey, Moms. What's up?" Her seventeen-year-old son was back

in his bedroom, but she imagined she could see him—headphones half on and half off his head, a video game controller in his hand.

"How was school?" There was no point in bringing her office problems and laying them at her son's feet. He had enough to deal with on his own. Instead, when he surfaced from his bedroom, Tonya listened to him talk about school. She washed the dishes that had been left in the sink—*Malik, I told you to wash whatever plates, glasses, or silverware you use so they won't be left here for me when I get home*—and began like single parents and mothers everywhere to cook dinner without ever sitting down to rest.

That night, when everything that could be done was done, she fell asleep before her body hit the bed, and she dreamed about Michelle.

The office looked the same, except Michelle's desk was bigger and more ornate than anyone else's desk. Tonya sat in her space, trying to do her work and mind her own business, but Michelle kept snatching everything she wanted. It was as though Michelle was able to follow Tonya's eyes, determine what Tonya wanted, then grab the item before Tonya's fingers could grasp it. Or she would check Tonya with her body to keep her from what she desired. When Tonya reached for a stapler, Michelle grabbed it before she could get her hands on it. Michelle snatched a folder, a chair, even a window office—all things that rightfully belonged to Tonya— the instant before Tonya could reach them.

Then, in that way that happens in dreams, they were instantly transported to Tonya's apartment. Michelle took pictures off the walls, hustled plates and food off the table, and took Tonya's car keys off the hook near the door. Michelle even took her husband.

That's when Tonya relaxed. That's when, even though she was still dreaming, she determined that she was having a nightmare.

Richard was already gone.

Chapter Eleven

onya pulled into her spot in the parking lot near the building where she worked, walked to the red metal slotted box at the entrance to the lot, and inserted her five-dollar bill to park for the day. *If parking gets any higher, I'll just have to stay home.* She smiled, thinking about her son. She'd enjoy getting to see Malik more. He was a good kid—he was going to be a good man.

As she got closer to the building, her breathing became more shallow and her palms began to sweat. *This is the day that the Lord has made, I will rejoice and be glad in it.* Tonya was glad for the solitary walk to the office building. It gave her time to shore herself up.

What a way to begin a week. Mrs. Judson was going to be boiling after the blowup on Friday.

"Tonya," she had said evenly on Friday afternoon, "one of the qualities I look for in managers is just that—that they are able to manage the employees they supervise. And that they, with decisiveness, be able to determine that an employee is unmanageable, whereupon the manager quickly takes steps to dismiss him or her."

There were lots of things Tonya could have said to Mrs. Judson. Things about compassion and about patience, not to mention that she was just a team leader with no authority, not a supervisor.

As though she'd read Tonya's thoughts, Mrs. Judson had gone on. "Of course, I know, Tonya, that you are not yet a manager, but I've observed your willingness to work long hours, to tackle difficult assignments, even to get along with difficult people. But this situation with Michelle must come to some sort of resolution. Quickly. I'm not prepared to make a decision this afternoon in the emotion of this situation, but I think we should meet Monday morning before our usual staff meeting."

I can do all things through Christ, which strengthens me. Tonya pushed the glass door of the office building and stepped inside. She spoke to the security guards like she always did as she walked to the elevator and pushed the button.

All weekend Tonya had relived what happened in the office. She tried to figure it out and explain it to herself.

One second Michelle had been smelling the flowers. She was smiling, even smiling at Tonya—something that almost never happened. Michelle had opened the card and read. She actually seemed to be glowing. Tonya was sure Michelle was glowing. Finally, she'd thought, something had broken through Michelle's hard shell.

None of the books or tapes she had given Michelle had helped—and Tonya had only given Michelle gifts and books that had actually helped her dig herself out of her *own* situations. The gifts only seemed to make Michelle angry.

But the flowers and the card had seemed to be working. *Thank You, God,* she had whispered to herself. She was happy she had been obedient and had bought the flowers. She'd leaned forward in her seat, enthralled by the enjoyment that Michelle's happiness brought her.

Just as soon as Tonya had relaxed, though, Michelle frowned.

And then Michelle was in her face, waving the card at her. Michelle was yelling, shouting and carrying on, and she was so dangerously close Tonya could feel the other woman's breath on her chin. Michelle was yelling something at Tonya about minding her own damned business, something about being "holier than thou" and about *kicking* something even if she was in an office.

The elevator door opened. She was glad the car was empty and that there were twenty-four floors to her office. She stepped inside. Normally the slow-moving elevator irritated her. Today she was grateful for the time. Maybe she would have it all figured out by the twenty-fourth floor. Right.

Cinnamon cappuccino. That's what she had smelled on Michelle's breath. Tonya felt her mind wandering again. What was happening had to be a nightmare. Michelle hadn't really yelled at her in front of everyone in the office. Mrs. Judson hadn't really stood in her doorway watching the whole thing. It had to be a dream.

Only it wasn't a dream.

Michelle had pushed up on her so close—hands on her hips, nails flicking in Tonya's face, jumping up and down, screaming like a crazy woman—and she had seemed to be trying to move even closer. It was fighting language. Fight-or-flight language. Either you were going to run from the yelling or you were going to stand and fight. Tonya knew Michelle had expected her to run.

That was the thing about being saved. It was the thing about being labeled. People didn't know who you were—or who you had been, for that matter. Some people seemed to think that her choice to live in peace and to minimize confrontation came from fear.

What Michelle didn't know was that there was a day—a day not long ago—when Tonya would have been more than happy to go to fist city with her, to knock her out. Tonya put her one hand on her hip and used the other to hide a quick smile as she remembered the old days. *Michelle better ask somebody! She better recognize!* Tonya sighed and dropped her hands. It was another one of those things people didn't understand.

Even she didn't know how to explain to people what having an intimate relationship with the Lord had done to her. Some days she didn't know herself why she wasn't slapping people when they got on her nerves, but something had happened after she had gotten closer to the Lord that had changed her life. Before, she would have pounded Michelle . . . joyfully. Now she cried to the Lord about her verbal beatdown—and she waited and trusted *Him* to work it out. Though more times than not, Tonya still thought she could give the Lord just a little bit of help.

Fourteenth floor. Going up.

Lord, maybe You want me to get fired from this job. That's where things seem to be headed. But what I'm hoping for is just some kind of sign, or some kind of breakthrough. Michelle doesn't have to be my best friend, Lord. But I need something. Something!

Fifteenth floor.

The elevator doors opened.

"Hey, baby girl!"

It was Shadrach. Tonya's shoulders relaxed.

"How's it going?"

Tonya didn't know why she began telling Shadrach everything, but she did. She really didn't know Shadrach well. But he seemed to be one of those people who took his job seriously—he was on time, he was always working and coaching other employees. There was a certain determined optimism about him. Determined because everyone knew, without saying it, that optimism and joy were not respected in the workplace. Comedies don't receive Academy Awards and joyful people rarely become executives.

She didn't know why the story came spilling out, but it did. Shadrach listened for a minute. Then he nodded.

"Let's push some of these buttons so that this thing will slow down while we talk." He punched buttons so the elevator would be forced to stop every few floors on its way up.

There was a joy vacuum where they worked. Some folks had never, it seemed, had any joy. Others had had the joy sucked right out of them, while others had just given it up, or packed it away in order to get promoted or to fit in. They had taken on the sour look, the turned down mouth that some CEOs—and even some preachers, for that matter—seemed to affect to make people think they were "serious" or "deep." Whichever the scenario, all the gladness was pulled out of any new people and out of the few that still fought to hold on.

Shadrach was different. There was something in Shadrach's eyes that said he knew the deal, knew the game, but he wasn't playing. He gave the company his time, his dedication, his loyalty—he had given them almost twenty years—but he was not about to give them his joy.

Tonya had watched Shadrach, year after year, serving people who thought they were better than he because of their position or title or because of the size of their paychecks. Shadrach found joy in serving them—which seemed to anger the people more. Tonya admired him for his servant's heart—something she would not have admired a few years earlier. "We don't want to serve," she remembered her pastor saying one Sunday. "We want to sign up for the Christianity that will get us a big car, a big house and servants. But we don't want to sign up for the Christianity that says that in order to reign, we must be servants to all." That was what she recognized in Shadrach—a servant's heart. He always seemed to listen, even when people were just responding to his hello. Shadrach seemed to focus on people and take in what they were saying. And he always knew the right thing to say.

As she talked, Tonya recalled how she had often seen Shadrach standing toe to toe talking to some young brother that didn't seem to have his act together—like he was trying to do with Tonya. But what she also observed was that the young men seemed to respect him and seemed to turn their lives around. What the young men didn't seem to be doing was cussing Shadrach out in the middle of his office. They didn't seem to be telling him where they would kick him. Of course, that might be because Shadrach looked a little more like a linebacker than she did.

Whatever the case, Tonya needed to get some things off her chest. So she let it out. When the door opened on the twenty-fourth floor, she was still talking.

"Michelle was yelling and screaming, calling me names, and she kept saying something about me being jealous of her boyfriends and of how she looks. Jealous?" Tonya looked down at her clothes. "Since when did I ever give anyone the impression that I was worried about how I look, or that I was worried about a man—"

"Hey." Shadrach had been listening patiently, but now he interrupted her. He shifted his packages, took Tonya's hand, and led her through the door marked *Stairs* near the elevator. "Well, we seem to be a little wound up, today." He smiled at his own understatement.

"I don't know why I'm telling you all of this. I just—"

"You just need to talk to somebody."

Tonya nodded yes and told herself that she was a strong woman and that she would not cry.

He sat his packages down on a step. "Well, what I can tell you is that it's not the end of the world. Look, you and me are old school. Jobs come, jobs go; people come and go, but we know we're going to be all right."

Tonya blew a shot of air from her mouth. He was right.

"Most people here don't know that, that's why they're so up-tight. We just have to remind ourselves not to get caught up in the madness."

She shifted her bag to the opposite shoulder. "I know." She sighed. "It's just . . . it's just that I was trying to help Michelle. I've *been* trying to help Michelle. And I don't understand what happened. How it went from flowers and a card on her desk and her smiling to her standing in my face cussing me out."

"Yeah."

"I don't get it. What was wrong with giving her something nice? And I'm risking my job. Mrs. Judson has been pretty clear that she thinks I ought to fire Michelle. She hasn't demanded that I do it . . . yet. So, I keep trying. I keep praying that something is going to get Michelle on track. I keep trying to help her get herself together—at least in the areas that I know people are watching, like getting here on time and staying off the phone. I'm trying to help and she seems to hate me for it." She looked down at her shoes and then back at Shadrach.

"You know what? I think you two sisters need to talk."

"I don't see that happening."

Shadrach shrugged. "Look, she's like a lot of young people. Michelle probably doesn't know who to trust. I think she's reading you wrong—I don't know why. But you won't know why unless the two of you talk."

"I've been talking. Every time I open my mouth . . ."

"Yeah, it sounds like both of you all have been talking, just not to each other."

Tonya didn't know what to say.

"Just try to keep your eyes and your ears open. See where she's coming from." Shadrach looked at his watch, then nodded toward the door. "Come on, baby girl. We're on the clock." He collected his packages and then held the door for her. "Don't give up. Your heart's in the right place—something is going to break."

Tonya nodded.

"We'll talk again later."

Tonya nodded again and watched Shadrach walk away. It was funny, but now that she didn't need a man, she could finally appreciate the value of a good one.

She turned toward her office and began to walk—dragging herself like a doomed man walking his last mile—in the direction of her desk. She hoped that what the old people said was right—trouble don't last always.

Chapter Twelve

he chair was old and stained, but it was still comfortable. It was the best chair to sit in to just sink away from the cares of the world. The piece of furniture was still gold in some spots, soft, and overstuffed. It had seen better days, but it was still the perfect place and Tonya looked at it hungrily.

Steam rose from the ground beef that she was browning in a skillet. She stirred the meat with one hand and reached in the cupboard for an onion with another. As she stirred, she listened for the washing machine to stop so that she could throw the load in the dryer. *Multitasking*. That's what it was called in business classes—doing several things at one time. The people who wrote books about management and business skills didn't know anything. If they really wanted to know about multitasking, they would interview mothers.

If she could abandon her tasks, Tonya would have been in the chair. Maybe the chair could help her forget what was going on in her life. Actually, what she really wanted to forget was work.

Earlier, at the office, Mrs. Judson had looked at her watch. "We will have to meet later in the week, Tonya."

Tonya hated the way Mrs. Judson said her name. It always sounded like she was saying *tan-ya* and not *ton-ya*.

"Tonya, you're going to have to absolutely get a hold on this situation with Michelle. Not only is it impacting productivity in your area, but you must realize that there are other managers—and team leaders—who have employees that are observing Michelle's behavior. 'If it's all right for Michelle, then it's all right for me,' they will say."

Mrs. Judson had looked down abruptly to check something on her cell phone. "I know this may seem like something that can be easily handled—her tardiness, her improper use of the telephone, and now this rude and insubordinate behavior—but one employee who behaves this way can ruin the morale of all the other employees."

She had clicked her cell phone shut and looked back up, speaking as though she was in a hurry to end the conversation. "As I've said before, I won't tell you what to do. But, in all honesty, I need to make you aware that her unchecked behavior is impacting how I view your performance as team manager." She smiled with her mouth, but not her eyes. It seemed that Mrs. Judson was enjoying toying with her. "And I know you don't want to jeopardize a promotion to manager." She stood, walked to the door of her office, and opened it for Tonya. "We'll discuss this later. Right now, I have to make a call and prepare for the morning meeting."

I know you don't want to jeopardize a promotion. It felt like a noose being flung over the branch of a tree.

Of course she would like to jeopardize a promotion, Tonya now thought sarcastically. She didn't have rent to pay or utilities. She wasn't worried every day that her car was going to stop and roll over, feet first. No, Tonya didn't need a promotion. Her son wasn't about to go to college next year. She definitely could do without the promotion—she would just live on her inheritance.

Tonya stopped stirring the beef and grabbed a paring knife from the green plastic container in the silverware drawer. It was a relief, even for a moment, to be sarcastic, at least in her mind.

She began to chop the onion. All this worry was because of Michelle, because of a woman—some ghetto-fabulous girl—who hated her. It didn't make sense. She didn't even know why she was trying to help the young woman. Michelle only thought of herself. She had no sense of responsibility to Tonya or anyone else in the office. It was all about Michelle—it was only about what she wanted.

Tonya scooped up the chopped onion and sprinkled it onto the browning meat. She dusted her palms together to get rid of any little pieces that were clinging, then turned on the faucet and held her hands under the cold running water. That's what she needed to do with Michelle. She needed to wash her hands of the girl. There had been no more screaming matches today, but she had looked up several times to see Michelle watching her. Several times during the day, Michelle had come near her desk, twice opening and closing her mouth as though she had something to say.

The third time, Tonya had turned her back to avoid her—what she didn't need was more confrontation. She had heard quite enough, thank you.

Yes, she needed to wash Michelle out of her thoughts, especially her home thoughts. That was something Tonya had always promised herself: she would never bring whatever was happening at work to her home.

The washer beeped and Tonya walked to it, raised the lid, and began to transfer the clothes to the dryer. The white sheets and towels were wet and heavy, but she loved the smell. She didn't like collecting dirty clothes or stuffing the things into the washer, but she loved what the washing and the water did—the clean, lightly citrus odor of the laundry at the end. The work was worth the reward.

"Malik?" He had been back in his bedroom since he got home. "Son! Can you come out here? I could use some help."

He appeared at the door. "Hey, Mom-ster. What's up?

Whatcha need?" He pulled his headphones off of his ears. Malik liked teasing Tonya. He liked changing her name into quirky nicknames. "It's your dashing, handsome, talented son to the rescue." He almost always made her laugh—almost. "Whatcha need, Mom?"

Tonya punched the *On* switch on the dryer. She put her hands on her hips. "What do I need? You know I have Bible study tonight. Why do I have to tell you what I need, Malik? It seems like you could look around and figure it out. Just do something to help me. I need you to take more responsibility, to think about somebody other than yourself. I'm trying to do everything—"

Malik's face went from excited to sleepy in two seconds flat. Then he raised his hands in the air. "Whoa! I surrender. What's up with all this attitude, Mom?" He stepped closer and put his arms around her. "Is something wrong, Mom?"

Tonya gave him a long hug back and took a deep breath. Malik wasn't Michelle. It wasn't fair to take it out on him. "It's nothing. I'm just rushing around trying to get everything done so that I can get to church on time, or close to on time. That's all."

Malik squeezed her one last time and glanced down so he could look into her eyes. When had he gotten so tall? "That's all? You're just rushing for church?" He laughed. "You're always rushing for church." His voice took on a more serious tone. "You're sure that's all?"

"Yes, I'm sure." Tonya wasn't about to dump her problems with Michelle and work on her son. She would leave it all in the office where it belonged. "I'm just feeling rushed."

Malik let her go. "Okay, Mom-ster." He nodded at the skillet. "Spaghetti and salad, right?"

"How did you guess?"

"It's Monday, right? If it's Monday, it's Bible study and it's spaghetti with salad." After washing his hands, Malik reached into the refrigerator for lettuce, tomato, and cucumber.

"Are we that predictable? Am I that predictable?"

"Yeah, pretty much so." He chopped the lettuce and tossed it into a plastic bowl. "You've got a lot to do, Mom-bo. It's hard to be spontaneous when you're carrying a big duffel bag on your back. Don't worry about it. Some day you'll get to click up your heels, again. I'll be on my own and—"

"Don't say that, Malik. I mean I want you to go off to school and to be everything you dream of being, but don't ever feel like you're a burden to me. You're the light of my life."

He leaned over and kissed her on the forehead. "Me, too."

After they had eaten, and the dishes were washed and put away, Tonya rushed out the door to make it to her class. It might have sounded boring to people that weren't there, but she found delight in listening to teachers bringing Bible passages to life. It was obvious that she wasn't the only person that felt that way—Monday Bible study always had hundreds of people in attendance.

Tonya found her usual spot on her usual pew and waved at the usual people. When the lesson ended, she grabbed her notes, her Bible, and exited out the usual door to the usual area where she parked on the church lot. She held her notes to her chest. It was all usual and predictable, but it was also safe. It made her feel secure. Too much had already changed in her life, and most of the change was disastrous.

God and her church family felt like two loving arms wrapped around her. The lessons at church, and seeing other people who had made the commitment to Monday nights, encouraged her. Maybe her life was too much of the same, every day, every week, every month, every year. But there was always hope. When her world was falling apart, she had found hope when she found something that never changed.

Besides, new good things might be just around the corner. Maybe.

She switched on the ignition and turned up the music. Shirley Caesar was singing "You're Next in Line for a Miracle." Tonya backed out of her spot and rolled over the gravel to the parking lot entrance, then slammed on the brakes.

It was Richard. He was driving by in a new car—with a new girl. The car passed quickly, but Tonya could see clearly. The girl was new and young. Tonya jammed her foot on the gas. Just as quickly, she moved her foot to stomp the brake again. The car rocked back and forth and she slipped the gear into *Park*.

Richard and a girl—it was just what she needed to put the cream on the rest of her day. And all Tonya needed to add to it all was to go chasing the two of them down the street as though she had lost her mind.

A new, young girl. That probably made Richard feel good; it probably made him forget his troubles—at least for a moment. But why did what made him feel better have to make her feel so bad? It had been over between them for a while. But seeing the girl re-opened the wound. What was wrong with her? Why wasn't she enough to satisfy him? Why couldn't she make him feel better?

She looked at herself in the rearview mirror and then down at her clothes. *Look at yourself.* She looked thrown away. She looked unloved.

She felt the tension creeping back up on her. It crawled up her spine to her shoulders and neck. It even found its way down to her ankles.

She never would have believed that her life would turn out like this. They'd had a happy family. They had a lovely home, two lovely sons, and a lovely marriage. She and Richard were, as Ashford and Simpson sang, solid as a rock. She was one of the few women she knew that had been able to be a homemaker while her husband made a decent living. Richard was a good and honorable man. They were the parents of two wonderful sons. It was all lace curtains, dinner parties, PTA meetings, and plays, friendships, Little League games, and barbecues.

Until the accident.

It took all the life out of Richard. The death of their son killed him. He'd tried to hold on; Tonya knew he had tried. But she could see him slipping away. He was surprised himself that the accident and the pain that followed had overwhelmed him. Richard had always been the man, the head of the house, the strong man. She could see it in his eyes—that he didn't know why he couldn't hold on, he couldn't explain to himself why he couldn't be the man he had always thought he was.

First, Richard began staying longer at work. There wasn't another woman then. Not being at home kept him from having to walk through the sadness, from having to look at the photographs, from having to look at her and Malik and see that he couldn't do anything about their pain.

Work was another world. It was a world where there were no dead bodies. At work, all the sons were accounted for in pictures on desks. At work, he didn't have to imagine his son falling from a bench in front of his school. When he was away from Tonya and Malik he didn't have to imagine how the bullets, on impact, must have made his son's athletic body jerk back and forward, side to side. At work, he could pretend the torn, bloodstained lettermen's jacket didn't exist. He could pretend that going to school, working hard, and moving to the suburbs was still the answer to keeping his children and wife secure from drugs and guns. Richard could pretend that what threatened little ghetto children each day of their lives couldn't somehow snake its way into his family and snatch their son from life in his senior year of high school.

At work, Richard didn't have to face that they still didn't know who shot their son or why—that they probably never would. At work, he didn't have to wrestle with reconciling what happened to his beautiful firstborn son, Richard Jr., with the all-knowing, all-wise, all-caring, omniscient God they had visited at church each Sunday.

It was funny—although maybe *ironic* or *strange* was a better choice of words—how Richard had fallen away. Almost like he was holding on to the edge of a cliff, or the rim of a ship. Tonya could see it in his eyes—had seen it coming for months. One day he just didn't have the strength to hold on anymore. Tonya could still see the shame, the panic, and the resignation in his eyes. Richard had let go.

His hands had reached for her as he descended into a deep, dark pit. He would call or stop by when he knew Malik wasn't home. He couldn't stand to see his other son. It was as though he couldn't bear to hold him, to wait for him to be snatched from life as well. So Richard pretended that Malik wasn't there. Even when Richard was still at home, he had stopped speaking to Malik or going to games.

It was hard to explain to Malik, but Tonya understood.

Richard tried to grab hold, but it was too late; gravity pulled him deeper into despair. He moved out of the house. He sent money home at first, so that she was able to maintain at least the outward illusion that things were okay. Then the money stopped. He plummeted. He quit his job. Soon there was no contact with him. He was like a tiny dot that grew invisible as it dropped to the bottom of a canyon. He was like a speck in the ocean that disappeared into the blackness at the bottom of the deep. Tonya saw him so seldom now that she had begun to believe that he never existed.

She had expected, after Richard Jr. died, that *she* would dissolve, that all that she was would melt and swirl together into some kind of strange nothingness. She had made a place in her bedroom and prepared to liquefy. It had surprised her, though, that she had instead become stronger.

Each time she had paid the bills or gotten a job or found an apartment, she was always surprised. She kept waiting for the "real" her to appear, and maybe it had. Maybe the real her was stronger than she had imagined. The things that Richard had run from so that he could survive were the things that she had run toward: her remaining son and her God.

"Things are going to get better."

"You won't struggle all the time."

"Weeping may endure for a night, but joy comes in the morning."

The promises spoken from pulpits, from tapes, and from books, kept her going. She grabbed hold of them like a drowning woman and pulled herself upward—her arms shaking and trembling, straining under the weight of what she bore on her shoulders. But she kept climbing, hand over hand—and she kept believing in the promise.

Each time there wasn't money to buy gas for the car, she meditated on the promise. When she didn't know how to raise her son to be a man, she leaned on the promise. When loneliness enfolded her and tried to pull her back, to send her spiraling down, Tonya held onto the promise.

For the first few years, it had been easy to wait and believe for the promise. She waited patiently for promotion. It was easy to find an economical way to get her hair and nails done. She even believed that there might be a man coming. So it was easy to buy little nighties and pack them away. The first few years, it was easy to keep shining so that the promise, the job, or the man that was looking for her could find her.

After a few years, it took a little more effort, a little more strength to keep believing. Each time there was a notice posted to the door about the water, the electric, or the gas, it took a little more strength to keep keeping on. Each time she had to pick up the phone and make sure there was a dial tone before she dialed, she had to dip into her reserve. The extra strength it required meant Tonya didn't have time to roll her hair in rollers every night. She couldn't spare the energy to lay out her clothes. She couldn't afford to expend the power it took to keep glowing brightly inside and out.

By the time seven years had come and gone—by the time Richard was a memory she questioned—Tonya had learned to sing "Just Jesus Alone," like the old folks. She'd learned to take joy in the private life, the private love she shared with the Lord. So she began to pray to Him that she wouldn't need anyone else. She was used to the struggle, to hanging on, and she had developed muscle. *Just Jesus Alone*. It was easier than hoping, more pleasant than watching and waiting. The Lord was perfect—dependable, steadfast, adoring. *Just You alone,* she whispered.

But somehow, though He strengthened her, God wouldn't give her leave to stop hoping. He required not only that she cling to Him, but that she keep waiting for the promise—for the fulfillment, in this lifetime, of her joy. It was having to hope—the hope and the anxious waiting—that had seemed to sap the last of her strength.

King David, in the days of old, said he would have fainted if he had not believed to see the goodness of the Lord in the land of the living. It seemed to Tonya it was the believing that was making her faint. She believed to see goodness for others. She rejoiced when she saw God work His magnificence and splendor on behalf of others. To believe for it for herself was something else entirely.

Perhaps it was fighting so hard against herself—while part of her steeled itself and committed to just holding on, the other part hoped and waited—that took the last energy she had to comb her hair, to go to the gym, to search for fashions, to shine her light. If God was going to keep His word and send her promise or send someone, it and he were going to have to find her dimmed, dulled, tired, and hidden amidst the rubble and the clutter of her life.

Tonya wouldn't let herself cry about Richard anymore. *I hope he's happy.* She eased her car back into *Drive* and pulled out into the street.

Michelle was wrong about her. It took more energy than she had to try to be desirable and exciting. Jealousy required an emotional mortgage she couldn't afford.

Tonya turned right off of the side street onto the boulevard that would carry her home. She started and stopped with the other drivers and moved forward down the street until her taillights became another pair of tiny red dots indistinguishable in the darkness from the others around her.

onya pulled off her pantyhose and reversed them so that the run would be on the back of her leg. That was good enough. She stood in front of the dryer and secured the end of her ponytail with pins to make a bun.

"Mom-bo, you've got to get a life!" Malik shook his head and smiled from the doorway. "Really, Mom, you have to stop going out of your way to look like you've been thrown away."

It was too early in the morning for this. She closed her eyes. *Jesus!*

"That bun is killing me. For real, Mom. Don't you remember when you used to get your hair done and fix yourself up? You don't have to hide, you know. It's okay for people to see that you're a beautiful woman. Look at those shoes, Mom-bo—they're breaking me down. Do something! You could get some new clothes, or just do something to your hair." Malik smiled, shook his head, and slurped at his orange juice. "I would be satisfied with a hair change. That bun is deadly."

Tonya started gathering her things—lunch, notebooks, purse. "Look, leave me alone early in the morning, okay? I don't have time to fool with my hair. I'm not trying to impress anyone anyway. Not to mention that we don't have—"

"Any money. Not to mention that we don't have any money." Malik laughed. "Mom-ster, that's the biggest excuse in the world. You can always find money for me to get my hair cut, get clothes, or whatever. Just admit you're hiding." He pretended to toast her with his glass. "This is freaking me out to say this to you as a son, but someone's got to do it. You're a good-looking woman and you still got a few hot years left and a few hot assets to show off. You're a beautiful person, and you work hard at that. Other people work out their bodies, but you work out your heart to be beautiful on the in-side. After doing all the work, though, now you're hiding. You've got to get a life. Really." Malik made his voice sound like his im-pression of a professional therapist. "Admitting you have a problem, Mom-bo, is the first step toward the cure."

She reached into a basket that sat on top of the dryer and threw a clean sock across the room. It landed on top of Malik's head. "I don't have time to fool with you, boy." She laughed as she walked to the door. "If you want to straighten out my life, Dr. Freud or whoever you think are, get to school on time and fold up this bas-ket of clothes when you get home."

Malik pulled the sock away and shook his head as she walked out the door. "That's okay. Don't listen to your offspring. I hope Dr. Phil's mom didn't treat him this way."

The office didn't look any less like the dead man's last mile than it had since the blowup with Michelle. Tonya, head down, made her way to her desk. She used to enjoy her job. Now it would be enough just to get through the day. She put her things away then caught her reflection in the mirror glued on the front of her filing cabinet. She patted her hair. It wasn't so bad—her hair wasn't really *deadly*, was it?

"Excuse me, can we talk for a minute?" Tonya almost jumped out of her seat. It couldn't be . . .

It was Michelle.

The elevator doors opened and shut as people got on and off. Most of them were stealing glances, pretending not to be as interested as they were in Tonya and Michelle's conversation.

"I just thought we needed to clear the air. You know, to bury the hatchet."

Tonya couldn't look at Michelle. She looked past her. "I don't know what that means: bury the hatchet." *Other than you want to bury it in my back!* "But if you want us to be civil, I always have been and I always will be." The sooner this was over the better.

"Well, I was thinking that maybe we should have lunch together, or something."

Tonya had to look. Michelle's face was drawn, like it was killing her to talk. "I might have made some mistakes. Maybe." Michelle stopped talking and waited as though she were expecting Tonya to own up to wrongdoing. She was going to be waiting a long time—some really hot places were going to freeze over if Michelle was waiting for her to say anything.

Michelle's jaws were getting tighter. "So, anyway, like I said. I thought we could get together and try to work this out. Maybe we could help each other."

Tonya didn't know how her hands got on her hips, but there they were. She didn't know how her neck got into motion, but it was moving. She forced herself to keep her voice low. "Help me? Me help you? Maybe you don't realize it, Michelle, but I've been *trying* to help you since you *got* here. I've been trying to help you get yourself together so that you can get promoted. Now my own promotion is on the line. Help you? Help you? *Girl*—"

Michelle balled up her hands and put them on her own hips. "Look, lady, I'm just trying to help both of us, okay? I don't know what your malfunction is, but I'm not the one." It was so out of character, but Michelle was actually keeping her voice muted.

"No, you are *exactly* the one. You're the one that stays on the phone—on personal calls—too long. You're the one that's rude to everybody like you don't have any home training. You're the one that thinks the sun and stars rise on your behind. You're the wannabe princess who is about to cost me my job." Tonya could feel her blood pressure rising. She was just going to have to go to the altar and ask God to forgive her later. "Oh, yes, Miss Thing, you're definitely the one!"

Michelle's neck went into overdrive. "Well, if you want to start slinging stuff, Miss Holier-than-Thou, what's up with all those books and stuff? What are you trying to say? Are you stalking me now? And as for the sun rising and setting in me, don't be mad because I love myself and my body and my self-esteem is intact." She looked Tonya up and down. "Don't get an attitude because I know how to dress. Just because you don't have a life except for this chump job, don't take it out on me. So sorry that you don't have a man and I know it bothers you that I don't have that problem, but don't be jealous . . . it makes you look ugly! What you need to do is fix yourself up, get a man, and get a life!"

Fix yourself up! Get a life! Tonya didn't need to hear that, again, today. She didn't need to and she wasn't going to. "Look, Miss Michelle—"

"Hey! Hey, ladies!" Shadrach stepped out of an open elevator. "Just the women I wanted to see." He grabbed them both by the arms, smiled like nothing was going on, and ever so quickly took them into the stairwell. Once they were behind the door, his smile faded. "I don't guess there's any point in asking what's going on here?" He dropped their arms.

Michelle pointed at Tonya and told Shadrach how she had been trying to make amends, to begin a new era of cooperation. "She got all huffy." Michelle rolled her eyes and turned her back to Tonya. "I don't know why she copped an attitude."

"She's the one." Tonya pointed at Michelle. She told Shadrach that Michelle had approached her, but that she came at her like she expected Tonya to apologize, and that was pretty clear or they wouldn't be in the stairwell now. "I'm just not going to take any more of her stuff. I've had it."

Shadrach looked from woman to woman and shook his head. "I guess I'll never understand women. Why can't you work together? Here are the two of you—both of you should be helping each other. What is the problem?"

He put his hands at his belt line and rocked back and forth as though he was about to start coaching. "Look, I know both of you got your own thing going on. But this—what you're doing in this office—has to be a team effort. You all have to work together. You all are the only two sisters in your office. You should be helping each other. You have to put aside your individual issues so that you can work together to help each other grow. You see what I'm saying?"

Tonya looked at Michelle, who turned her eyes away toward the wall above Tonya's head. Tonya followed suit.

Shad sighed. "No, I guess you don't. Well, I'm going to take control of this situation." He shook his head. "You two grown women, you two shining examples of beautiful black womanhood need a coach? Well, I'm signing on for the job. The two of you are going to get together and we're going to work on this thing like you're running drills to play in a game. You are going to get it together here." He took their right hands in his two hands. "The first thing you're going to do is shake hands."

Michelle jerked her hand away. "I'm not shaking her hand. I tried to bury the hatchet."

Tonya pulled her hand away from Shadrach's hand. "Yeah, you tried to bury the hatchet all right. Right in my back!" She finally said out loud what she had been thinking before.

Shadrach grabbed their hands again. "That's the last of that. You two are going to work together or else. I'm not asking you. I'm *telling* you. Now, you two shake hands."

Michelle didn't move, so Tonya didn't move.

"I didn't *ask* you ladies to shake. I'm *telling* you. Now, shake hands."

Tonya and Michelle shook hands like something was going to rub off—some foul-smelling thing was going to transfer, some slimy substance was going to be exchanged when they touched each other. It was more of a hand touch or slide than a shake.

Shadrach slapped one of his hands to his forehead. "You two are worse than two little kids fighting on a playground. But I tell you what, I'm going to get you two together, or my name is not Shadrach Malone. Now, go to your separate corners—your separate desks—and we'll meet tomorrow for lunch. And don't bother bringing a note from home little girls. No excuses accepted."

All that day, Tonya could hear Michelle whispering on the phone. The telephone would ring, then Michelle would begin whispering and looking in her direction. Tonya watched as she slammed drawers, pounded the stapler, and banged cabinet doors. Once her cell phone even went off. "I told you don't call me on this phone during the day. You're using up my minutes. Call me back on the other line." When the phone rang, Michelle answered and began whispering again. Tonya couldn't make out the words, but she knew Michelle was talking about her.

Tonya thought of approaching her about using the phone for personal calls. Really, for just being on the phone all day. She had the authority to write Michelle up—she should document it, write a memorandum for record—it was what she deserved and Mrs. Judson would approve.

No excuses accepted. She had done everything she could to make things work with Michelle. It was impossible. But she would wait. If Shadrach wanted to try to coach them to some sort of reconciliation, she wasn't going to be the one to mess it up—Michelle would take care of that. Shadrach would see soon enough what was going on

with the ghetto princess. Tonya looked at Michelle, who was looking at her and still whispering on the phone.

No one would be able to accuse Tonya of casting the first
stone . . . or of backing down this time.

Chapter Fourteen

he note, on a piece of white spiral notebook paper with frayed edges, lay in the center of the kitchen table.

Hey, Mom-bo!

I know you remember, but I wanted to remind you anyway that I left early this morning for the football trip.

Really, I'm writing because I hope you are thinking about what I said, okay? You know, about getting a life—a new life. You want great things for everybody else. You want everyone you come in contact with to have the best. You put your whole self into making everybody's dream come true—with your prayers, your money, and your advice.

You know what makes me sad, though, Mom-bo? It's that you give the best to everyone else and you barely give yourself the leftover crumbs. I want you to live, Mom.

If you can't do it for yourself, do it for me. Just like you're happy to see me explode—to see good things happen for me—I feel the same about you. I want to look at my Mom-bo and see her happy, you know? I know God wants to see you happy. And I think both of us want to see you get rid of that bun! Just kidding there, Mom-ster.

But seriously, Mom, I want to see you smile again. You owe it to me to let me see my mother shine. Let me see you come back to life. Come on, Mom. Don't be afraid. Live! Let me see that there really is life after death—even after the death of a son.

Peace, love, and hair grease!

Malik

Tonya stuffed the note into her purse. It kept her all the way to work, into the building, and through the morning. The note made her feel good. It made her feel real good. Tonya didn't know if she could explain to anyone why.

Maybe it was just having someone care enough about her to take time to write a letter. Maybe it was seeing God do what He promised—to see Him turning her little boy into a thoughtful, considerate man was a blessing. It might have been that in her son's note she felt the caress of a new wind. Malik, like Isaiah the writer and prophet in the days of old, might be heralding that good news was on the way. He might be singing a praise of new life to come.

Whatever the case, despite the fact that Michelle still frowned and Mrs. Judson still threatened, Tonya felt herself responding to her son's words. She walked down the aisles with just a little more spring in her step. She lifted the phone from its base with just the slightest bit of a flourish. She turned on her radio and started to hum—the faintest traces of a song had begun to bubble up from her heart.

Malik's letter, his act of love, carried her through the morning and even walked her to the restaurant booth to meet with Michelle and Shadrach. "Good afternoon," Tonya said when she slid into place.

Shadrach had chosen well. The restaurant was quiet and the eating spaces—surrounded by plants—had an air of privacy. The booth was *u*-shaped and Shadrach sat in the middle. The State Department could have made use of his diplomatic skills.

He looked back and forth at the two of them. "It's good to be eating lunch with both of you ladies." His eyes kept lingering on Tonya, as though he was trying to figure something out. "Did you do something differently, to your hair or something? For some reason, you look different."

Tonya smiled. "No, just the same old routine."

Shadrach looked again. "All right, then." Michelle glared, but Tonya ignored her. Shadrach waved at the waitress. "Let's get on with lunch and our meeting." He checked his watch. "We're still on the clock."

He dipped a tortilla chip in the bowl of salsa that the waitress placed on the table. "So, do either of you have any ideas about how we ought to handle this?"

Michelle looked at Shadrach. "I thought you had all that worked out, Shad. I was looking to you to take care of it."

He nodded. "What about you, Tonya?"

"I'm following you."

"Okay, ladies. Well, I'm a straight-up kind of man. I don't believe in sugar-coating things. You both know that about me. So, I figured the best approach was to face this head on. You know—to figure out what it is that you two are beefing about. There's no way to do that without just coming at each other with the truth."

Tonya nodded. Michelle pursed her lips.

"So, what I figured was we need to have some order to it. It doesn't get anywhere going back and forth, doing the he said, she said thing. You all feelin' me?"

The waitress came back to the table to refresh their chips and their drinks. "Is everything all right?" She was a pretty girl. "Are you ready for me to take your order?" They nodded and made their selections.

When the girl walked away, Shadrach resumed. "So, like I said, one at a time. One person says what they don't like. The other person responds, not by telling the other person what's wrong with her, but by responding to the comments. The last thing, is to come to some common ground."

Michelle dipped a chip in the salsa. "What do you mean by common ground, Shad?"

"I mean areas that you two can agree need to be changed and ways that you're going to get that change. It means finding the places where you *respectfully* agree to disagree. Ain't no point in sitting here just jerking your jaws. You sisters are in trouble, whether you know it or not. You need something real to happen before somebody gets fired, locked up, or both."

Tonya reached for a chip. "What we need is prayer."

"Yeah, no doubt about that. You won't get a fight from me on that one." Shadrach nodded. "But you need more than faith. You're going to have to do something. What is that saying about faith and works?"

Tonya spoke quickly. "Faith without works is dead." Michelle frowned and looked away from the table. She looked as though she was feeling excluded.

"Yeah, that's the one. Faith without works is dead. I'm going to leave you two ladies to let faith be your homework. From where I sit, you're going to need faith to get you out of this one. Mrs. Judson don't play, and I think the shoe is about to fall. But . . . you know, you all pray about it."

Tonya stared at Shadrach while he spoke. She had never heard him say anything about God. He was a good person, but she had never heard anything from him about the Lord. You never knew about people.

You still got some hot years left. Tonya thought about Malik's letter. Could Shad find someone like her attractive? But, she and Michelle had more important things to think about—like whether they were going to be able to keep their jobs. Tonya moved her attention back to the conversation.

"So, like I said, you two ladies let that be your homework. What we're going to deal with here is the works part. And you're going to have to leave your attitudes and your feelings at home or at your desk. You don't have time to waste, and I sure don't. So, are we agreed?"

"Yes." Tonya watched and waited for Michelle's response. She was sure to show her true colors before it was all over.

Michelle rolled her eyes. "I guess so. But who's going first?" It was unbelievable how much attitude flowed out of the girl.

Shadrach smiled at her. "Why don't you go first, Michelle. It looks like you got the biggest issue at the moment."

Michelle adjusted her seat. "Be up front, right?

"Right."

"Just let out what's on my mind?"

"Let it out, sister."

"Well, since you brought up faith and praying, let's talk about it." Michelle glared across the table at Tonya. "I'm tired of being insulted, like nobody knows anything about the Lord or about the Bible but you. You don't know me. You don't know anything about me or where I come from."

Tonya felt like her face had been slapped. She looked at Shadrach, expecting him to say something. He simply looked back and forth between Michelle and her. Tonya cleared her throat. "I don't know what you mean."

"I don't know what you mean." Michelle mocked her, widening her eyes and dramatically pressing her hand against her bosom.

Shadrach folded his arms across his chest and looked at Michelle. "Okay, let's set some ground rules here. You can be as blunt as you want to be, but don't be mean just to be mean. I'm not here to watch you all just do what you can do without me." Shadrach took a drink of soda. "Okay, let's try that one again." He nodded at Tonya.

"I said, I don't know what you mean." Maybe this was a worse idea than she'd thought. There was no point in sitting here being insulted. She didn't have to use her lunch hour for that.

"What I mean is, you act like you're the only one who knows anything about the Bible. And like you're the only person who knows how to pray."

"That's not true."

"Well, why would you buy me all those little books and that Bible and leave them on my desk like the Easter Bunny?"

Shadrach raised an eyebrow. "Michelle?"

"Okay. Tonya knows what I mean." She looked at Tonya. "So why would you do that then?"

"I was trying to be nice. I was just trying to show you that I cared about you. I knew you had been going through a tough time lately—"

"And that's the other thing, Tonya! You are always nosing in my business!"

Shadrach grunted and threw down an imaginary flag. "One thing at a time, ladies. Finish what you started, Michelle."

Michelle huffed. "Okay, then. So, why all the books and stuff if you're not trying to tell me I need to be more holy? More like you?"

"I just thought . . . I just . . . the books helped me. I thought they might help you. I felt like I was supposed . . . Oh, what difference does it make?"

Shadrach blew the whistle. "You can't just stop talking because you feel uncomfortable. You have to stay in the game."

"What's the point? Michelle hates me. She's already made up her mind. It doesn't matter what I say."

"You're just feeling defensive. You just want to play defense, or the safe martyr, but you got to talk back. Okay, Tonya, so tell Michelle what you were doing."

The waitress came with their plates. "Be careful, please. They are very hot." They waited until she left to begin talking again. It gave Tonya time to think.

"I don't know, Michelle. When I was in trouble—not that I'm not still having trouble—those books helped me. One of the hardest things about going through was going through alone. I just wanted you to know that I cared. That I wasn't just someone you worked with, that I was here for you." She looked down at her plate. "I didn't know how to say it to you, I guess. I gave you what helped me." She looked Michelle in the eye. "I really wasn't trying to insult you."

"Mm-hmm." Michelle was still giving much attitude. "Well, I do know the Bible. Okay? I used to go to church. If I do or don't go now, that's my business, okay? I didn't come here for friends. I came here to work. That's all."

Tonya bit her tongue. It wasn't her turn.

Michelle looked at Shadrach. "Can we go on to another point, now?"

"Okay. It just sounds like a small misunderstanding that happens all the time. Maybe Tonya tried to give you a gift, but what she gave you was something that she liked. But you weren't feeling her. Every time she gave you another gift of the same kind, you got madder and madder, right?"

"You got that right." Michelle jabbed her fork into her tamale.

"So is there something you two ladies could do different next time? Like maybe, Michelle, you could tell Tonya how you feel about the gifts—just tell her you don't like them."

Michelle waved the fork—sauce, shredded pork, and corn cake on the end—back and forth to emphasize each word. "I don't like them!"

Shad looked exasperated. "I mean, next time tell her before things get this bad. And next time, Tonya, talk to Michelle, right? Didn't you notice that she didn't like what you were doing?"

"I just thought she didn't like me. I didn't think." Maybe she hadn't thought about anything. Like maybe she hadn't considered that this—this meeting, this roasting—was really a bad idea.

Michelle looked like she was biting her tongue. The blood rushed to her face. She took a deep breath, collected herself, and looked back at Shadrach. "Can we move on now?"

"Yes." He took a forkful of food from his plate.

Michelle's narrowed gaze settled on Tonya. "The other thing I don't like is how you watch me. When I come in, you're looking at the clock. When I'm on the phone, you're going back and forth in front of my desk. What is up with that? I hate that. I came in here to work, not for you to be my slave master." Shadrach's face said, "Oh no she didn't?"

Tonya looked down at her plate. Why had she agreed to this? What about this had made it seem like it was going to be a good idea? "Look, Michelle, I know you don't believe this, but on my own, I could care less when you go or come. Really. Talking about people, if you really knew me, you would know that's the last thing I worry about. But Mrs. Judson—"

"We're not talking about Mrs. Judson. I'm talking about you."

Tonya put her hand in her purse and moved it about until she found Malik's note. "But that's just the point. It *is* about Mrs. Judson. This is her office. It's her rules and her judgments that get us promoted or fired. Because I listen to her, because I'm in meetings with her, I know what she likes and what she doesn't like. What she doesn't like is employees who don't come to work on time. It doesn't matter that it's okay with me. Mrs. Judson doesn't like it and it's my responsibility—" Michelle rolled her eyes in disgust at that. "No, honestly. In all honesty, I'm trying to look out for you. I guess I'm trying to protect you from yourself. Mrs. Judson is not going to promote anybody who can't get to work on time and who takes personal phone calls habitually. What I call myself doing is trying to cover for you without saying anything. I'm trying to give you big hints that you need to get to work on time and get off the phone."

Tonya frowned. "I guess I just need to be like Shadrach says. I just need to be straight up with you."

Shadrach nodded.

Tonya rubbed Malik's note back and forth between her fingers. She needed courage. "Okay, here's straight up. If you think I'm trying to mind your business or be in your personal life, you are wrong. I got enough issues and business of my own to keep me busy for a lifetime. Personally, I don't care what you do. Business-wise, Mrs. Judson hates it, and she pays me to take care of it so that she doesn't have to deal with it." She looked squarely at Michelle.

"Get to work on time and get off the phone, Michelle, or Mrs. Judson isn't going to promote you; she'll fire you. Those behaviors, she feels, let her know how much respect you have for the people around you and how committed you are to working here. Do it, or I'm going to have to start writing you up, because my job, as long as I'm here, is to make sure that you do what Mrs. Judson wants done. That's as straight up as I can get."

Michelle looked away from the table.

"I don't want to make you feel bad. I really am trying to help you get promoted, Michelle. I want to be your friend. Maybe that's impossible at this point—but that's what I want. Everybody in authority is not trying to hurt you. I'm not against you. There are some rules you just have to follow. If I insulted you giving you the books and sending you flowers, I won't do it anymore. But the other—the phone and getting to work on time—is not negotiable. That's the deal."

Shadrach looked at his watch. "Well, ladies, it looks like Round One is over." He chuckled, as though he was attempting to lighten the mood. "I thought this was football, but I see both you ladies are wearing gloves. Move over, Muhammad Ali." He pointed at their plates. "I say we box up this food. Handle up on this conversation and think it over. See you tomorrow, same time, different restaurant."

He mimicked ringing a boxing-match bell. *Ding! Ding!*

Chapter Fifteen

onya dragged into the chicken wing restaurant where they had agreed to meet. Why was she even doing this? She rubbed Malik's note, which was tucked into her jacket pocket. None of this was feeling like a new day to her. It was feeling like hard work. Wasn't walking into your season supposed to be easy?

Shadrach waved her over to a table in the far corner. Michelle was already sitting. "How are you two ladies today?"

Tonya forced herself to smile—just barely. Michelle looked at her and then looked away.

"Making progress and changing ain't easy." Shadrach looked down at the menu. "That's why most people never do it. That's why most people just talk about it. Building relationships is just like building a body—no pain, no gain. Being successful takes a lot of hard work."

He flipped the laminated menu over. "I don't even know why

I'm looking at this thing. It's a chicken-wing place. What else is there to order?"

A waiter took their order—wings and several different sauces. After the waiter brought drinks and left, Shadrach wove his fingers together and laid his hands on his chest. "Round Two."

Tonya kept rubbing on Malik's note. She looked around the room.

"Tonya?"

"I really don't have anything to say, Shadrach. I mean, I said all I needed to say yesterday." She shrugged.

"You're in the game, Tonya. You got to play."

"I don't see how this—"

"Tonya, baby, you got the ball. It's your round. Whatever."

She kept fingering Malik's note and playing with her napkin with her free hand. "Well, what I don't understand is what all this attitude is about. All this anger. Where does all this anger come from?"

Michelle waited before she spoke. "I'm not angry, okay? I'm just taking care of myself. I'm letting you know what's on my mind."

"Can't you let me know what's on your mind without yelling at me, without disrespecting me?"

Michelle looked like she was ready to leap over the table. Her expression said that what was on her mind was a beat-down.

"Yeah, I suppose I can talk to you without yelling." She looked around the restaurant, then back at Tonya. "Anything else?" Her eyes spat anger.

"Well . . ."

"Look, the sooner we do this, the sooner it will be over. Just spit it out, okay?"

Shadrach stepped in again. "Give her a chance, Michelle. She gets to run her offense like she chooses. You let her bring the game to you."

Michelle moved her fork to the other side of her place setting. "Yeah. Whatever."

"Go ahead, Tonya."

Tonya cleared her throat. She might as well plunge in. "I really feel like part of the reason you don't like me is because I'm trying to be nice to you. It's not just the books; you resent the idea of anybody being nice to you. Or maybe you just don't trust people that are trying to be nice to you."

Michelle looked at Shadrach. "What does this have to do with anything?"

"It's Tonya's offense. Let her bring it."

Tonya cleared her throat. "You said yesterday that you didn't come to work looking for friends. It might be that you really can't *accept* anyone who wants to be your friend. That you have a problem with anyone who wants to be good to you—you have to find a way to make what they're trying to do bad. You have to make it be about the person trying to hurt you in some way."

Michelle glared at Tonya, then looked at Shadrach. "I thought we couldn't say things to hurt each other."

"Tonya's just saying what she thinks. She's not being mean. I'll check her when I feel it's needed. You let me be the referee, okay?"

Michelle frowned at Tonya. "Anything else?"

She was too far out in the water to turn back now. "Michelle, it just seems that . . . okay, the other day you said I was jealous of you. It just seems like you have all these feelings about me that don't have anything to do with how *I'm* feeling. What do you mean, I'm jealous of you?"

Michelle looked at Shad. "Can I answer that?" He nodded. "Let me be real. I think you're jealous of the way I look."

"Michelle, you're kidding yourself. You look very nice all the time. I might think some of it is just a cover, but I give you that. You look nice, but why would you think I'm jealous?"

"Okay, you want to know? You act like everything you're doing is because of Mrs. Judson. But truth be told, I think some of it is you. I think you *are* jealous. I think you're jealous because I'm still young and your life is fading away. You're jealous of how I look, that I get attention from men, and that I have a life."

Hot spots exploded on Tonya's cheeks. "I have a life!"

"Where is it?"

"I don't have to talk to you about this." Tonya looked at Shadrach, but he was silent.

The waiter returned with the order. When he left, Michelle took a wing from the plate and resumed talking. "You can bring me books and a Bible because you're worried about my private life—my spiritual life—but I can't tell you about your issues. Don't you think something is wrong with that?"

"Look, Michelle, I'm not trying to run your life."

Michelle trailed her wing through the barbecue sauce. "We're not talking about you running my life, we're talking about you not having one. What are you saying? You can look at me and see my faults, but you're too good, or I'm not good enough to see yours?"

She leaned forward. "You know one of the things that makes me most not want to go to church? It's women like you. Why would I want to go to church if it's going to make me shrivel up and die? Isn't God supposed to give you life?"

Tonya looked away. She felt invaded, violated, under attack.

"Why would I want to read the books you read if I'm going to end up all washed out, lonely, and tired? I mean, does being saved mean you have to look so sad? I don't care what you're wearing, if it's a long dress, or whatever—do you have to look bad all the time? Does it mean you have to stop having fun? Because if that's what it means, I don't want it. If that's what it means, stop trying to put it off on me."

Michelle jabbed at the table with the index finger of her free hand. "Tonya, you keep telling me what Mrs. Judson likes. Well, I also know that she likes for the people in her office to look profes-sional. You come in here with your hair barely combed and wearing stockings with runs in them. How do you think Mrs. Judson feels about that?"

Tonya folded and unfolded her napkin. She was not going to let Michelle make her cry.

"You said you could see that I was going through a hard time? Well, I can see that you're going through a hard time, too. I might cover mine up, but you wear yours all over you. Or maybe you use your hard times to cover up having to have any real feelings."

Michelle's wing waved wildly as she spoke. "Did it ever occur to you, Tonya, that I don't like seeing people push you around and walk all over you in the office. I get mad because I want to see you stand up for yourself. You may be fighting for me, but I don't see you fighting for yourself. Why are you a team leader? You're doing the same work as the managers, taking the same heat, but I don't see you demanding the same money. What about that?"

Tonya squeezed the note in her hand.

"I never had anyone in my life who looked like me that was in charge. I want to be proud of you. I want to see the other people in the office watching you and be proud. Maybe I'm shallow, but I want to see you look good. I want to see you look happy. You're the only representative I have in the office—I want to see you look like you're in control. Maybe I'm not being realistic, but I want to see you look like a sister that has it all together."

Tonya rubbed Malik's note with her thumb. "I—I've been through a lot. My son . . . and my husband . . . my marriage . . . Everything is on me, now. You don't understand."

"There's no excuse, Tonya. What you don't understand is that I've been through stuff too in my life. Okay? I'm younger than you, but I've been through things you couldn't even imagine. I may not have it all together, but one thing I know. I am not going to die. I'm not going to roll over and play dead. And I'm sure not going to bury my own self."

Tonya could feel tears burning her eyes. She was not going to let them fall. But her mouth, despite how hard she fought to keep it from happening, turned into a frown.

Michelle wasn't finished. "You might be having a hard time, but you're not having a hard time every day. You could do something with yourself *sometime*. And you may be right, Tonya, I may be having a hard time accepting friendship from people. Maybe I am running from the Lord—not that that's any of your business—but maybe the only love *you* know how to accept is from the Lord. Maybe I am trying to hide behind the way I look. Did you ever think that you might be doing the same thing? That you might be covering up with your tiredness and sadness? Did you ever think that you might be hiding? Tonya, when was the last time you had a conversation with a man?"

Shadrach signaled to the waiter. "Check, please?" When the waiter left the table Shadrach looked at Tonya and Michelle. "I think we just finished Round Two."

Ding! Ding!

he stood in Malik's doorway and watched him playing a video game. The animated character he was controlling rode a motorcycle on a track that dipped and dove, that had all sorts of obstacles. At one point in the run, the character had to make a jump. Each time Malik attempted the jump, the rider fell, and the game sent them—Malik and the character—back to the beginning of the run. Tonya shook her head and leaned against the doorway. "How can you stand to keep doing that? How many times are you going to do that?"

Malik looked at Tonya and smiled.

"Until I get it right, Mom-bo. I just keep doing it until I get it right. If you want to win, you have to keep trying until you get it right."

Changing is hard work. She could hear Shadrach's voice. "Someone said almost the same thing to me today."

"Must have been a great mind." Malik grinned at her and touched a finger to his head. "Great minds think alike."

She laughed and looked around for a sock or something she could throw. "Whatever, Malik." She watched him try the round again. "Malik, can I ask you something?"

He leaned forward to try to make the killer jump in the video game. "Sure, Mom-ster. What's up?"

"That's okay. You go ahead and play. I shouldn't be bothering you."

His character fell again, and he switched off the game and turned to face her. "All right, Mom, I'm all yours."

"That's okay, Malik." She turned and walked toward the kitchen, but he followed and sat on the edge of the table. "Malik, get off of there. You know we don't sit on the table." She popped at him with a dish towel.

"Stop! Police! Help!" He slid off the table onto a kitchen chair. "You got to stop being so violent, Mom-bo!" He laughed and held up his arms as though he was fending off blows. Then he dropped his arms. "Okay, Mom. What's the deal? I'm all ears."

She lifted the lid to check on the squash she was cooking. "I shouldn't be talking to you about this."

He looked around the room. "Unless you see somebody that I don't see, Mom-bo, I don't see that we got much choice here."

"Boy, if you don't stop that smart-mouth." She laughed and swatted at him with the towel again.

"Why so much violence, Mom? Why? Can't we all just get along?" Tonya laughed and turned back to the stove. "So what is it, Mom? For you to even bring it up, it must have been bothering you for a while. Go ahead, Mom, I'm man enough; I can take it."

"It's just something that happened at work."

"Work? Is that why you've been so uptight? That's how it always is, isn't it?" He pretended to have a hangman's noose around his neck. "They make you mad at work, so you come home and take it out on the kids."

"Malik, give me a break. I don't know why I even brought it up."

"Okay, I'm through kidding. Come on, Mom-bo. Spit it out."

She sat down across from him. "Malik, do you think I'm dead?"

He threw back his head and howled. "Mom. Come on."

"I don't mean literally. I mean, you know?"

"You mean like what I've been talking to you about? Like the hair and everything?"

Tonya held her breath and nodded.

"I don't think you're really dead, Mom. I think you've just gotten tired of trying. I think you're just stuck in a loop and it's easier to stay where you are, than to work to get out. You're not dead, you're hibernating."

"So you think there's something wrong with me?"

"No, I think you're human, Mom. Humans tend to do what's easy, what takes the least amount of effort. I think you're tired, and I think it's been a long time—maybe you've lost a little confidence. It's been easier to be tired than it has been to change it." He shrugged. "We usually stay where we are until someone or something happens that makes it harder to stay than it is to move forward." Malik rested his elbows on the table. "So, what's the matter, Mom-bo?"

"Nothing really. Just someone at work that was saying I should fix myself up. Look out for myself. That's all."

He sat back. "The same kind of stuff I've been saying. Good. He or she must really like you. I'm glad you're making friends." Malik smiled. "You're going to need something to do when the nest gets empty."

Tonya wasn't about to tell Malik that Michelle wasn't her friend. She certainly wasn't going to tell him that Michelle didn't like her at all, that they had been arguing. *"She must really like you."* That was an overstatement if ever she had heard one.

He raised an eyebrow. "Is it a man?"

"Malik!" She certainly wasn't going to tell him about Shadrach—not that there was anything to tell.

Tonya didn't tell Malik, but she thought about the afternoon's conversation—Round Two—and about what Malik, Michelle, and Shadrach had said to her as she washed dishes. She thought about it on the way to prayer meeting, and she thought about it on her knees.

God, if this is You, if this is You troubling the waters—then, okay. Help me to know that it's You. Help me to see myself. You are magnificent. You are mighty. You are the God of the whole universe. Nothing is too hard for You.

Maybe I have been stuck too long. It doesn't seem possible that somebody could get used to being tired and miserable, but if that's what I've done, or if that's who I am, then help me to see myself. If You want me to move forward, then show me how. Show me where to go. All I know how to do is what I've been doing.

If I'm hiding out, being safe instead of casting out to deep water, then give me the courage to change. Give me the determination to keep doing it until I get it right. You are glorious and there is no shadow of turning in You. Help me to reflect Your beauty and Your light.

Lord, I don't want to be sad and tired—I want to give You glory. I'm sick and tired of being sick and tired. Let all that I am reflect who You are. Don't let me miss my season. Help me to see any doors that You are opening for me. Help me to see doors that You are closing.

God if I'm not where You want me to be, then move me. Don't leave me alone in the wilderness of grief and complacency. God You are the God who heals. If You don't change me or heal me, nothing will be changed. Move with me and show me the way to go. Be a pillar of cloud before me in the day, and be a pillar of fire before me at night.

And, God, while You heal my broken places, while You look after my son and me, look after Michelle. Bless her where she needs to be blessed. Help me to show her love that she can accept. Help me not to be offended, so that I can hear the truth in what she's trying to say to me.

And, God, You are our Banner, our Protector, our Strong Tower. You are the God who can turn the heart of a King. Lord, turn Mrs. Judson's heart. Lord, in Jesus' name, lead me and help me to get it right. Amen.

Chapter Seventeen

rs. Judson's office seemed infinitely wide and deep. Her desk was sterile and mammoth. Everything in the room bespoke wealth and power. The gray-haired woman sat behind her desk in a rich, chocolate-brown leather chair and peered over her glasses at Tonya. It felt like she was lost in the ocean and a wave was about to come crashing down on her. "I had hoped to speak with you this morning about Michelle—to see if we might quickly resolve the matter and move forward. However—" She looked at her cell phone. "—I have some pressing business that won't wait." She set the phone down. "I also have a week-long meeting out of the country. We'll have to resume this meeting in two weeks when I return."

Mrs. Judson's face told Tonya she was dismissed. "Perhaps this will give you some time to strategize and to solve this dilemma, in the manner that best serves the company—and yourself."

Tonya left the office with the same feeling she always had: Mrs.

Judson's office tried too hard. It was too big, as though it was intended to compensate for something else. It was too plush. It seemed to be hiding something.

Two weeks. Well, at least it was two weeks more than what Mrs. Judson had intended. It would give Tonya a chance to work things out with Michelle, to try to get things in order before Mrs. Judson got back.

She looked across the room. Michelle had come in on time.

And I bought new stockings.

Of course, that didn't mean everything was okay and settled. It might be a start, but it might not be. It was too soon to tell.

As she left Mrs. Judson's office and passed by Michelle's desk, she could hear her talking. "Todd, I'm not trying to give you the brush-off. You'll have to call me at home." Michelle paused. "I know I've been doing it all this time." Another pause. "Things have just changed, Todd. Don't read a lot into it, okay? Instead of talking at work, you're going to have to start calling me at home. I don't know how many different ways I can say it. I'm not trying to get rid of you. I just can't talk about it here. Not now. Not anymore. Call me tonight."

Michelle hung up the phone and glanced up at Tonya. Neither woman said anything.

Tonya and Michelle worked hard that morning—at least they worked hard at staying out of each other's way. If one went to the copy machine, the other waited until she had returned. There were no tandem bathroom runs and no twin retreats to the coffeepot or to the water fountain. They were cavalierly, intentionally distant. That is, until five minutes before twelve.

Tonya rose coolly from her seat, hoping Michelle wouldn't hear her heart pounding or see her knees knocking. She only had two weeks—someone had to take a chance. She might as well get it over with. She walked across the burning desert, across a gully of quicksand, across a long and terrible tundra to reach Michelle's desk. "I was hoping we could walk downstairs together."

Michelle looked wary. "Okay." Tonya could feel other people in the office watching them as they talked, then as they walked to the elevator. She could imagine the speculation. *Do you think Tonya's firing her? How do you think Michelle will take it? Who's going to call security?* They were professional observers—they would watch, but no one would lift a hand, not even a finger, to help.

Tonya pushed the button to send the elevator down. She wasn't sure what to say to Michelle. *Help me, Lord.* Michelle's shoulders were stiff and she stared straight ahead. She looked tense, as though she was ready to leap at the first opportunity.

When the door opened, they still hadn't exchanged any words. Someone had to say something. "Shadrach said to meet at the Chinese food restaurant, right?" Of course he did, but she had to say something.

Michelle nodded. "Yes, the Chinese food restaurant."

Tonya took a deep breath and plunged. "I know this hasn't been easy for either one of us—at least, it hasn't been easy for me. But I appreciate Shadrach trying. I appreciate what he's trying to do."

"Yeah."

"Mrs. Judson is gone away for two weeks. She told me, before she left, how she wants this situation handled—" *Easy does it. Not too much, not too little.* "—and I want you to know that I've been thinking about it, and I've made a decision—"

"Look, Tonya, why don't we wait until we get to the restaurant. I don't want to do this on an elevator. I would appreciate if you said whatever you have to say to me in front of Shad." Michelle folded her arms.

They were quiet the rest of the way down, when they entered the restaurant, and when they were seated. After Shadrach was seated, he held up three fingers. "Round Three," he said. "I think you two have worked through a lot. You might be feeling a little tender, but I think when the bruises heal—I think you all have a chance to do something real. So today why don't you just let it flow? Just talk—whatever you want to talk about."

Michelle frowned and crossed her legs. Her shoulders looked even more stiff and tight. "Tonya started telling me something on the elevator." She looked at Shadrach and avoided looking at Tonya. "I told her whatever she said, I wanted her to say it in front of you." She tossed her head. "You know, it really doesn't matter. I'm going to survive, no matter what." Michelle refolded her arms across her chest. "It just seems to me that we should see this through to the end before we start making decisions about things. What's the point of doing this, or starting this, if we're not going to see it through to the end?"

Shadrach just listened. He leaned back, folded his arms, and looked at Tonya.

Why was Michelle always so uptight? "Yes, I told Michelle—or I started telling her that Mrs. Judson was going to be out of the office for two weeks." Tonya turned her attention to Michelle. "Mrs. Judson made it pretty clear what her opinion was, but I've been praying, Michelle."

Michelle rolled her eyes. "What's new?" Shadrach looked at Michelle but remained quiet.

"It's probably not professional, and it's probably not what any management consultants would recommend." Tonya laughed softly. "It's not even what my pocketbook recommends. But . . ." She couldn't believe she was about to say what she was about to say. "I . . . it's all or nothing, Michelle. When you got hired, I was part of that. I thought you were smart and qualified. I still think you're smart and qualified. But . . ."

Michelle did a kind of sitting swagger. "There's always a *but*."

Tonya went on. "But like we talked about, some things have to change."

"It's only been a day. What do you expect in a day?"

"Michelle, I'm trying to tell you something. I'm just having a hard time saying it."

"You want me to say it for you? I'm a big girl. I been through worse before and I might have to go through worse again. You play the hand you get dealt." Michelle threw her hands up in the air. "Big news! Mrs. Judson wants me fired! So what's new?"

An older woman came to take their order. "You want hot tea?" Tonya nodded. "Just one tea?" She looked at Shadrach and Michelle. "You want cola, ice tea, ginger ale?" Michelle and Shadrach both indicated cola.

When the old woman walked away with the order, Michelle resumed speaking. "Mrs. Judson wants me fired? Okay, you work for her. I got it figured out, okay? I'm smart enough to figure it out. Why should you put yourself out for me? It's okay, *sis-tuh*. You don't have to feel uncomfortable saying what you have to say—I can make it on my own."

See? I told you so, Michelle's eyes said to Shadrach.

What was all the attitude? Tonya looked at Michelle then at Shadrach. There was no figuring it out; she just needed to say what she had to say. "Like I said, I'm having a hard time saying this. You're right, it's just been a day, or two days. That's not enough time to make a judgment on something that can impact a person's life—or, really, the lives of all the people that are linked to that one. You're right, it's not enough time. But we don't have time. After meeting with Mrs. Judson, I realized that."

She might as well get it over with. "So I've made a decision and I need to tell it to you now."

Chapter Eighteen

he waitress walked to the table balancing a tray on her shoulder. She carried a small collapsible stand with her, which she unfolded with one hand. She set the tray on it and began to lift lids off the covered plates. "Shrimp fried rice." She nodded at Shadrach and set the steaming plate in front of him. "Chicken with mixed vegetables with tofu." She slid the hot plate in front of Tonya, then she nodded at Michelle. "You gonna like this one. Pepper steak, extra onion."

Michelle nodded, but made no move to touch her food. She kept her arms folded.

"Enjoy." The old woman nodded and walked away.

Tonya laid her napkin across her lap and lifted her fork. "You're right, it's not enough time. But sometimes, you have to just go with what you feel. There's been a lot of friction between us. I understand some of it better now. Not all of it, but it's some better. We started two days ago. Mrs. Judson doesn't know that. She doesn't know about any of this. She just knows that she has a situation she doesn't like and she wants me to take care of it. That's my job. That's how I keep the roof over my head. That's how I feed my son."

Michelle unfolded her arms and adjusted her jacket. She touched a shimmering hot pink baby fingernail to the corner of her mouth, as if to move something away—something she could feel that the other two could not see. "Yeah, well, we've all got responsibilities."

"Exactly. So I thought about our conversations, about what it would take to change and make things better. You came in on time, today, Michelle. I appreciate that. That doesn't mean you're going to come on time from now on, but I appreciate what you did today. I saw you on the phone when I walked by—"

"See, Shad? See what I mean? She's looking all the time to catch me doing something wrong." Michelle turned her head away from the table.

"Let her finish, Michelle." He touched her on the arm. "Let her finish."

"Michelle, I couldn't help but hear when I walked by. You were trying to get off the phone." Tonya picked at her food with her fork. "You know, Michelle, I only had the energy—or the courage—to buy new stockings. I started putting on an old pair this morning. But I heard your voice talking to me. I stopped at the store on the way in and bought a new pair. I wouldn't have done that if you hadn't talked to me. I can't promise anybody that I'm never going to just put on a pair with a run and twist them around. I hope I don't, but I might slip. But today I tried."

Tonya patted her hair. "All night I thought about my hair. I thought about changing it, but I didn't. Maybe I didn't have the courage. It might have been too public a change—or it might have brought me too far out in the open. But I thought about it, which is progress. I didn't have the courage to change my hair, but I do have the courage to take a stand."

Michelle looked at her. "And?"

"And you had the courage to come in on time and to change

your telephone habits, even though you might not have the courage to try to trust me. You have to work on trust; I have to work on my hair. But I do have the courage to tell Mrs. Judson that this is all or nothing."

Michelle frowned. "What do you mean, all or nothing?"

"I mean if I'm the team leader, then I need the autonomy and the authority to do what I think is best. If I fail, then she's right to remove me. But I have to have the space to try. I can't take a chance on myself and believe I can change and not believe the same thing for you. Michelle, I'm not willing to let you go. If Mrs. Judson makes the decision to let you go, then I've decided that I'm going with you. It's all or nothing."

Michelle stared. She opened and closed her mouth several times. Finally, she found her voice. "So you're going to give up your job for me?" Her words dripped with cynicism. "I wouldn't do it for you."

"Maybe not. But I don't think anything happens by coincidence. I don't think we happened to work together by accident. I don't think we've had tension by accident. The Bible says—"

Michelle rolled her eyes. "Here we go."

"The Bible says that as iron sharpens iron, so one man sharpens another.[3] We're both strong women, in our own ways, and maybe we needed each other to help us become better. We just didn't see it on our own, so Shadrach—"

"Yeah, Coach Shadrach." Michelle pursed her lips.

"That's exactly what I think. I think Shadrach is a coach— maybe a divine coach. The Bible says that all of us have gifts. I think this is Shadrach's gift—to coach us into working as a team so that we can be what we're supposed to be. If I'm right, I don't think there's any way the Lord is going to let Mrs. Judson fire us. If I'm wrong, then we'll both be fired, but maybe I will have persuaded you that you can trust someone."

---

[3] See Proverbs 27:17

Michelle looked at Shadrach, then back at Tonya. "So what's the hook? What's in it for you?"

"What do you mean?"

"I mean, nobody does something for nothing. What's the pay-off for you?"

"Just what I said, Michelle. I don't think I can transform me all by myself. I need to see me through your eyes. I need you to help me. You do your work—you can do that with your hands behind your back. You can do that talking on the phone and coming in late, for goodness sake. But I think that we have more than just work products to offer. Maybe that's how it is with a baseball or a football team. Guys join the team to play and, hopefully, to win. But they obviously get much more out of it. They grow, they build friendships and bonds, and they help each other become better men. Maybe we can do the same thing for each other."

"That's it?"

"That's it."

Shadrach shook his head in amazement. "Wow!"

Michelle's eyes were full of doubt. "We'll see, okay? We'll see." Suddenly she reached out to shake Tonya's hand. "Together we stand, divided we fall—at least until I hear otherwise." She leaned back in her seat. Her lips pursed and Tonya wasn't sure if what she read there was sarcasm or the beginnings of a friendly smile. Michelle's eyes were roving in mild disapproval over her features. "But, seriously, Tonya, if we're going to try, you got to do something to your hair. Girl, that bun is killing me!"

Shadrach collapsed with laughter. The three of them sat talking while people hustled and bustled around them. In the midst of all that was around them, surrounded as they were by hundreds of people, enclosed in a building, enfolded by a teeming city, the Holy Ghost found them and breathed on them the breath of life, the breath of renewal, the breath of change.

It was a new day. A glorious new day.

Part Three

Winter – Delores Judson

Chapter Nineteen

elores Judson sat in the office waiting for the principal and waiting for her granddaughter. The office wall was made of blocks that were faced with the color of wood, but there was no mistaking that they were concrete, granite, or some other similarly strong material. There were certificates on the wall that Delores could not read without her glasses. Most likely, they were the same certificates that had hung on the wall when she was a girl. There was also student artwork on walls—artwork that was supposed to convince the students that the school belonged to them, that it was their place.

It was like so many things she did in the office to get the employees to buy in; the bottom line was that the school administrators ruled, just as she ruled her office. It was all governance by stealth.

She resisted the urge to check her watch. There was no point in getting upset over something she couldn't control. Since Delores had been there, several buzzers had gone off and there had been an occasional announcement over the public address system. She was in charge at work, she was even in charge in her home, but being in school—even to retrieve her granddaughter—always made her feel as though she were losing control.

Of course, Claudia might have something to do with her discomfort. Things might have been different if Dolores had come to see her granddaughter get a citizenship award. She might have been able to maintain the cool interior to match the trained calm of her exterior if Claudia was the lead in a school play or a soloist in the school choir, but such was hardly the case.

Her darling thirteen-year-old granddaughter had already been expelled from three exclusive private schools, which was why the child was even attending a public school. Word had gotten out, and no one else—no other private school—would have her. Since Claudia had come to the school, Delores had been summoned to retrieve her on numerous occasions for numerous reasons: smoking, cursing teachers, not doing homework, failing tests, skipping school.

It was because of Claudia that Delores now carried a cell phone. She despised the invention; no one needed to be in constant communication with anyone. However, it was less embarrassing to have the school contact her at the cell phone number than to have the calls come through her receptionist.

Before the cell phone, she had been interrupted in business meetings, during negotiations, and at private conferences. The schools always insisted that they needed to speak with Delores immediately, it was an emergency. Her receptionist had dutifully broken in on her meetings. Matilda never made a comment, but her eyes said it all—that she knew a secret, that the head that wore the crown had an uncontrollable weakness . . . that weakness was named Claudia Judson.

So Delores had gotten a cell phone. Only the school had the number. The thing had changed her breathing pattern. She held her breath because she was always afraid the cursed thing would go off. Of course, when it did, she answered it casually. She begged the pardon of anyone who might be present; she was so sorry to be rude, but other, more important business, called. The cell phone seemed, somehow, to raise her stature in other people's eyes.

But it was giving her an ulcer. Not much more than a week ago Delores had had to leave work to come to the school. She hated the digital pulsing sound—she hated even more what the sound meant. It meant the school was calling. Something was wrong, again, with Claudia.

The door opened. It was the principal. He stuck out his hand. "Mrs. Judson, I'm sorry to have to call you again."

Mrs. Judson leaned forward and coolly shook his hand. She never rose to shake hands; she was a lady. She was compromised, but she was not going to surrender to the shame of it all.

"Of course, Mr. Carter. I'm certain there was nothing else that could be done." Let him figure out for himself whether she was being sarcastic or not.

He nodded. "We've been trying to work so hard with Claudia, all of us partnering together—the administrators, the staff, the teachers—" He nodded at Mrs. Judson. "—and you, her family. The only one that doesn't seem to be committed is Claudia." He sat in his chair behind his plain wooden desk. "I hate to have to call you. I hate to have to tell any parent about something like this."

"Indeed." If he was waiting for her to say more, he was going to be there until the next day.

"Well, this time . . . I don't know if we're going to be able to continue to work with Claudia. Maybe our school isn't the place for her. Our resources are strained as it is. We've focused so much on Claudia that, I hate to say it, but there are many times we're neglecting some of our other children. If they aren't giving us any trouble, we have been ignoring them . . . in order to devote resources to children who need more help. Claudia, I'm sure you would agree, is one of those children who need more help."

"That appears to be the case."

"Well, we're willing to make the sacrifice and expend the extra effort. Each child is important to us. But the child has to be motivated to change. Of course, we need the parents' support, but the child has to play his or her part."

"Of course." Delores nodded. She had given enough bad appraisals that she knew when one was coming. This report was going to be bad, no doubt about it. She just needed to minimize the damage.

"Mrs. Judson, we don't see Claudia exhibiting behavior that says she's interested in changing or even that she wants to be in this school." There were beads of sweat on the principal's upper lip. It was definitely going to be bad.

"Mr. Carter, please excuse me for interrupting." Delores gave him her most magnanimous and charming smile. "As an employer, I can fully appreciate your position. Because I'm dealing with adults, I have certain expectations that they will come to the workplace with certain skill sets and at a certain level of responsible behavioral deportment. I manage a workforce of adults, but even in that case, I don't want to have to throw anyone away."

He was nodding. Sweat was dripping from his forehead, but he was nodding. Now was the moment to sucker punch him.

"Of course, since you are dealing with *children,* you must be even more circumspect and committed to restoring them, rather than taking the easy out. Which is, of course, disposing of them."

Delores flashed another smile at him. She made her voice sound as though it was dripping honey. "It's obvious that you are a very caring man."

Dark, wet circles had appeared under Mr. Carter's arms. They were widening. "I am, Mrs. Judson. I am. Which makes this all the more difficult." The principal cleared his throat. "There's no other way to say this. One of the teachers happened to be checking the girls' restroom. Claudia was there. She was drunk."

Delores kept her game face. "Who would give a child liquor?"

"The bottle belonged to Claudia. She admitted to it and she admitted to giving whiskey to some of the other children. They were impressionable sixth graders. Of course, their parents are very upset."

Delores searched for a way to minimize what had happened. She couldn't think of anything.

"The school nurse has reason to believe that Claudia was also intoxicated with some other substance. So we're recommending that you take her immediately to your family doctor. But she's going to have to leave here." Mr. Carter used the back of his hand to wipe his lip. When he realized what he had done, red crept into his cheeks. "I've called the board and I'm completing paperwork to have Claudia transferred to a county alternative school. It's not within our district, but it is within the county—it was set up as a last chance for children who are having behavioral problems." He looked down at the papers on his desk and then back at Delores. "I'm sorry, Mrs. Judson. Claudia has left us no other choice."

Delores pushed the button that powered down her cell phone. Claudia's pediatrician had agreed to see her immediately. *How did my life get so out of control?* Delores tried to collect her thoughts while she drove.

Claudia looked totally unconcerned. She had seemed surprisingly upbeat leaving the school. "I was sick of this place anyway. It's so dull, so banal." Claudia had smiled brightly at Delores. "What now, Grandmama?" she'd asked as she plopped into the back seat of the Mercedes. She said *grandmama* with a European affectation that she knew especially irritated Delores. The child was always turning the screw.

As she drove, Delores stole glances at Claudia in the mirror. The child had a plump, cherubic face that didn't match her small, thin body. The top half of her thick hair was stiffly gelled into magenta-colored spikes. The lower half was died a wretched gothic black. Claudia was actually a bright child who had had all the best opportunities. What had gone wrong?

There was no conversation between them even after they were

inside the doctor's office. Delores whisked her granddaughter past the receptionist's greeting area. She spoke pleasantly but efficiently to the staff, watched them lead Claudia to a room, and then returned to sit in the waiting room. It was such a waste of time. There were so many other things she needed to do.

She pretended to be engrossed in a home-decorating magazine until the doctor came to the waiting room door. Dr. Green appeared youthful. But she supposed that was a benefit in his work; he spoke to his young patients in their language.

Dr. Green smiled sadly. "Could you come back here for a moment?"

Delores wanted to strangle Claudia. What now? Why couldn't she just cooperate with the staff? Whom had she slapped, kicked, or cursed now? Delores followed the doctor into his office. He pressed the door closed behind them, leaving it just slightly ajar as he moved to sit at his desk.

Dr. Green was a straight shooter. "The school was right. Claudia is drunk. They were also right about the other. She's hopped up on Ecstasy. You do know what Ecstasy is, right?"

"Not really, Dr. Green. I am vaguely aware of the drug."

"Let me make this as simple as possible. It's a synthetic drug that is similar to, or can be categorized as, an amphetamine. It can be deadly—it raises the blood pressure and can cause dehydration. I don't want to get too clinical, but it's a drug that has found some use among therapists for patients in psychotherapy. What draws kids to it is that it's supposed to heighten sensual and sexual responses. They claim that Ecstasy gives them a sense of emotional euphoria, a sense of connection, it gives them loving feelings. Ecstasy gives them a sense of emotional well-being that they're lacking. That sense of emotional openness and euphoria, the stimulation, and the sense that everything is right with the world can lead to diminished inhibitions, including diminished sexual inhibitions."

"I don't see why Claudia would be attracted to something like that. Carl and I took her in—she's not isolated. And she's only thirteen. She's not sexually active."

Dr. Green got up and firmly closed the door. "I'm surprised at how many parents have no clue what's going on with their kids. We work, you know, so that we can take care of them. Only we get so caught up in our work that we don't have time to care for them." He sat down and leaned his elbows on his cluttered desk. "Forgive me, Mrs. Judson, I don't mean to lecture. I know you are giving Claudia the best care you can, but I see so many children going down the tubes." He paused. "But we aren't here talking about them, are we? We're talking about Claudia."

He leaned back in his chair, tenting his fingers. "We wanted to check your granddaughter thoroughly." He touched the tent to his mouth. "There's no point in mincing words, is there, Mrs. Judson? I'm sorry . . . Claudia's pregnant."

Claudia's pregnant. Delores felt something break inside.

There was nothing for her to say. Delores just hoped that the doctor couldn't see that on the inside she had slumped to the floor. All the wind had been knocked out of her. All she could see ahead was trouble and darkness. Utter darkness.

Chapter Twenty

here had the honey blonde gone? Her hair had been one of her most prized assets. First there had been a few white strands here and there. Then more . . . and more. Finally, she had had to surrender. Delores touched her silver gray hair. If she couldn't fight it, she could certainly enhance it.

She looked beyond her husband to her image in the gilt-framed mirror behind him. She touched the wrinkles on her face and on her neck. Being thin had held the finger of age at bay for awhile, but it was rapidly beginning to take its toll.

She refocused from her image to her husband. "Carl, I'm tired."

He nodded. "Yes, dear. I know."

"I'm too old for this. We're too old for this. We've already raised a daughter—only God knows where she is. I didn't think we would be raising a child at this age." She lowered her voice to a whisper. "I have no room in my life for a child."

"No, Delores, we don't have room." He lifted his pipe from where it hung at the side of his mouth, tapped it on the large crystal ashtray in front of him, and then returned it to his mouth. "Old age is not the optimum time to raise a teenager."

The rosewood table between them spanned almost the entire length of the room. A chandelier hung from the ceiling and sparkled above their heads. She lifted her drink—scotch on ice.

"And add to that, Carl, that she's wild and out of control. What is she doing drinking? She's only thirteen. And Ecstasy? Why does she need that?" Delores shuddered and took a drink. "We have to do something. And what are we going to do about the pregnancy? We can't raise another child."

"No, we can't raise another child. There's no room in our lives for the one we have."

Delores took another sip. "And I don't even want to see the boy responsible. Maybe *responsible* is the wrong word. I can just imagine. He probably has green hair to complement hers."

Carl shook his head and puffed on his pipe. "Well, she *is* attending public school."

"Drugs and sex? She's only thirteen. But I guess the apple doesn't fall far from the tree. Claudia was so sweet and docile when she first came here. I thought we had gotten her in time—before her mother's warped behavior rubbed off on her." Delores laid her head in her hands. "I guess we were too late."

"Too late."

"Carl, I didn't work as hard as I have—*we* didn't work this hard—to have it all unravel because of a careless child. I will *not* have my life wrecked." She took a deep breath. "I will send her to a home, a boarding school, or even just put her out before I let her bring us down. This is my life and I'm not going to see it ruined."

"No, dear."

"If there's any consolation, at least Carl Jr. seems to have escaped all the madness of this age. He's settled and has his business. Carl Jr. even did for Claudia what her own mother has never done.

He's going to be devastated when he finds out all the time he spent taking that child to the opera, to the theater, and such was just a waste of time." She rubbed her hand across her face. "I really don't want to deal with this."

"I can handle it, dear, if you like."

"No, Carl, I think I better take care of it."

"As you like."

She lifted the decanter and refilled her glass.

Drink in hand, Delores grabbed the tail end of her caftan and climbed the stairs to her granddaughter's room. Claudia lay across her bed, wearing earphones. Her eyes were focused on the video screen in front of her, and her fingers tapped skillfully on the controller.

"Claudia, I need to speak with you."

The girl ignored her.

"Claudia, I need to speak with you, please." Delores drew herself to her full height. "Now."

Claudia turned and smiled at her. "Are you speaking to me, Grandmama?"

"Claudia, I'm in no mood for foolishness. Remove the headphones and turn off the game. Now."

Claudia moved casually, humming to herself. She removed the headphones and touched the button on the remote that powered down her stereo system. She grabbed a smaller, sleeker remote that turned off her video system. "Yes, Grandmama."

Delores reminded herself that she was an entrepreneur, that she managed adults, and there was not one among them that intimidated her. She was at her best, and her most skillful, resolving problems. Right now, Claudia was her problem. "There is a solution to each predicament that life hands us. First, you must determine the nature of the problem and then determine the most efficient solution."

"Yes, Grandmama." Claudia batted her eyes. Coyness was going to get the child killed.

"There is an issue with your abusing alcohol and some drug usage."

Claudia continued to smile.

"Claudia, you're only thirteen years old. I can't imagine. I wasn't drinking at thirteen. Why would you want to drink?"

"I like the way it tastes?"

"Claudia, this is not the time for games. We have some serious problems that we must address quickly."

"I drink to drown my sorrows." Claudia beamed at her grandmother. "You don't mind if I lie down while we talk, do you, Grandmama?" Claudia flopped across the bed. "For some reason, I'm very tired."

"Please don't go out of your way to be disrespectful, Claudia. This is not the time for foolishness." Delores moved inside the room and sat on a chair near the doorway. "I didn't bring you here for you to become a drug addict like your mother."

"X just makes you feel good. In thirty minutes, you're rolling. Besides, it isn't addicting." Claudia looked up at Delores and added, "Grandmama."

"That's not what Dr. Green says."

"Who cares what doctors say. How would he know?" She smiled at Delores. "Do you think Dr. Green might have tried it? He looks like a cool guy."

Delores tucked her caftan beneath her. "I am not going to have this inane conversation with you, young lady. I came up here to try to help you solve *your* problem. I don't have to bother with this, Claudia. As easily as you came, you can also go. I took you in—Carl and I took you in, because your mother wasn't capable of taking care of you. Who knows who your father is? The idea of a Judson becoming a foster child was unacceptable. So we agreed to be responsible for you. However, we never entertained the idea that you would go out of your way to make our lives miserable.

"You've been expelled from more schools than I care to enumerate. You've embarrassed us to no end. Now we have to deal with this pregnancy. If I were you, I would stop making light of this matter now."

Claudia's face looked hurt and frightened. Her eyes widened and her lips trembled, but only for a moment. Within seconds, she was smiling again. "Yes, Grandmama."

"I don't guess there's any point in asking who the young man is? I'm sure we don't know his family."

Claudia didn't respond.

Delores sipped her drink. "You know I never considered it. But maybe *you* don't even know who the father is. I hope this isn't one of those situations like on television, where the girl has been sleeping with so many boys she has no idea who sired the child."

Claudia didn't speak.

"Do you know who the boy is?"

"It wasn't a boy." Claudia smiled as though she were playing a game.

"Well, you may not want to call him a boy. You may consider yourself an adult, but you're not. You can't take care of yourself, let alone a baby." Delores shook her finger at Claudia. "You can laugh now. But you'll be sorry about all this. What you *can* count on is that your grandfather and I are not going to sit around picking up after you. We've covered enough of your mistakes. So don't be flippant, young lady. You're hanging on by a very thin thread."

Claudia was silent.

"Tell me, how could you have sex and not protect yourself? If you were going to have intercourse, you're a bright young lady, how could you let it come to this? Why didn't you make provision?"

"I wasn't planning it, Grandmama. I wasn't planning to have sex."

"Well, that proves that you're not an adult. Neither is the miscreant that you were bedding with. And I hope you don't think he's going to be of any help to you. You've been had, is what I would say." Delores looked down at her feet and then back at Claudia. "Did you give him money?"

"No, Grandmama. He didn't want money."

"So he got what he wanted?"

Claudia shrugged.

"This is all so sordid and embarrassing. Aren't you embarrassed?"

Claudia said nothing.

Delores touched her cool glass to her face. "And your poor uncle. I am not going to break his heart by telling him. He thinks so much of you. What do you think Carl Jr. would say if he knew?"

"I don't know, Grandmama."

Delores waved her hand, waved away the dirtiness of it all. "Well, there really is only one solution. You'll have to have an abortion. You're too young to raise a child. Your grandfather and I certainly are not going to do it. It's the only way for you to avoid humiliation. Not that you're capable of experiencing such an emotion. But you are not going to embarrass us and make us laughingstocks." Delores rose from the chair. "Well, that's settled." She turned toward the door and then turned back. "Do you have any other ideas? Do you have any objections to an abortion?"

"I wouldn't dream of defying you or your solution, Grandmama."

Delores turned and started down the hallway. She stopped. She had a right to know. She and Carl had a right to know. If they were going to pay for it, they had a right to know. She returned to Claudia's doorway. Claudia lay facedown on the bed.

"Tell me, Claudia, who was it?"

"You don't want to know, Grandmama."

"Stop the *Grandmama* nonsense. I deserve to know. Your grandfather deserves to know. Who was it, Claudia?"

Claudia pressed her face further down into the bed.

"If you don't tell me, I can make it very difficult for you."

Claudia lifted her head. Her eyes sparkled, hard, almost maniacal. "Uncle."

Delores grabbed the end of her caftan and turned to leave again, but turned back. "I am not going to put up with this discourteous behavior. I demand to know. You will tell me, now."

"I said *Uncle*, Grandmother. The father is my uncle."

Delores dropped her glass and slumped to the floor.

he tub of hot water felt good. Delores closed her eyes and pretended she was on a tropical island—an isolated island. There was no one around—no tourists, no servants, not even any family. Especially no family. She stretched all the way out so that she could lie back. The water closed up over her shoulders. She let it cover her ears. It edged up to the corners of her eyes and then finally covered the tip of her nose. There was no other person in the world. Her cocoon of water separated her from anything that might hurt her.

It worked. The tub of water distracted her as long as it was hot enough to burn her, as long as it was hot enough for her nerve endings to keep her mind occupied. When it cooled, everything came flooding back. Not that Delores could make any sense of it. She didn't want to make any sense of it.

She lifted her head out of the water.

She thought of calling Carl Jr. on the phone so he could put the whole sordid lie to rest. But she didn't want to call him. She didn't want to hear the disquieting silence on the other end of the phone while he tried to think of a clever lie. She didn't want to hear that peculiar sound—that note in his voice that only a mother could hear, would know—that would tell her that he was lying. She didn't want to think back on other things in the past, things she might have overlooked.

When Delores had come to, after hearing Claudia's terrible news, Carl was holding her and yelling for Claudia to call for an ambulance.

"No, I'm fine," she had insisted until Carl calmed and decided she was right, he didn't need to call. When he was sure that she was fine and had gone to his study, she tiptoed to Claudia's room.

"We mustn't tell anyone. Especially not your grandfather, it would kill him." Delores had scratched at her elbows and rubbed her hands together. *"It would kill him. We'll just keep this to ourselves."* She couldn't look Claudia in the eye. *"Not that I believe you for one minute. Why should I believe you? It's not as though you haven't lied about a thousand things. I don't even know why I'm trying to help you, when you've made up such a horrible lie about your uncle. Particularly when he's been so attentive to you, when he's been your champion on so many occasions."*

Delores had scratched her scalp and then wrung her hands. *"No, we won't tell anyone this horrible story. You don't have to tell me who the father is. I won't ask you anymore. What difference does it make? There won't be a baby, so there's no need to even inquire about the father."* She had grabbed Claudia's arm. *"But you will not, under any circumstances, mention this to anyone, especially not your grandfather. We'll just take care of this little problem and we'll find you a new school. A private school so we won't ever have to deal with anything like this, again. You'd like that wouldn't you, Claudia? A new school—a new start."*

The hot water was her reality now. The pins and needles dimmed the pain of her granddaughter's revelation. It wasn't possible was it? It wasn't possible. Things like this didn't happen to people like them. Claudia was simply trying to deflect trouble. Delores pushed away the temptation to consider that Claudia might be telling the truth. She pushed away thoughts that tied the time Carl Jr. became so attentive to his niece with the time that Claudia began to act out in school.

It wasn't true. Delores didn't want to think about it. It was all a lie.

"And you won't create a lot of emotional histrionics over this. You won't cry or throw tantrums. This will all just go away. No one will know. It will be a vague memory—if you remember it at all. I will forgive you for the things you said—accusing your uncle—and we won't speak of it anymore."

If it were true, she and Carl would have to call the police, wouldn't they? The police would have to arrest Carl Jr., wouldn't they? Her beautiful, brilliant, upstanding son would have to go to jail, wouldn't he? A jury, because he was rich, would no doubt convict him, wouldn't they? He would spend his life in prison with murderers, liars, thieves, and perverts, wouldn't he?

If it were true, Carl Jr. would be the bad one. Claudia would be held up as a poor little victim. The world would turn upside down.

Carl Jr. was innocent. But even if he wasn't, what was the point of reporting him? Claudia was already on the road to ruin. It made no sense to sacrifice his life for hers.

If Carl Jr. did do it she wouldn't be able to hug him anymore. She wouldn't be able to look at him and be proud. Carl might despise his son. There would be a scandal. The people at the club, the people at work—everyone would point and whisper. *Did you hear about Mrs. Judson?* They would laugh and call her names. *There must be something wrong with her, something wrong with her family.* They would be happy to see her taken down a peg.

Delores turned on the hot water, again, and sank beneath the liquid veil. She and her granddaughter wouldn't talk about it ever again. Claudia would keep her mouth shut and everything would be fine.

When she drove to work Monday morning, Delores went right through a stoplight. When she walked into the office, she had difficulty determining what was real. Was what happened Friday real? Had she really gone to the school for Claudia? Did Dr. Green really say her granddaughter was pregnant?

"My uncle is the father."

It was hard to tell. If all that was reality, then how could people be sitting at desks? How could the clocks still be ticking?

"Good morning, Mrs. Judson."

Delores walked past without speaking.

She didn't turn on the lights in her office. She just sat with her coat still on, in her chair behind her large desk, and looked out her window over the city. Her appointment book lay closed.

The buzzer had been sounding for a while before she answered. "Mrs. Judson, are you all right?"

She didn't respond.

"Mrs. Judson, Tonya is here for your nine o'clock meeting. Should I send her in?"

Delores didn't want to talk to Tonya. She didn't want to talk to anyone. She opened her appointment book and flipped through the pages. Why were they meeting? She couldn't remember. She wanted to curl up on the floor until it was all over. Her training, forty years of practice, took over. "Of course, Matilda. Give me just a few moments and then send her in."

By the time Tonya entered Delores's office, all appeared to be right. Delores sat behind her desk, pen in hand, as though she was preparing to take notes. "Good morning, Tonya."

"Good morning, Mrs. Judson. I hope your time away went well." Tonya looked at her strangely. "Should I turn on the lights?"

Delores nodded and forced herself to smile. "Yes, of course. Thank you. I was resting my eyes."

After Tonya turned on the lights, she sat in the chair across from Delores. "Mrs. Judson, I've been thinking about Michelle. I know you want me to take care of the matter quickly, but I don't believe that I can. Two weeks hasn't given me enough time to judge by."

Delores nodded. "It's been a while now with Michelle and there doesn't really seem to be any improvement."

Tonya moved her hand up and down forcefully, emphasizing each word. "What I would like is a few more months. As her team leader, I need the autonomy to make that call. I don't want to throw anyone away—"

"There doesn't seem to be any improvement."

"Well, Mrs. Judson, I beg your pardon, but while you've been away, Michelle has made some changes. We just need more time. A few months would be—"

"How many months, Tonya?" Delores didn't have the desire to fight.

"Well, I think that I would be able to make a decision within two or three months."

Delores forced herself to scribble in her planner. "Which would you prefer, two or three?"

Tonya's eyes widened. Clearly she was surprised. Her look said something was out of sorts. "Well, I think two months would tell me. If everything goes smoothly we could submit the papers for her promotion."

"All right, Tonya. We'll meet then. Get on my calendar." Delores willed herself to look pleasant as Tonya rose to leave. Just before Tonya left the doorway, Delores called to her. "Tonya?"

The woman looked bewildered. "Yes, Mrs. Judson?"

"Would you turn out the lights?" Exhausted, she buzzed her receptionist. "Would you hold all my appointments and calls for the next fifteen minutes?" Delores Judson closed her eyes and laid her head on her desk.

Chapter Twenty-two

here is something about having no one to talk to that slowly siphons away life. A burden that one cannot share grays the hair, furrows the brow, and bends the back.

Delores Judson had built a safe life behind the walls of success, wealth, and power. No one came into her life that she did not let in; she carefully orchestrated each encounter. The walls made her secure from any thieves, any pains, and any complications that might try to insinuate their way into her life.

She worked at her success to make it strong and impenetrable. Delores had started small as a struggling secretary. But each promotion brought her in contact with a new businessman, industrialist, or czar and she learned from them. She studied their needs—what was missing, what they needed to make their kingdoms complete. What they didn't have, she became or learned. It was her mission to acquire what they needed.

She stacked each one of those needs like bricks. When she had gained enough experience and savvy, when she had built enough connections and the right network, she used those elements like mortar to seal the bricks together. Her wall was firm and sure. Others could come and see it. They could touch, even, but she gave nothing away.

Delores learned the value of each of her bricks. She calculated the worth of her knowledge and her skill and bled the price from each one she encountered. She used her wealth to make her inaccessible to things distasteful and contrary. Her riches stalled off the approach of those who could not meet a certain acceptable standard of attractiveness, intelligence, or giftedness. Delores used her wealth to fortify her wall.

Her success, her bricks, and her wealth, conferred upon her a certain amount of power—power to make the rules. Because Delores was intelligent and resourceful, she took the seed of power her successes gave her and cultivated it. She nursed it, watered it, weeded it, and even pruned it when need be. Soon her seed grew into a vine, laden with purple, delicate flowers. A vine that stealthily approached others and, where it detected a suitable place, wrapped itself around the unsuspecting tenant. After the tenant was strangled and died, Delores's pretty vine took its place. The further her vine spread, the greater her control grew. And her power extended the protection of her wall beyond its physical barriers.

Delores knew all this might seem mean, ruthless, and uncaring. But at the end of the day her motives were simple: she just didn't want to be hurt. She had promised herself, as a child, that when she grew up she would not be hurt. So, Delores built a wall.

She planned hard and she worked long. Behind her wall, she planned for success, wealth, and power. She planned for a husband and two children. What she *didn't* plan for was an addicted daughter. She didn't plan for a pregnant thirteen-year-old. She didn't plan for a prodigal son.

Because she had drawn her life's conclusion as a child, it didn't contain truths that only come to the most mature adults. If she had been a little older when she formed her determination, Robert Burns and John Steinbeck might have told her about the best laid plans of mice and men. She might not have avoided keeping company with those who had less than she did. A little older, and she might have learned it is often the weak, poor, rejected, and disenfranchised—the silent, most unlikely people—whose stories point the way to hope and healing.

And so it was that Delores sat in her office alone, certain that her life was over. Assured that all she had worked to build was crashing down around her.

Delores had not studied the stories of women like Mother Teresa. There were no men behind her walls like Nelson Mandela and Elie Wiesel. What she needed, in her despair, were people like them. People whose lives and memories would have assured her that she had the strength to survive and endure. Unlikely heroes who could remind her that suffering, even extended suffering, does not have to dehumanize. Delores could have used a friend like Jesus to tell her, "In the world ye shall have tribulation: but be of good cheer; I have overcome the world."[4] It would have helped her to lean on the shoulder of a psalmist like David, to listen as he sang, "Weeping may endure for a night, but joy cometh in the morning."[5]

But her plan and her defenses kept her from such comfort.

In her sorrow, Delores could have used the embrace of a mother. If not her own, then the embrace of a surrogate, a handmaid, or a nurse mother. Not someone famous, not some media darling, but Delores could have used a down-home mother. She needed the arms of a woman full of wisdom and hope—a woman aged like herself, but a woman tempered by grace. That woman's stories of survival could have strengthened Delores. That heavenly minded mother's example could have shown her that there is solace in music, that there is eternal hope in prayer, that there is divine strength

---

[4]John 16:33 KJV
[5]Psalm 30:5 KJV

available in faith, and that there is great comfort in family . . . fellow-ship . . . and love.

Such an old woman's personal stories of renewal and restora-tion—of living through the Depression and World War, of her mother and father's survival during the Jim Crow era—might have been just the thing to give Delores the courage to go forward. She could have used a mother like Sarah to tell her that she might be cry-ing now, and that it might take a long time, but that God was going to make her laugh again. She could have used a woman like Ruth to tell her that no matter how bad it looked, God was not going to leave her alone—that God specializes in restoration.

In all Delores's confusion, a child might have helped her, too. A child might have been able to whisper deep into Delores's spirit that the least of us may have the wisdom and compassion to save us all. There are children who walk to school every day in war-torn urban areas—Kosovo, South Central LA, Harlem—children who are not certain that they will live to reach adulthood. Those brave chil-dren, unlikely heroes, might have been a comfort to Delores. Those children might have convinced her that she could still dance, write poetry, and sing in a world in which she no longer felt safe. A boy like Solomon could have told Delores that if one asks, God will grant, to even a child, wisdom and understanding.

There are survivors of abuse and disease, wounded warriors who could have told Delores stories of how they have pressed for-ward to squeeze life and hope from each day during times of uncer-tainty and tribulation. Maybe if Delores had sat a while with the infirmed woman or with the woman with an issue of blood, the sis-ters could have told Delores that God has the power to loose, and that there is nothing too hard for Him.

Delores worried that her wall was about to come tumbling down, that her kingdom was about to come down in ruins. Some-one could have comforted her. Maybe the homeless could have taught Delores that she was so much more than any wall, business, or building that she might erect or in which she might dwell. Perhaps, if she had leaned in closely, they might have told Delores how to feel safe and keep her dignity when her wealth, her wall, or the other symbols of her safety were lost. The patriarch Joseph might have told her that it is neither the pit nor the palace that determines the depth of a man's character, but character is determined by virtues like forgiveness and enduring faith.

If Delores had sat with Mary, she might have told her that the Master really would come. Mary might have reassured Delores that no matter how putrid and stinking things might appear to be, God specializes in resurrecting dead things.

When the vines of Delores's own existence began to choke her, a Canaanite woman might have comforted her and reassured her that God would transform the rules, if He had to, to get her a blessing.

But Delores had formulated her life's plan as a child—a nugatory plan to build and live life behind a wall. So when life crashed around her, there was no one to help. Delores was alone. There was no Paul to counsel her that the solution to her problems was to renew her mind, to put away childish thinking. He wasn't behind the wall to tell her intellect and all she knew wouldn't save her when her back was against the wall, but that she needed to rely instead on eternal hope.

The walls Delores had built were so true, so high, and so wide there was no one she could call. So, she wondered in her heart if there was a God and if He could hear. If He did exist, Delores wondered, could He or would He send someone over the wall.

everal weeks had passed since Delores had returned to work. That's how she referred to it: *since she had returned to work*. She didn't mention—even to herself—about her granddaughter or about the nastiness with her son. The key to coping, she had determined after she returned to work, was to create two separate lives. There was a work life and a home life—and never the twain would meet. It kept her afloat. She was still Mrs. Judson. In fact, all might have been settled.

Except for Carl.

Her husband didn't know everything she knew. So he kept talking about the right thing. *"Do you think it's the right thing for Claudia? Shouldn't we think it over? We're not religious people, dear, but do you think abortion is the right thing?"*

Delores had been making the decisions all these years. Now Carl wanted to talk about the right thing. He would grow weary of it, though. She would just wait him out. There was still a little time.

She pushed back from her desk, stood, and stretched. They still called her *Mrs. Judson* here. She still had an office with a view of the city. She still made the rules.

She reached in her cabinet and grabbed her purse, then into her desk drawer for her shades. She left her office and nodded to her receptionist. "I'm going to go get a bite of lunch." Delores never ate in the restaurants in the building. She usually ordered in or dined with other bigwigs in exclusive restaurants. Familiarity with subordinates breeds contempt—she had learned that at an executive women's leadership seminar.

As she walked through the office, she noticed Tonya standing at Michelle's desk. Since Delores had returned to work, Michelle hadn't been much on her mind other than that she noticed Michelle had been much quieter. It was still unusual to Delores, though, to see Tonya and Michelle smiling together. The two women seemed more . . . carefree—happier. Something about the change seemed unnatural and made Delores feel uncomfortable. Besides, today there was something else about Michelle—

Delores looked at the young woman from behind her shades. That was it—shades. Michelle was wearing shades in the office. She was a most peculiar girl.

Delores rode the executive elevator to the lowest level, got off, and walked into the nearest restaurant. The waitress seated her in a booth surrounded by ferns and ivy. Her waitress took her drink order and then walked away. It was like sitting in a secluded paradise. She sat back and enjoyed the moment.

Removing her glasses, she closed her eyes, pretending she was far, far away. Until she heard her waitress' voice nearby.

"Is this booth all right?" She recognized the two women's voices as soon as they answered. She checked the plants around her to assure herself that she could not be seen. *Why, of all places, did they have to eat here today?* The last thing she wanted to see was someone from the office. The last thing she wanted to hear was Tonya and Michelle.

"It seems funny eating without Shadrach. Without Coach Shadrach."

Delores could hear Michelle laugh. "You got that right, Tonya girl. He's coach—a big, old, mean coach, too."

"Not so mean, though. Just serious, don't you think?"

"Yeah, Shad is good people. He said that about you, too, Tonya—that you were good people. I didn't want to hear it then. But he was right. You are. And I appreciate all that you have done."

"Oh, girl."

"You didn't have to do it. You didn't have to stand up to Mrs. Judson for me, Tonya. You didn't have to risk your own job."

"Michelle, the funny thing is, I didn't have to risk my job. Mrs. Judson was so easy about it. Like there was something else on her mind. I didn't have to do anything—I guess I just had to be willing."

"Well, whatever you did, girl, I appreciate it." Michelle laughed. "I appreciate you and I appreciate Shad, with his big old self."

Tonya laughed. Not convincingly, but it was still a laugh. "It sounds to me like . . . I didn't know you liked Shadrach."

"Why not? What have I got to lose? I've bombed out with everyone else in my life. I might as well mess it up with him, too."

"Have you all—are you all dating?"

"Dating? Nobody dates, anymore, Tonya girl. You really are old school, aren't you? No, we're not dating, but the way things are going—" Delores could hear Michelle tapping on something. "—I might as well give it a whirl."

"Does he know?"

"There's nothing to know. I'm in search of a good man, and after this—" Delores heard the tapping sound, again. "—he's as good as any."

"What? Is there something about your glasses?"

"Come on, girl. Why do women usually wear shades at work?"

Delores heard Tonya make a clucking sound. Her own eyes widened as she realized Michelle was talking about bruises.

"I'm sorry," said Tonya. "I didn't even think about that. I didn't think Todd was that kind of man."

"Todd? You must be kidding. That man is straight as an arrow. All he knows how to do is love me and watch over me. Todd would cut off his own arm before he would hit me. No, this is Trench's handiwork—the lover extraordinaire. I guess him talking to me like I was crazy wasn't enough. He figured he had to hit me before I could get it. A woman can't build her life just around a man."

"We can't build our lives around anyone. And we put too much on men, like they can make everything wrong with us turn right. They can't always be perfect or strong either. But you're right, we can't build our lives around men. That's the truth."

Delores could hear Michelle laughing. "What do you know about life? What do you know about men?"

"I may look like it's been just Jesus all my life, but that's not true."

The waitress came back to the booth to take Delores's order. She pointed at her drink and then waved the girl away. The last thing she needed was for Tonya and Michelle to think she was listening to the two of them. Even if she was.

Tonya lowered her voice. "I guess you know about my son and about my marriage? Why wouldn't you—everyone in the whole office knows. But before then—I went out with some boys, some men before I was married."

"Who? Dudley Doright?"

"Right, Michelle. Thanks." Tonya laughed, too. "I went with a boy in high school."

"And how long ago was that? Was *Soul Train* even on television then? What about *American Bandstand*?"

"Don't be smart-mouthed, Michelle. I'm trying to tell you something."

"Okay, girl, spill it."

"I was so in love with this boy, girl. I love-ded him! I mean I looooov-ded him!"

"I like that, girl."

"Well, I liked it, too. But I was naïve. I didn't know a lot about the world."

"Which you do now?"

"I know more now than I did then." Tonya stopped speaking for a moment. "Things got serious, too serious. I got pregnant."

"Tonya, I didn't know you had a baby that old."

"I don't."

"What?"

Tonya's voice dropped almost to a whisper. "I had an abortion. We were just kids. We didn't know what to do. I don't even know where he got the money from. It was illegal where we lived, so we had to go to another state."

Delores froze, her glass held to her mouth.

"You know you hear all of this stuff about how gruesome the procedure is. People try to use scare tactics to keep women from doing it. But fear won't stop a desperate woman or a desperate girl. You're already trying to get an abortion because you're afraid. Somebody else trying to scare you just makes you run more.

"What nobody told me was about the emptiness that I would feel. I couldn't put my finger on it. I didn't even associate it with the abortion, but it was like something had died in my life. Because of what I've been through with my son Richard Jr.—when I look back, I realize that I was in mourning."

Tonya's voice sounded teary. "And nobody told me about the guilt. You deny that you feel guilty, but you have this secret shame that follows you for years and years. Think about it: you're having the abortion because you don't want to deal with the shame, but the silent shame gets you anyway. Even after I got deep into following the Lord—I was going to Bible Study, I was even married—I couldn't talk about it. If I told my husband, the father of my sons, what would he think of me? If I told the people at my church, what would they say? Can you still be holy and have had an abortion? Is it like adultery for a man—is it an unforgivable sin?"

Michelle whistled softly. "Still, nobody knows?"

"One day—I know some people don't believe in feelings—but this feeling of peace swept over me. It was like the Lord was telling me that He had forgiven me. It didn't matter what people thought. 'You don't serve people, you serve Me,' I could feel Him saying to me. It was forgiven and forgotten. And He wouldn't ever bring it up again, because that sin—think about it, Michelle—that murder didn't exist anymore. It was covered on Calvary.

"Now I tell people that I'm led to tell. You can't tell everyone your business; lots of people aren't strong enough and weren't meant to carry your burden. But I don't have to carry it anymore. There's no more silent shame."

Delores could hear them rustling in the booth. She held her breath and told her heart to slow its beating.

"I never would have imagined, Tonya."

"That's what I thought I recognized on Mrs. Judson the other day. That same kind of fear and deep sadness."

Delores's head jerked as though she had been slapped. Her cheeks reddened.

"Fear and sadness on Mrs. Judson?" Michelle laughed. "The Iron Maiden?"

Delores could feel her face grow warmer.

"Tonya, there's no way Mrs. Judson could be struggling or sad. Girlfriend has enough money and enough bling-bling for everybody. Mrs. Judson's white and she's running things—ain't no master on her back. What does *she* have to be upset about?"

Delores could feel the color draining from her face. She self-consciously lowered her glass.

"You know, Michelle, you're right. Mrs. Judson has money, she's in charge, and it doesn't look like anybody's breathing down her neck. But one thing I've learned—pain's not prejudiced. Sorrow and grief don't care if you're red, yellow, white, black, or brown. You can be unhappy rich just as well as you can poor. And the only remedy I've ever found is available to all. That's why I love the Lord so much. That's why I keep getting on your nerves talking about Him."

"Oh, Tonya, all that is over, okay?"

"The Lord really looked beyond my faults and saw my needs."

Delores sat quietly. She was afraid to even breathe. Not more superstitious mumbo-jumbo.

"Tonya, it's over about the books and everything. All this time that we've been meeting I've been looking at the books—taking peeks and reading little portions of them. I didn't want you to know. But I feel guilty. It really wasn't you. There are some things about my family . . . about my mother. I really don't want to go into all the details. But there are some things . . ."

Michelle cleared her throat. "I got saved once. I believe in God. It's just that I could never figure out how God could let that happen to me. How could He sit by and watch me be raped? I never knew my father . . . I still don't know him and I haven't been able to forgive my mother for letting it happen to me. I don't understand why she would let that man talk to her that way, beat her, and then do what he did to me. Why she would let him use me? She knew it. My mother knew what he was doing to me. I can't forgive her for pretending that her boyfriend didn't . . . I was supposed to go along with it and pretend it didn't happen. I was supposed to accept her worrying about him instead of me."

Michelle spoke in hushed tones. "But I've been reading that Bible you gave me, Tonya. One day I asked God to help me. To answer me if He was listening to me. I picked up the Bible and it just opened to a page." She sounded amazed. "There was this passage that caught my eye. I read it and now I can't get it out of my head. 'When my father and my mother forsake me, then the LORD will take care of me.'[6] It was the same passage you sent to me in the card, right? It had to be God, don't you think? It *had* to be God, Tonya."

---

[6]Psalm 27:10 NKJV

Delores turned back to her coffee. She didn't want to hear anymore. She didn't understand it, but she just didn't want to hear anymore.

When the two women left, Delores paid her check and quietly slipped from the booth as though nothing had happened.

Chapter Twenty-four

hey knew that I was there! Michelle and Tonya had followed her to the restaurant. They had to have known she was there. It was the only explanation. How else could they have known to say the things they did? They had misused her favor and betrayed her.

Delores paced back and forth in her office. She had been thinking about it all night. She had been thinking about it all day.

Could He or would He send someone over the wall?

It was too pat. It was the kind of thing that people believed and shouted about at tent meetings—and at revivals where the ministers spoke with Southern twangs and wore pomaded hair. There was no God that involved himself in anyone's life.

If there *was* a God, why would He have been so concerned with Delores that He arranged for her to eat lunch in a restaurant she never frequented? Out of all the tables in the restaurant, why would an all-powerful God bother to have two women sit beside her—women who had stories that touched her life? Delores rubbed one hand back and forth on top of her head. She didn't even believe. She wasn't shouting about God or sending offerings. If there was a God, why would he be bothered with her?

Delores was a powerful person. She knew and had studied the behavior of powerful people. No person, let alone a god, would expend the energy it took to set up this afternoon's coincidental little passion-filled play.

Those two women hated each other. She had seen and heard them arguing in the office herself. Something was going on; something was rotten in Denmark, and she was going to get to the root of it.

No one—least of all someone who worked for her—was going to make a fool of her. No one!

"I had an abortion."

What kind of fool did they take her for? No one—not even a fool—was going to believe that Tonya had had an abortion. If they wanted to make it convincing, they should have let Michelle play that part.

"That's what I thought I recognized on Mrs. Judson the other day. That same kind of fear and deep sadness."

Fear and sadness? She wasn't afraid of anyone and she wasn't about to let life make her sad. Tonya had toyed with the wrong person. Delores would teach her what fear was all about.

And Michelle was going to be sorry.

"Why would she let him use me? She knew it. My mother knew what he was doing to me. I can't forgive her for pretending . . ."

How convenient—did they actually expect her to believe that her Claudia and Michelle had lived the same life? She was going to make Michelle eat those words.

Delores didn't know how they knew, but somehow Tonya and Michelle had discovered her secrets. They knew about Claudia and Carl Jr. They knew about the baby and the planned abortion. They knew she had been feeling uncertain. Maybe they had intercepted the signals from her cell phone. It really didn't matter how they knew; the two of them knew and they were scheming to use it against her.

Tonya had probably intended to use the information against her when she came to her office that Monday morning for the meeting. They had planned, Delores deduced, to extort promotions from her for their silence.

Tonya and Michelle were working together against her . . .

"Pain's not prejudiced . . ."

Maybe not, but something had brought the two of them together. Delores hadn't built a successful business because she was foolish. She wasn't about to let the two of them undo her.

Could He or would He send someone over the wall?

Delores sank into her chair. No one in her life had ever cared enough to go out of their way for her—not unless they wanted something from her. She had done everything for herself. She had made her own fortune. She had built her own family. Delores had learned early that she could only rely on herself.

Could He or would He send someone over the wall?

There was no one coming to save her—no knight in shining armor, no super hero, and certainly no caring, benevolent God. No one was coming to rescue her.

Delores rested her elbows on her desk and laid her head in her hands.

"My uncle is the father."

Delores could see Claudia's face and her trembling chin.

"Do you think it's the right thing?"

Carl was bewildered and full of doubt. And she could see Carl Jr. All of it was on her. All of it. All of them were counting on her to make some sense of what was senseless. No one was coming over the wall. Delores was going to have to pull herself together. There was no Savior coming. The only answer was within her.

She reached for her buzzer and spoke to her receptionist. "Please send Tonya and Michelle to my office immediately. Thank you."

Chapter Twenty-five

hen Tonya and Michelle walked into Delores's office they were all smiles and laughter. Delores played along. "It's good to see that things are so much better between the two of you." She smiled and nodded at both of them. "I just thought it was time for us to have a heart-to-heart about how things are going. Have a seat, won't you?"

Tonya and Michelle sat down in the seats in front of her desk. They were just as sweet and innocent as lambs before the slaughter. Delores needed to do something to make them uncomfortable, to set them off balance. "Michelle, do you mind removing your sunglasses? I want each of us to look the others in the eye." She forced warmth into her smile. "Like a visit between old friends." She leaned back in her chair.

Michelle's face registered embarrassment as she removed the shades. She turned her head and looked down.

"Michelle, is something wrong with your eye?" Delores was pleased with the compassionate tone of her voice.

Michelle shifted uneasily in her chair. "I had—I had an accident, Mrs. Judson."

"Really? Did it happen here in the office?" She looked at Tonya. "Did you report it?" Then back at Michelle. "Would you like to talk about it?"

"No, Mrs. Judson, it wasn't work related. It happened at home."

"At home? Well, Michelle, you know we're all family here. There's nothing you can't discuss with Tonya and me. Isn't that right, Tonya?"

She was enjoying herself playing the magnanimous leader. It felt good toying with them.

"It's all right, Mrs. Judson. We don't need to talk about it."

Delores smiled. "All right, if you're certain." She shuffled some papers on her desk. "Why don't the two of you go ahead then and give me a status report?"

Tonya looked mildly confused but still confident. "I'll go first if you don't mind, Mrs. Judson."

"You go right ahead, Tonya."

"Well, Michelle and I have been meeting regularly and attempting to learn to communicate with each other more effectively."

Delores smiled brightly. "That certainly seems to be working. You appear to be quite the little team."

"It has been, Mrs. Judson. Since we began meeting, there haven't been any more incidents between us in the office—in fact, neither one of us have been involved in any angry discussions with anyone in the office. The meetings have cleared the air."

"Well, isn't that wonderful. Do you think God might have done it?"

Tonya brightened. "Well, we both have been praying, Mrs.

Judson. Thank you. Thank you for asking. I didn't know—thank you for asking."

"You didn't know I was a religious woman? You're right, I'm not. Of course, that may be why I've been looking fearful and deeply sad."

Tonya's smile faded.

"Anything else, Tonya?"

Tonya cleared her throat. "The other issues concerned tardiness and personal phone calls—neither of which is an issue anymore."

"Are you sure of that, Tonya? I mean at this point, not yet two months later, can you say that tardiness and phone calls are not an issue? Or are you saying what you need to say to get your friend promoted?" Mrs. Judson smirked. "Why don't you pray about that, while Michelle speaks?"

Michelle held two fingers to her face; they favored the mouse on her eye.

"Are you sure you don't want to talk about that?" Delores pointed at Michelle's face. "Was it a doorknob or something?"

Michelle's face showed her agitation, but her voice sounded controlled. "No, Mrs. Judson, I don't care to talk about it."

"Well, why don't we talk about why I shouldn't fire you, then?"

The room was still for a moment. Then Tonya interrupted the silence. "Mrs. Judson, you said—you promised a two-month trial and that I had the authority to make the decision."

"Well, I guess I changed my mind, Tonya. It is a woman's prerogative, isn't it? And I believe that I was addressing Michelle." Delores turned her attention back to Michelle. "Tell me, Michelle, why I shouldn't fire you?"

"Mrs. Judson—" Michelle looked at Tonya. "—I thought you were giving me a chance to improve my performance." She looked back at Mrs. Judson. "I thought we were being open and honest with each other. I don't understand."

Delores stood up from her desk. "Open and honest? You mean open and honest like you were with me yesterday?" She was certain that her smile looked wicked. The spectacle had begun—she was going to shred them, bit by bit.

Tonya and Michelle looked at each other like they were confused, as though they didn't understand. They were missing their calling in her office; they were quite the actresses.

"Are you feeling uncomfortable? The feeling is mutual. You know, *pain is not prejudiced*."

The two women looked as though they were ready to stand and leave. "Oh, don't leave yet. Your little charade is over. Did you actually think that I would fall for your little act?" Delores didn't even try to hide her anger. "I don't like betrayal and I like extortion even less."

Tonya finally found words. "Mrs. Judson, I don't understand."

"I didn't understand myself for a while. I tossed and turned about it. For a moment, I actually considered that some God might have intervened. But today, I faced the facts. You two connived to do this. You followed me to the restaurant and arranged to sit in the booth next to me. I heard everything. Everything! I don't know how you know about my life, about what's going on in my family, but you will *not* use it against me." Delores shook her head. "What sickens me most is that you would use the information against me, to try to hurt me when I was attempting to help you." She sneered at them. "Well, you two ladies should know that I have undone much more worthy opponents. You both made a big mistake this time."

Tonya and Michelle stared at her for several minutes. They were silent and appeared to be stunned. They were probably thinking about how costly their miscalculation was going to be.

Tonya spoke first. "Mrs. Judson, I don't know anything about your life. I'm really not sure what you're talking about."

Michelle was more agitated. "You know what?" She stood and

put her hand on her hip. "I'll be doggone if I'm going to let some-body go off on me like she's lost her mind. Especially for some job. I don't know what you're talking about, and frankly, I don't care."

They were good. The two of them were very good. Delores probably would have believed them if she hadn't been there at the restaurant and heard it for herself. "I heard everything. Of course, I was supposed to, wasn't I? Yesterday at lunchtime, you two saw me leave and you followed me to that restaurant."

"We didn't follow you, Mrs. Judson." Tonya looked very calm; she looked as though she knew the answer.

"I suppose it was just a coincidence that we ended up at the same restaurant and that we were seated in booths next to each other."

Michelle looked ready to jump. "I don't know *what* you talk-ing about, woman. I didn't see you no where."

"So it was just coincidence that you were talking about abor-tion and about child molestation? Do you think that I'm stupid enough to believe that?"

Michelle put both hands on her hips. "I don't know what you're stupid enough to believe. But I know you're stupid enough to be in my business. Lady, you are messing with the wrong woman. *That's* what I think." Michelle lifted a hand and pointed at Tonya. "She's the one that always speaks like she's got honey in her mouth." Michelle pointed at herself and stepped forward. "I'm the one that will go to town on your—"

"Michelle, wait a minute." Tonya stood between them. "Wait a minute, okay?" She looked at Mrs. Judson. "I understand now. You overheard Michelle and me talking in the restaurant yesterday."

Mrs. Judson glared at Michelle and spoke to Tonya. "How very perceptive of you."

"You think that we made up the whole conversation—that we knew about problems in your life and we made up the whole thing."

"Of course. How else would you know about Claudia and

Carl Jr.? How else would you know that she's going to have an abortion?"

Michelle lowered her fists. "Oh, my goodness. Oh, my goodness, Tonya. This is just like in the Bible!"

Tonya waved her hands. "Jesus!" She looked at Mrs. Judson and then at Michelle.

"I think we all need to sit down."

Chapter Twenty-six

onya and Michelle sat down. Tonya waved her hand, again. "Mrs. Judson, I think you need to sit down."

Delores stood behind her desk trembling. What was going on? "This is my office. You can't tell me to sit down."

Michelle whistled. "Girl, this is just like the woman at the well."

Delores could feel her knees weakening. She sat down. Did they think she was going to actually fall for this Three Stooges routine? She played along. "What woman at the well?"

"There was this woman at the well in Samaria that they talk about in the Bible. Jesus came by and he was able to tell her all about her life. It was a miracle. That's how she knew He was real. I can't believe what just happened. God is really real!"

Delores looked at Tonya. "What is she talking about?"

Tonya radiated tranquility. "Mrs. Judson, I know that you know that I believe in God."

"We *all* know you do. You make certain of that."

"Mrs. Judson, I say before God that Michelle and I didn't know you were in that restaurant. We didn't know your life story—we still don't know. I assume Carl Jr. is your son, but I don't know who Claudia is. Mrs. Judson, you are a very private person. How would Michelle and I know the details of your life?"

"You could have intercepted my cell phone calls."

"Have you talked about your family situation over your cell phone?"

Only the school knew Delores's cell phone number, and she hadn't used it since she'd returned to work. "Maybe you listened to my land-line telephone calls."

"Mrs. Judson, your line isn't accessible on our phones."

Michelle chimed in. "That's right, it sure ain't."

"Mrs. Judson, we don't know anything about your life. That's how you want it, and that's how it is. I respect you, Mrs. Judson, but I wouldn't tell you my personal business. I wouldn't tell you that I had an abortion—well, I have told you, I guess. But I didn't do it intentionally. You're my employer, not my friend."

Michelle rolled her eyes. "I know that's right. It ain't no way in—no way in the world I would tell you about my momma and . . . ain't no way in the world I would tell you that . . . about her boyfriend. You can take that to the bank!"

Delores felt her stomach cramping; the muscles felt like they were forming into knots. "You're trying to tell me that all this was coincidental?"

"No, Mrs. Judson, I'm trying to tell you that it was divine. When you look at people who believe and wonder why they keep holding on, why they believe when times get hard, or why they believe when books and men all around us tell us we're foolish, it's because of things like this.

"God keeps showing up in our lives. It would be easy to dismiss Him if He showed up in neat, tidy little ways. If God were just a little breeze it would be easier to dismiss Him.

"It would be coincidence if we ended up at the same restaurant. Maybe still coincidence if we were seated next to each other. But Mrs. Judson, how could my story and Michelle's story just happen to be your story? If you think back through your life, there are some things that just cannot be explained away as a random event."

Michelle nodded. "Just like the woman at the well."

Delores combed through the events, trying to put the pieces together. It couldn't be. She sat forward in her seat. "I don't even believe in God. Why would a God go through all of this for someone who didn't believe?"

"Most of the miracles that the Lord did when He was here, He did so that people would believe. God wants you to know that He's real, Mrs. Judson. He wants you to know that He's watching over you. God wants you to believe."

Michelle had bowed her head. She was weeping. "Maybe He didn't do it just for you, Mrs. Judson. Maybe God did it for me, too. He did all this just so I would know that He loved me, and that it was safe to come home. The Lord wanted me to know that no matter what I have done, He knows, and He still wants me to come home. He wants *me* to know that He's real!"

It was disconcerting to see Michelle cry. Delores looked at her while she questioned Tonya. "If God really exists, why would He bother doing all this for me? He's God of the whole universe. How could such a busy God have time for me?"

"Because, Mrs. Judson, God says that He knows every hair on our heads.[7] He says that He knew us before we were formed in our mother's womb.[8] The Lord is not like we are. He makes time for us and He says that He longs to draw us under his wings like a hen gathering her baby chickens.[9] He says that He is the Great Shepherd and we are the sheep of his pasture. No matter how many sheep He

---

[7] See Matthew 10; Luke 12
[8] See Jeremiah 1
[9] See Luke 13; Matthew 23

has, if one is lost there is nothing He won't do to find that one lost sheep. We may not mean much to ourselves. We may not mean much to each other. But we are precious to God. The Lord came here to earth and walked among us as a man so that He could gather the lost sheep. He is still doing it today."

Delores put her hands over her face. She pressed her fingers against her eyes. "But I have nothing in common with the two of you. Why would God choose you two as examples for me?"

"Maybe because God enjoys using the least among us. The Lord uses the least likely people to show the way. Jesus chose lepers, prostitutes, and swindlers to show other people that He was real. He chooses the foolish—the least likely—to confound the wise. He shines His spotlight on the people that everyone else would like to overlook."

Michelle lifted her head. Her face was wet. "Maybe He wanted all of us to know that we make too big of a deal out of the small things that separates us. We may not have the same amount of money. We may not be the same size or the same color. We may not come from the same neighborhoods or the same kinds of families, but we share the same heartaches. We all feel alone sometimes. We all feel rejected sometimes. We all are sad sometimes. We all feel like our world is falling apart sometimes. We all feel misunderstood.

"We need each other, we can help each other. We all need answers. The answer, no matter what our differences, is the same: Jesus' name is still the same."

Delores was tired and confused. Nothing was making sense. She looked at the clock. It was late; everyone else had probably gone home.

Could He or would He send someone over the wall?

She needed time to think. It was best not to commit to a decision under these circumstances. She needed to take control.

She cleared her throat. "It's getting late. It would be best to finish this discussion at a later date. I'll have my secretary put you ladies on my calendar. In the meantime, I will consider our meeting. I'm not convinced that I shouldn't fire both of you, but I'll weigh everything that we have discussed here. I will be fair. When we meet again, I will give you my decision."

arl tapped his pipe on the ashtray. "I just don't think it's the right thing, Delores. I've tried to make peace with it, but I don't think it's the right thing. I don't think it's the right thing for Claudia." His cheeks sagged and his mouth turned downward. His hair seemed more gray. Carl looked weary. "I know what you think is best. It would be convenient, Delores, but I don't think it would be the right thing."

She could tell that making the statement had taken the wind out of him. Carl never defied her. He never disagreed with her. How many hours, how many days, had he rehearsed what he was saying? How many scenarios had he run through in his mind? How many times had Carl thought, *I will say, then she will say* . . . ? Delores knew it was hard for him. Carl loved peace. Maybe, even more than that, Carl hated conflict.

It was hard for him. She should make it easy. She should, but she couldn't. "What do you mean, exactly, by *it*, Carl? Do you mean the abortion? Are you afraid to say *abortion*?"

Carl flinched and his face flushed. Would he give in? She hoped he would, so that she wouldn't have to hit him again. She hoped that he would cover his head and stay on the floor. Delores didn't want to destroy him. The argument was emotional, but its toll felt almost physical.

He put his pipe back in his mouth and adjusted his glasses. "I don't think Claudia should have the abortion. I don't think we should do it."

"What do you mean you don't think *we* should do it, Carl? You're not having a baby. No one's going to be pointing at you. Claudia's the one that's pregnant, or have you forgotten that? I'm just trying to help her so that she can move on with her life. She's thirteen, for heaven's sake! What is she going to do with a child?"

Delores hoped that Carl would take the count—that he would take the count and walk away still a man.

"That's exactly my point, Delores. She's a child; we are involved."

Carl staggered to his feet. He threw a punch even though he could barely see. "We're responsible for her, and since she can't be responsible, we're also responsible for her child."

"Carl, you said yourself that there wasn't room in our lives for a child. We were sitting right here in this room, right here at this table. What is this—some fit of conscience? Some holy crusade? Don't tell me you've found God since the last time we talked about this?" It was not right, she knew, to hit him with what had been troubling her. It was not right to try to shame him into denying God because she was ashamed of her own uncertainty.

God keeps showing up in our lives.

Tonya and Michelle were common women who didn't know any better. Delores knew better than to turn to religion. She wasn't going to turn to an opiate out of desperation. It was not right to shame Carl, but all was fair in war.

"Of course not." Carl looked away from her. He did not, Delores could tell, want to look her in the eye. "Religion has nothing to do with this." He looked back at her. "I'm talking about making a logical, rational decision. I don't think we've considered the full ramifications of this. There are issues beyond scandal, Delores. We have to think about Claudia's emotional, physical, and mental health."

"Do you think it's going to be healthy for her to have people talking behind her back or even calling her names to her face? Do you think it's in her best interest to ensure that no decent man of any potential is ever going to want to marry her? Do you think it's in her best interest for her immature body to be stretched and damaged trying to give birth? Tell me, Carl, how is this going to help?"

He looked over the top of his glasses. He was so open to her. He was so vulnerable. Delores could see the water pooled in his blue eyes. "I don't know that anything is going to help, Delores. I just don't want to do anything that will hurt. I just want to do the right thing."

"Here we go, again. The right thing. *The right thing.* The right thing is whatever we think it is—if you're really just making a logical decision, Carl, *we* determine the right thing."

"Of course, I agree with you Delores." His shoulders curved and his body slumped. "I don't want to fight about this. You know I hate fighting with you."

"We're not fighting, Carl." She lied, hoping that he would stop resisting. "We're just discussing our options."

"I don't feel good about this, Delores . . . it isn't right. We can't do this just so people won't know that we aren't perfect. There has to be something more to who we are as a family, who we are as people, than our reputations."

She didn't want to tell him. Why was he forcing her? Why couldn't he just let go? Why couldn't he do what he always did and just lie down?

"I never defy you, Delores. I love you. I want to make you

happy. I have loved you since the moment I saw you. I love your strength." He cleared his throat. "And I can't imagine living my life without you." Carl paused, looked at his right hand lying flat on the table. "But I feel strongly about this."

He looked into her eyes. "I'm prepared to take Claudia and live with her alone." He looked around the room. "I don't know where we would go." His voice pleaded. "I don't know where we would live or how. I can't imagine . . . But I feel it's that important."

Delores didn't respond right away. She was angry with Claudia for ruining their lives. For taking away the one person in her life that she could always count on. She was angry with Claudia for forcing her to break Carl's heart.

"Maybe you're right, Carl. Maybe our reputations aren't that important. But while you're saying this, there's something you don't know. There's something I haven't told you. Something I didn't want to tell you because I didn't want to hurt you. I'm not the bad guy in all of this. I didn't get Claudia pregnant, remember that. I'm just the one who has to take care of the mess.

"I don't want to tell you now, Carl. So, please, let this go. Just let it go. It's painful now, but we'll all get over it. Trust me. You love me? Then trust me. Let's just put this nastiness behind us and move on, Carl. I don't want to make it any worse."

Carl looked down and then into her eyes. "I can't budge on this, Delores. I want to—I tried for weeks now to convince myself. I'm not really sure why, but I can't move."

Delores pulled a knife in what had, up until now, been a civilized fistfight. She got up from the table. Carl called out behind her, "Delores, wait."

She walked to the foot of the stairs and yelled for Claudia. Her granddaughter appeared at the top of the steps. "Come down here." As Claudia walked down the stairs, Delores could see her life, her marriage, and her happiness tumble down the stairs ahead of the girl.

She steered Claudia into the room where her grandfather sat. Claudia stood at the head of the long table, while Delores returned to her seat across from Carl. She looked at her husband. "There's still time to stop this, Carl. We can just do what needs to be done. We don't have to finish this. Let's just let it be done."

Carl shook his head. "We have to do the right thing."

Delores took a deep breath. She had always been the one willing to do the hard thing. "Claudia, tell your grandfather."

The girl looked tiny standing at the end of the table. Her smile was gone. It had been gone for weeks. She was pale, which made her hair even more stark against her skin. Her eyes looked almost hopeless. "I don't know what you mean."

Claudia had stopped calling her *Grandmama*. Now she just avoided her. Now she was just a ghost.

"I want you to tell your grandfather what you told me."

Claudia said nothing.

"He needs to know. I know I told you to never tell, but your grandfather needs to know." Delores reached for a magazine that was lying on the table near to her. She flipped it open for effect. She pretended to browse a few pages. Then she turned back to her granddaughter and lowered her voice. "Tell him, Claudia. Now. Tell him about the father."

She didn't want to hurt Carl, but he was bringing the pain on himself. He wouldn't submit. The news about Carl Jr. would be the final blow. It would wrench his heart apart like it had hers. It would knock the wind out of his lungs, just as it had done her. The news would flood his eyes with tears and render him speechless, just as it had her. The news about Carl Jr. would lay her husband out flat on his back, just as it had done to her. Only she was certain Carl wouldn't be able to get back up.

Carl shook his head. "You don't have to do this, Claudia." He shook his head at Delores. She could see it in his eyes. He knew it was something he didn't want to know. It was something that might kill him—the blow that she was striking might be fatal. "Don't do this, Delores."

It was too late. She had pleaded with him before. It was too late now. "Tell him, Claudia."

Carl looked at his granddaughter. "You don't have to tell me." His voice was tender. "It doesn't matter who the boy is—what he is. We'll deal with it. You can go back to your room. You don't have to tell me."

She loved him. She didn't want to have to hurt him. She had tried to warn him . . .

She looked at Claudia. Her granddaughter's eyes were begging. "Tell him, Claudia. Tell him now."

Claudia began to cry. "I'm sorry, Grandfather. I'm sorry."

"Don't tell me, Claudia." Carl began to cry, too. "Don't tell me."

"Tell him, Claudia. He deserves it. He's trying to protect you and he needs to know."

"I'm sorry, Grandfather. I'm sorry." Claudia looked to Delores for clemency, to be spared striking the fatal blow.

"Tell him!"

I'm sorry. Claudia mouthed the words as her face wrinkled in pain. "My uncle," she said. "My uncle is the father."

I'm sorry, she mouthed again. Her young body crumpled to the floor.

"What do you mean?" Carl choked out a laugh and looked at Delores. "What does she mean?"

She was through crying—she had to protect herself, right now. She had to preserve their way of life. "Her uncle. She's talking about your son." Delores delivered the information like a cobra strike.

Carl clapped both of his hands to his face. His shoulders convulsed and a wail shook his body. He writhed in agony. Delores could almost feel the pain of the strike and the venom moving through her husband's veins. She looked down at Claudia, who lay transfixed on the floor, watching her grandfather with misery in her eyes. Delores felt like ice.

After a moment that seemed like years, Carl slowly lowered his hands and removed his pipe. He looked on the table for some-thing—maybe a handkerchief, tissue, or a napkin. He first wiped his face with his hands, and then yanked them through his thinning hair. He began to cry again. He turned his head and gave Claudia a fee-ble smile.

"It's all right, darling. Don't worry. It's going to be all right."

Claudia broke down then, weeping silently with her face pressed to the floor. Carl tried several times to control his sobbing. He slumped forward and then straightened himself again.

Delores would not let herself feel. She was numb inside.

Carl sighed as though he had aged a hundred years. "Go up to your room. It's going to be all right." His face was pink and his hair was disheveled. "Claudia, it's going to be all right."

No matter what happens, I'm going to be all right. Delores squared her shoulders and straightened her back. She sat and waited for the end.

Part Four

Spring
~~Winter~~ – Miz Ida

iz Ida danced around her kitchen with a jar full of water—
a quart-sized mayonnaise jar with no label—in her hand.
She sang along with John P. Kee, "I believe." She shook
her head and her hips. No one was watching, so she moved every
body part she could. It was her way of thanking the Lord for the ac-
tivity of her limbs. She even tried to cut a few new hip-hop steps—
what she could do without wasting the water. Every foot or so, she
stopped to water a plant. More accurately, she incorporated the watering into her dancing.

No one at church knew it—because church people don't have
to know all her business—but when the Spirit hit her, Miz Ida could
still kick her right leg up over her head. She danced and waved her
free hand over her head. It didn't matter what things looked like; she
knew that God was moving.

Miz Ida planted lots of seeds and her kitchen was full of lots of
plants. It wasn't the season, but the plants didn't seem to know it.

Nothing withered and blooms showed up everywhere. Miz Ida broke into a praise step.

She was a firm believer that everyone needed a little time alone to dance and praise the Lord. 'Course, she left room for those who weren't as spry as she was. Miz Ida was willing to agree to disagree.

There wasn't much for an ordinary person to shout about in her old kitchen. The walls and even the refrigerator were old and yellowed. The tile on the floor had cracked. There were only two good eyes that still worked on the stove. Most folks would have said the things in the kitchen didn't have much use anymore. Of course, many folks would have said the same thing about Miz Ida. But Miz Ida wasn't ready to give up on the kitchen and she wasn't ready to give up on herself.

She kept the kitchen clean, but try as hard as she could, every once in a while a roach passed through. She always let each one know not to unpack its bags—it didn't pay rent, it wasn't welcome, and she wasn't fixing it anything to eat. Still, sometimes the six-legged trespassers tried to test her resolve. The bugs were always sorry because Miz Ida had a little something deadly waiting for them.

But she just wasn't willing to let any of it get her down. *Hallelujah anyhow!* She hoofed around and imagined that she was singing in a gospel video. She moved from side to side and shook her head.

Someone looking in her window—which was of course impossible because her kitchen window and apartment were so many stories up from the ground that someone would have to be a giant, or Tom Cruise hanging from a wire, to see in—would have thought Miz Ida was crazy. But that's what she did, that's what kept her fueled when other people said she should slow down—crazy praise.

People who didn't know her would have thought she was two or three bricks shy of a full load. But people who knew Miz Ida knew she believed that spring was liable to break out any time and all over.

Once it broke out one place, it just seemed to spread. Miz Ida believed that just because someone said it was winter that didn't mean that the sun couldn't shine and things couldn't grow.

Miz Ida was a fountain of hope. That, a lot of prayer, a good measure of faith, and a lot of love, she believed, was why her kitchen was always green. In Miz Ida's kitchen it was always spring.

She watered one more plant and stopped to pray. "Lord, You and me been at this a long time. We've seen sinners turned into saints, sick bodies healed, and broken hearts mended. And You know I'm glad about it. Lord, I'm old, but I know You can still use me. It's good to be on the Lord's side.

"You said, Lord, if I would delight in Your law—in Your word—and if I would think about You day and night, You would do something special for me. Well, Lord, You know Ida thinks about You all the time." She laughed to herself. "Some people might get sick of someone calling on them as much as I call on You. I'm glad You ain't like people. Lord, I love Your word and I can't get it off my mind or out of my heart. 'Course I wouldn't try it if I could.

"So, Lord, do what You promised. I'm calling on the favor that You have give me. There so many people all over who just need a new day! They're tired and worn out. They're sick of just being sick of themselves. They been hanging on waiting for a change to come. Lord, let this be the beginning of a new day. Let this be the day when the seeds they have planted come into their season and bear good fruit. And make their lives like my kitchen, Lord. Even when it's winter, let it always be green."

Miz Ida knew something that Sarah, the wife of Abraham, had known: The winter of a woman's life isn't a time for sadness and despair. The winter of a woman's life is a time to rejoice. Miz Ida knew that winter was the time of miracles, that twice it was mentioned in the Bible that Sarah laughed. The first time, Sarah laughed at God. The second time, in the winter of her life, Sarah laughed with God. The first time she laughed at the impossibility of God's promise to give her, a barren woman, a child. The second time she laughed because she learned that God is faithful and even in winter He keeps His promises.[10]

People forget, when they complain about winter being cold and lonely, that Christmas comes as a signal of the new day. People forget, when they're counting all the ways that winter gets on their nerves, that winter ushers in a brand-spanking New Year. People forget that it's winter's right to always introduce the spring.

So, Miz Ida laughed with winter. She enjoyed her winter years because winter was just spring painted frosty white. God gave new life, even in the winter years. "Lord, I just get tickled seeing You break out all over. Do Your thing, Lord. Show off if You want to, Jesus, You know Miz Ida ain't mad at You. Show off, Lord, and let us see the goodness of the Lord in the land of the living."

The old woman danced, sang, laughed, and watered until the doorbell rang. She stopped and peeked in the mirror, just to make sure she was presentable, on her way to the door. She squinted and looked through the peephole. It was Michelle.

"How are you, baby?" She wrapped the girl—the woman—in a great big hug. There was a time when she'd had to bend to embrace Michelle. Now Michelle was bending to hold her. It was funny how the seasons and the times changed.

"Now you come on in here." She took Michelle's hand. "Ain't nothing like a visit from a real good friend."

They sat on the couch and Miz Ida caught hold of her hand. "Honey, I was just thinking the other day. Remember when you and me used to play Uno? I remember the first time you told me about that game, I thought you had lost your little mind." She was bubbling over, just happy to talk to her young friend, until she realized they weren't conversing. She was talking, but Michelle was having nothing to say.

"Cat got your tongue?" She nudged Michelle playfully, but the

---

[10]T.D. Jakes, *Woman, Thou Art Loosed* (Tulsa, OK: Albury Publishing, 1993) 175–176, paraphrased.

younger woman had nothing to say—she barely smiled. "What's wrong, Michelle? You know you can tell me."

Michelle stood and walked to a window. She looked outside for several minutes and then turned back to Miz Ida. "Either everything is getting better, or else everything is falling apart, Miz Ida, and I can't figure which one it is. What it feels like is everything is falling apart."

Miz Ida patted the couch. "Come and tell me about it, baby."

Michelle plopped down beside her. She pointed to her face. "I guess you can't see my eye anymore. Trench walloped me good, Miz Ida. And I thought it was good enough to end it. It was good enough for me to see what you've been trying to say to me all along, that I'm following in my mother's footsteps. Like I've just brought to life the same man to do the same thing to me that was done before. I see it, and I thought it was over. I'm a smart woman and I know better."

She looked away. "But I let him back in. I let him back in my house, knowing who he was. Trench is not staying there; I wouldn't let him stay over. And I told him not to come back—not that I haven't said that before. But I can't figure out why I even let him in, why I let him touch me, again. He didn't scare me, Miz Ida. I scared myself.

"And then there's Todd. God knows that he is a good man. And, Miz Ida, I can't even tell you that I stay away from him and keep him away from me because I don't love him. I love Todd. But I don't understand why, or what is going on in my life. Even when I don't mean to push him away, I push him away. But, I keep thinking if I don't get this together soon, I'm going to lose my husband. Todd is going to get tired of waiting for me."

Michelle looked at Miz Ida. "I sound like an old, whiny stereo don't I?"

"No, you sound like a woman who has been thinking. You sound like a woman with a lot on her mind."

"Well, you're right, Miz Ida. I have been thinking. I been thinking about Todd and Trench. I been thinking about my job. Miz Ida, things have been going so good at my job. Me and that lady, Tonya, that I been telling you about—things have been work-ing out so much better between us.

"She told me that I've been helping her be a better person. She's saved—good and saved Miz Ida—and she's tell me that I'm helping her. I never had *anybody* ever tell me that." She laid her hand over her heart and her voice sounded as though she could not be-lieve what she was saying. "I've always been somebody's hurt. I've never been anybody's help before."

Michelle shook her head. "Then something crazy happened. It was just like in the Bible, Miz Ida."

Ida listened as Michelle told the story about Mrs. Judson and about her overhearing the conversation in the restaurant.

"She thought we were tricking her. But it couldn't have been nobody but the Lord. But now she's mad at us. She is threatening to fire both of us. How can we defend ourselves against something that the Lord did? Now that things seem to be working good, it looks like I might not even have a job. How can God let it be so good on one hand, and so bad on the other?"

Michelle held Miz Ida's hand and laid her head back on the couch. "But one thing I know for sure is that God is real. Not that I doubted He was real. You know that, Miz Ida. But I could see Him, so strong, working to speak to me this time. When the thing happened with Mrs. Judson, I knew He wasn't just trying to speak to her, He was speaking to me. All these years, I never had the Lord speak to me that way. It makes me wonder why He wasn't speaking to me before."

Ida patted the younger woman's hand. "He was speaking be-fore, Michelle. Your heart just wasn't ready to listen. When you were a girl and your mother was lost, God situated you in a building where the three of us could meet. When you were heartbroken and away at school, feeling like you weren't worth a red cent, God sent Todd into your life. That boy loved you with a supernatural love. Now that he's a man, he still does. God was in that; you just weren't ready to see it. Think of all the things He brought you through—abuse, drugs, and prostitution. Baby, just think how many people never make it out of that alive. God was in your getting delivered and coming out; you just couldn't see it.

"If you really sit back and think about it, God's been working for you and trying to tell you that He loves you all along. You were just so hurt and brokenhearted you couldn't accept His love. Most of the time we don't recognize God because He just doesn't look like what we expected. I'll bet when you were a little girl and you were looking for God to send someone to help you, you were looking for a superhero in a cape or a big policeman with a gun. The last thing you probably expected was a little black woman with gray hair in some funny-looking clothes."

Michelle laughed, "You were dressed funny, Miz Ida, the first time you came to our door."

"See what I mean? And when you were a young lady, after being used by men and after selling yourself to men, the last thing you expected was for the Lord to send you a man to rescue you."

Michelle raised her head from the couch. "Miz Ida, I never thought about it that way. But you're right. I never expected a man to try to help me. I think I've always been waiting for Todd to show his true self, to turn around and hurt me and use me like the other men in my life did. I didn't expect God to send a man to rescue me."

Miz Ida squeezed Michelle's hand. "When the Lord came, people didn't believe it was Him because He didn't look like what they expected. Nothing has changed. And something else—that woman at your job, is she about your mother's age?"

A strange expression came over Michelle's face. "I hadn't thought of it that way, Miz Ida. I never expected God to send me help from someone who was like a mother, either."

"And you know, Michelle, something just came to me. God said where two or three gather in His name, He would be there in the midst of it.[11] God talks to us when we're alone, but He speaks in a different way when we sit or gather with other people. You and

---

[11]Matthew 18:20

that lady Tonya were in that restaurant talking, and one of the things You were doing was lifting up the name of Jesus. When you were in Mrs. Judson's office, His name got lifted again. It seems like to me that He was in the midst of you, and that He was doing what He promised—opening His arms to draw you near to Him."

Michelle sat up on the couch. "So what do I do now, Miz Ida? I don't know how to fix all this. I don't know if I *can* fix it."

Miz Ida looked calm. "Well, baby, you know the hotline is always open. God knows us. When we are angry or rebellious, when our hearts are hard, we can't hear His voice. But He's always there waiting for us with open arms. If we need wisdom, all we have to do is ask. He'll teach us just like he taught David. Listen to this." Miz Ida grabbed her Bible off the table. She adjusted her eyeglasses on her nose. "Let me see, now, I think it's Psalm Twenty-five. Yes, here it is." She began to read at verse four.

> Show me your ways, O LORD,
> teach me your paths;
> guide me in your truth and teach me,
> for you are God my Savior,
> and my hope is in you all day long.

Miz Ida lowered the book. "David was praying the same thing, thousands of years ago that you are praying today. God listened to him then, and He listens to you now. David needed the same thing you need then that you need now—the answer to a life or death question. All he was saying was 'Lord, help me to tell the good from the bad. I can't figure it out myself. Make it clear to me when it's You speaking and moving in my life, Lord. All I can trust and count on is You.'" She handed Michelle the Bible. "You read for a minute."

> Remember, O LORD, your great mercy and love,
> for they are from of old.

Remember not the sins of my youth
and my rebellious ways;
according to your love remember me,
for you are good, O LORD.

Miz Ida closed her eyes and nodded. "That's right, Michelle. It's like David and you were going through the same thing. He was saying 'Lord, forget about my past all the things I did wrong. But when you think of me, Lord, think about love and mercy—don't think of what I did wrong, just think of how much you love me.' And don't you know that it's like that with parents? Your children can do wrong, but when you look on them sometimes all you can think about is love." She tapped Michelle on the shoulder. "Read that other little bit to me, baby."

Good and upright is the LORD;
therefore he instructs sinners in his ways.
He guides the humble in what is right
and teaches them his way.[12]

"Isn't that something, Michelle? It just does something to me to think that thousands of years ago someone prayed the prayer that is still perfect for us today!"

She put her arm around Michelle. "Don't you worry about a thing, honey. God has done major surgery on your wounded heart. Now He is renewing your mind. You keep praying in your heart. You keep the Lord with you. When you feel like you about to step wrong, you remember that I'm sitting here praying—and no matter what, God is with you."

Miz Ida smiled, slapped her knee, and then squeezed Michelle's arm. "If you could feel coming what I feel coming, honey, you would want to get up and dance with me. Girl, get ready, get ready, get ready! You keep watching, you keep believing, and you keep praying. Something good is about to come!"

---

[12]Psalm 25: 4–9 NIV

Chapter Twenty-nine

hen Miz Ida answered the phone, it was Michelle. She was laughing to beat the band. She couldn't stop laughing long enough to say hello. "What is wrong with you, girl?"

"Nothing, Miz Ida. I just had to call and tell you." Michelle was still laughing. "You know me and Tonya been meeting for lunch, and I told you about that man Shadrach? Well, we took some extra time and went to lunch at the train station today." Michelle sounded as though she could hardly catch her breath.

What on earth had gotten into the child? Miz Ida couldn't help smiling. Whatever was going on with Michelle was contagious.

"When we got back, I wanted to call you so bad! But you know I'm trying to cut down on the calls at work. It was all I could do to hold it until I got home. I just have to tell you what happened . . ."

Michelle, Tonya, and Shadrach decided to meet for lunch outside of the building. Sometimes it's good, Shadrach said, to go somewhere different, and to try a little something new.

The restaurant was inside the old train station. Walking inside the station was like walking into a palace. The ceiling arched way above their heads and was covered with paintings of people, intricate plaster shapes, and gold detailing. Michelle, Shadrach, and Tonya, like all the people, restaurants, and shops around them, were swallowed inside of the structure. The design was so elaborate that they wondered amongst themselves how regular people like them could have dreamed dreams and birthed visions so divine.

They found a restaurant on an upper floor, closer to the ceiling, where they could watch people beneath them come and go. It was good, Shadrach said, to keep changing perspective.

There waiters were dressed in white coats with gold buttons and they wore crisply pleated black pants. The light—soft and diffused—came from antique-looking wall sconces. The wallpaper was an elaborate pattern of what looked to be red velvet and gold.

One of the waiters, a young Hispanic man with his hair combed like Rudolph Valentino, walked by and winked at Michelle. She looked at Shadrach and Tonya. "I think I've decided. I'm giving up men."

Shadrach laughed first. "Shoot, girl, what you talking about?"

"I'm talking about giving up men. You know, I just can't figure it out—I can't get the man thing together. So I figured the best way is to just let it alone."

Shadrach pretended to be offended. "So, the brothers are responsible? The brothers got to suffer?"

Michelle looked across the table. "You know what, I really don't want to talk about me. I want to talk about this new 'do our girl is sporting."

Tonya patted her hair. "You like it?"

"Girl, when you walked in today, I barely recognized you. I thought we had a new sister in the office." She laughed. "When you said change, you meant change. Tonya, girl, with a hairdo like that, you can take your place among the *divalicious*!"

Tonya blushed. "The divalicious? What are the divalicious?" She laughed.

"Yeah, what are—who are—the divalicious?" Shadrach turned in his seat.

"Well, you know nowadays everybody and her mama is a diva. It's diva this and diva that. The divalicious are the best of the best, the diva of divas. The diva-licious are the most luscious and delicious of divas. You know, the sister with the biggest hats, the biggest hair, the baddest suit—whatever the woman is working, she's working it to the '-est degree'! That makes her diva-*licious*!"

Shadrach shook his head. "I've heard it all now. Where did you come up with something like that?"

Michelle laughed. "I told you I was giving up men. A sister has a lot of time on her hands."

Shadrach leaned closer to the wall. "Please don't let that word get out anywhere. I'm going to choke you, Michelle, if I hear it again out of anybody's mouth because I will know where it came from."

Tonya patted her hair. "So, you really think I'm divalicious?"

Shadrach groaned. "I signed up to be a coach. I didn't sign up for this."

Michelle ignored him. "Girl, ain't no doubt about it. The bun is dead." Michelle began to sing softly to the tune of "Ding Dong! The Witch Is Dead!"

Hey, yo! The bun is dead.
Which old bun?
Tonya's bun.
Hey, yo! The killer bun is dead!

Shadrach leaned away from her and stared. "What is into you today, girl?"

Michelle waved him away and smiled at Tonya. "Girl, you got

to celebrate when stuff in your life that has been holding you back is now dead. That bun had you in bondage—or *bun-dage*—for years. We got to sing it away so it won't try to come back!"

She stood up and started lifting and lowering her arms and legs like she was performing in a Broadway play.

Shadrach pulled at the edge of her jacket. "Girl, sit down! People are looking at you like you are crazy! They're going to kick us out of here."

Tonya was laughing so hard she started snorting.

Michelle refused to sit down. "These people don't know me. What do I care what they think? Sometimes, you got to make your own party. My sister is coming out! The girl is divalicious and the bun is dead! If they can't get with that, if they're too dried up and dead to join the party, they should have stayed home."

She waved her arms and started singing again. The waiter passed by; instead of winking, he just lowered his head. Michelle sang louder.

Hey-yo! The bun is dead!
Which old bun?
Tonya's bun!
Hey-yo! Tonya's bun is dead!

She grabbed Tonya's hand. "Come on and sing it with me!"

Hey, yo, the bun is dead.
Which old bun?
Tonya's bun.
Hey, yo, the killer bun is dead!

Shadrach shook his head and covered his face.

It's gone where the bad weaves go,
No mo', no mo' no mo'!
Hey-yo! Let's get on up and sing out loud because . . .

Michelle grabbed the waiter when he passed by, again. "Dance, boy. Sing and bounce with me."

Hey yo, the merry-oh,
It has died! It ain't no mo'!
We're singing cause the killer bun is dead!

The maitre d' came to the table. "Ladies and gentleman, please. Is there some way that we can help you?"

⌒

Michelle's delighted laughter rang in Ida's ears.

"Miz Ida, when I told him what was going on and showed him how beautiful Tonya looked, the maitre d' got caught up in it too! The next thing I knew, most of the folks in the restaurant were singing. We had a kind of congo-line thing going around the restaurant. Tonya was leading and laughing. You would have never recognized her. She was like a new person."

Miz Ida laughed out loud trying to imagine the scene.

"It was crazy, Miz Ida. Poor Shadrach kept trying to hide out, but pretty soon, he was caught up in the whole thing, too."

Miz Ida laughed with Michelle for a while. "That was a good thing you did, today, baby."

"I didn't do anything, Miz Ida. Tonya has done so much. It just seems like it happened suddenly. She told me she was going to start working out. And I laughed at first because she said she was just going to sneak in ten minutes or so here and there. But Miz Ida Tonya is looking good. Then after she killed that bun, I had to say something. I just had to. But that wasn't all Miz Ida . . ."

⌒

By the time everything settled down in the restaurant, and Michelle and the others had returned to their booth, Tonya was smiling—she was actually glowing. "I want to thank both of you.

You have made so much difference in my life. Even my son has noticed. I couldn't see that I had just laid down and given up." Her
eyes filled with tears. "Thank you."

Shadrach smiled and looked slightly uncomfortable. "That's all
right. Don't worry, you'll get the bill for my consulting fees."

Michelle elbowed him. "Whatever, Shad."

Tonya gave them both an effervescent smile.

Shad leaned forward. "So, now that you're working on this
new hair, this new look, and this new attitude, why don't you take
it all the way?" His eyes sparkled. "You could get you some spike
heels." He smiled. "Wine just gets finer with age, you know. I don't
know why women—especially church women—have to give up and
start trying to make what still looks good look bad. A sister that's
taking care of herself can still pull off something that shows some
curves, something that shows she's still got it. The spirituality in a
woman makes her more exciting. Now, if you can get the outside to
where it's pumping, too, then you got something. You could try
something like Michelle wears. Maybe something short and spicy!"

Tonya blushed. "Oh, Shadrach, stop teasing me." She lowered
her voice. "I tell you what, though. If a man wants to be with me,
he's going to have to use a little imagination. The bun is dead.
Michelle just made sure of that, so the hair is not an issue. He might
be able to get a little higher heel out of me. But it ain't but so tight
and so short that I'm going, brother! I am not going to become
some hoochie look-alike."

Michelle laughed, then stopped and looked back and forth between them. "Wait a minute. Should I be offended?"

Shadrach and Tonya ignored her. Shadrach leaned back. "Well,
Tonya, you're right. A woman and a man both have to know who
they are and what they want out of life. You know, like what they can
tolerate and what they can't."

"For example?"

"Like, for example, a man can't be with a woman who makes
too much money. A woman has to think about a man's ego."

Tonya adjusted the way she was sitting on her side of the booth. "The thing is, Shadrach, I don't know how I feel about that. I mean, suppose I get promoted—not that I'm going to because Mrs. Judson is still not speaking to me and Michelle. But if I did get promoted are you telling me that being successful could mean that a man might just fade out of my life?"

"Well, a man needs to be the leader, the provider, the head of the household. It's a touchy subject with a man."

"I can understand that."

Michelle stared at Tonya. She had never heard her talk this way to a man. Even the timbre of Tonya's voice changed—it was purring and smoky.

"I understand it, but don't we have to grow beyond that kind of thinking? I mean, whatever money I have, God gave it to me. I wasn't really seeking it. I didn't have a plan in my life that I was even going to be working. God gave me this to bless me and take care of my needs and to bless people that are in my life. Are you telling me that because God blessed me I have to be lonely?"

"I'm just saying it's a sticky situation with a man."

"I hope that you're not saying that I have to be lonely because I'm blessed. Because the Bible says that God's blessing makes us rich and He adds no sorrow.[13] It would make me really sad if God put the perfect man for me in my life, but he rejected me because I was blessed. That wouldn't make sense would it? That would make me sad—that would add sorrow."

Shadrach stared into Tonya's eyes. "No, it wouldn't make sense, but it's still a sticky situation with a man."

"Maybe what a woman would need to do is to reassure her man that what gives him value in her life is not the coins in his pocket, but the richness of his character."

Shadrach's smile was slow and approving. "That might help."

"Maybe what a real woman would need to tell a man, the real

---

[13]Proverbs 10:22

man in her life, is that she is striving to be a virtuous woman—a virtuous woman, like the woman in Proverbs Thirty-one."

Shadrach was staring at Tonya as though Michelle wasn't there. "I've heard a little bit about that. The virtuous woman is strong, wise, trustworthy, and supportive of her man."

Tonya nodded. "But Shadrach, not only is the virtuous woman a spiritual blessing to her family, not only is she so much woman that her husband and her children praise her, she is also a wealthy woman. Now how can a man find fault with that?"

"I hear that. It sounds like a good thing, believe me, but I just don't know how it plays out in the real world, Tonya."

"Well, the Lord didn't have trouble traveling with wealthy women. He visited their homes and they supported his ministry."

"It's still a hard thing for a man. A man needs to be in control."

Tonya smiled. "Well, a man needs to know the heart of the woman that he's thinking about marrying. He should know, if he's going to be with her, that the key to his authority in her life is not his platinum credit card. He needs to know that he is her king because of her admiration for the generosity of his wise and understanding heart. He is her lover because of his intelligence, which is spirit led and without price. A woman would have to reassure her blessed man that he is her husband because she has found him to be her match—body and soul. I think that a blessed man and a blessed woman would have to believe that the spirit of the Lord would intercede and work out the rest."

Michelle looked at Shad. What had just happened? Shadrach grunted. "Why do women always ask questions to just tear down your answers in favor of their own?"

❦

Michelle fell silent for a moment, and Ida waited. She knew the story wasn't over.

"Miz Ida, I was looking at those two people and I think I just disappeared. For a minute, I got this funny feeling. You know, like I wanted to say something or do something to make Shadrach pay attention to me. He's a nice man, you know. I was thinking for a minute, why would he want her instead of me."

"That was just the old Michelle talking. You know, the old Michelle that just needed attention from any man. You're not that woman anymore."

Michelle's voice sounded as though she had just discovered she had some new treasure. "You're right, Miz Ida. I'm not that woman anymore. And it came to me that Tonya is my friend. I never was able to say that before about a woman, but Tonya is my friend. I want her to be happy. She and Shadrach would make a good match. So I didn't have to try to get his attention."

"No, you're not a needy woman. Michelle, you're a blessed woman."

"I am blessed, Miz Ida."

"Not only are you blessed, but you're blessing others—because you blessed that woman today. Yes, you did, baby. You made that woman laugh. It ain't no telling how long it's been in her life since she had a good stomach laugh. Michelle, you were a blessing to her. People think the only way to bless someone is to hand out money or material gifts. Don't ever let anybody tell you that you're nothing, again. From here on out, you sing a song for yourself. God has blessed you to be a blessing!"

"Besides that, Miz Ida, when Tonya was talking to Shad, I thought about Todd." Michelle's voice was lighthearted and full of amazement. "You know, Miz Ida, I do love Todd. Through all that's been going on he's stood by me. And I love him for the very reasons that Tonya was saying. All this time I've been listening to crazy stuff—that a man is something just because he has money, because he is fine, or because he's supposed to be some kind of super lover."

Miz Ida could feel herself blushing. "Well, do tell?"

"Today, Miz Ida, I realized I been listening to the wrong people. I been listening to women who don't know no more than I do—maybe even less. I been listening to women because they're famous instead of because they're wise. I been listening to them, and I've been about to throw my good thing away. Now ain't that nothing?"

"That's nothing, baby."

"Tonya's right. I love Todd because he is wise and understanding. He is a good man and he loves me. He is a man of God, Miz Ida, and he's been praying for me and singing God's songs to me. He is my match body and soul."

"All right, now, Michelle! I think we're getting somewhere."

"That's just it, Miz Ida. *Now* I know and I hope it's not too late."

When she and Michelle had said their goodbyes, Miz Ida hung up the telephone. "Lord, my Lord." She waved her hand in the air. "My Lord, have Your way. Hallelujah!"

iz Ida rocked back and forth with the tiny baby in her arms. He wrapped his little fingers, the nails so miniscule and translucent, around hers. Miz Ida talked to him. "You're a strong little fella, aren't you? The way you're holding my finger, you're going to grow up to be another Samson. Yes, you are."

As she rocked him, Miz Ida recalled the first time she had walked in the Children's House of Peace. When her feet hit the black rubber of the sensor pad that automatically opened the door, she had thought about turning back. She hadn't known anyone at the center. She hadn't even known too much about what she was trying to do.

She had stopped at the information desk and got the directions, then taken the elevator to the fourth floor and followed the red line to the high-risk nursery unit. She was a little nervous—people told her it was time for her to settle down, she didn't need to be pushing herself—but the children needed somebody. She had heard it on the TV and then read about them in the newspaper—border babies. The Children's House of Peace was a haven for them.

They were babies born to mothers who were HIV positive or who had AIDS.

"Some of the babies who are born test HIV positive because babies carry the immune system of their mothers. Many times, though, when their own immune systems begin to function those same babies become HIV negative," the nurse that worked with volunteers had told her. "People are so afraid of them. We need people who have hearts big enough to care. We need people who have love that will overcome their fear."

Miz Ida loved rocking baby José. They had been meeting twice a week since she first came. "We always try to assign the babies to the same volunteers because we hope that they will get even some small sense of normalcy in their lives," the nurse said. "Some of the babies are with us because their moms are in jail and there's no one else to care for them. Some, like José, have mothers who are just too ill to care for them. Whatever the reason they're here, they need love. Most of them got here because the people before them lived lives without enough love. We're trying to draw the line in the sand for these babies right here."

They needed love and Miz Ida had plenty to give. When she held José, she couldn't help but think about Michelle. Not many people would ever have thought that child would make it. Not many politicians or social scientists would have predicted that Michelle would have become the woman that she was. When she met Michelle, the girl was what they called now *"at risk."* Hallelujah! Michelle had made it over, but there were plenty other children in need.

Miz Ida came out twice a week because her soul was fat. She had heard lots of good preaching, had lots of good teaching, and she regularly studied the Word. She was full. She was so full, one tiny touch from the Lord, one iota of the Lord's goodness just made her cup of tears overflow. The folks already in the church, Miz Ida felt, were healed or on their way to healing. There were lots of folks— grown-ups, babies, and children—on the outside, though, who were starving.

"We've come to worship and now we leave to serve," her pastor always said after the benediction. *You can't feed the hungry sitting in your living room,* Miz Ida told herself. Starving folks didn't always have the strength to make it to church, so Miz Ida figured it was her duty to go to them.

There was nothing about Michelle, about José, or about any of the babies at the House of Peace that God couldn't handle. Miz Ida knew the Lord could do whatever needed to be done. So she didn't spend a lot of time, when she held José, praying for God to heal him. That was settled and done as far as Miz Ida was concerned.

The reason she came to visit José twice a week was to hold him, to love and serve a new life that needed her. But she also came to pray about broken hearts. Miz Ida figured that broken hearts were about the hardest thing, it seemed, to mend. So she prayed every week for all the children who didn't know their fathers or who only saw them once in a blue moon. She rocked José and prayed for all the children who didn't know their mothers, or who felt that their mothers had made the choice to give them away. She prayed for all the families separated by crime, by war, and by death.

God, we got to break this thing somewhere. We got to draw a line here somewhere. It's too much heartache and we got to stop it now and say, "No more!" No more heartbroken girls growing into heartbroken women. No more boys carrying heartache with them until they die as men. No more, Lord.

She rocked the baby and smiled and sang to him while she prayed in her heart. *Lord, I'm holding this little baby, and I'm praying. But don't just do it for him. Lord, I'm praying for all the babies who don't have anybody to hold them. Don't just heal bodies, Lord— mend broken hearts.*

Right now, Lord, there are some grown women walking around every day smiling and working. Everybody around them thinks they're okay. Even their best friends, husbands and boyfriends don't know. They don't know that sometimes these women steal away to cry. Some of these women just want love from any man, from anyone. But some of them, Lord, are so cold it's like winter in their souls. They're sitting alone right now telling themselves and the world they don't need love—but it's like the pins and needles of cold weather pressing into their hearts.

Lord, I'm praying for a new day. I'm praying that new healing and new deliverance starts right now. I'm praying that they would begin to weep healing tears that will thaw their hearts. Tears that will clean and heal the wounds that they've been carrying with them for years. God, let them feel Your sweet love for them. No matter what they've been through, no matter what they've done, Lord, let them feel Your sweet, sweet presence. Lord, touch right now, from the jailhouse to the White House. Lord, move in women's lives wherever they are—in school, in the home, at work, in the air, on land, and at sea. Let these women, these girls, know what it means to be loved. Let them know how it feels to climb up on Your lap and how good it feels to call you Daddy. God, I know You're able. I'm looking for a new day.

Ida paused a moment to smile at José. She clucked her tongue at him and then resumed her prayer.

Lord, there are so many heartbroken men. Men whose hearts are as fragile as this tiny baby's heart. They're pretending to be strong on the outside—they got so much to take care of and so much weight on their shoulders. Some of them are trying to be men when they never had a father of their own to teach them how. They're hard on the outside and afraid to let anyone get near their hearts because they're wounded. They're afraid to love or be loved, even by children, because all they've known is heartache. God, I know that You're able. I know that You are the heavenly Father who can speak healing to the heart of a man. You're the Daddy big enough to wrap Your arms around a man and touch that place in him that is in need. God, I need You to heal these men. There are so many men locked away in so many prisons—physical pris-ons, mental prisons, emotional prisons, sexual prisons, spiritual pris-

ons—because of heartbreak. Heal them good so they'll be able to turn around and heal others. There's no one like You, Lord. I'm looking for a new day.

In the new day, Lord, I'm looking for new hearts for all mankind. I'm looking for families that looked like they would never be together to get together. In the new day, Lord, I'm looking for hearts that have been bound up for years, for generations, to suddenly be healed and free.

Just like You're blessing José, Lord, You know we're all Your babies. We're all Your children. Hold us real tight. Bless us and heal us like You're healing him. We're looking for a new day, Lord. We're looking for a new day.

Miz Ida got on the bus, singing and praying for people as she rode home. She got off the bus and walked down the street blessing and praying. No one knew it. She didn't wave her hands or speak out loud, but the Lord heard just the same. Miz Ida stopped at the door to her building, and looked at the young man curled up near the door.

"You better leave that man alone, Miz Ida! He's on drugs, and there ain't no telling what he might do to an old woman like you."

His clothes were torn and his hair was matted; there was dirt on his face. It was the same young man she had been seeing for months. The one she promised Michelle she was going to do something about. Somebody had to do something. "You all right, young man?"

He didn't answer.

She bent over him. "Young man, I said are you all right?"

He lay still, but opened one eye and growled at her. "Get away from me, you old bag. It's bad enough I got to be out here without looking at something as black and ugly as you."

Miz Ida stood up and stepped back. "Young man, you don't know who you talking to. This is the last day you going to talk to me like that."

He rolled over on his side. "Go ahead, old lady, cuss me out. Makes no difference. What's new?"

"I'm glad you asked that question, young man. The whole day is new. It's a new day." Miz Ida drew herself up to her fullest height. "I said this is the last day you going to talk to me like that cause your life is about to change. The Bible says—"

"Oh, no! Leave me alone, old lady. I don't want to hear that Bible mumbo jumbo."

"You may not want to hear, young man, but you gonna hear it just the same. The Bible says if I got faith as small as a mustard seed, I can ask anything in the Lord's name and it will be done. Well, if I can tell a mountain to move, I can tell *you* to get up. Get up, young man. Get up and get loosed! Rise, shine, and give God the glory! From this day forward, in Jesus' precious name, your life is forever changed. Some woman needs a good son. You gone be the man. Some woman needs a good, saved husband. You gone be the man. Some child needs a good father. You gone be the man. It's a new day, my son. You gone be the man. Amen, amen, and amen!"

Miz Ida clapped her hands together and walked away. While she walked, she spoke to the Lord in her own language of praise.

"Hey, lady!" She could hear the young man calling behind her. "Hey, lady!" Miz Ida turned back for a quick look. The young man was sitting up. "Hey, lady! Whatever this holy-roller stuff is you trying is not going to work." Miz Ida kept walking. She could still hear him when she reached her door. "You hear me, old lady, I said it's not going to work."

Miz Ida laughed to herself. "Too late now. Can't nothing stop the power of God." She couldn't wait to tell Michelle.

t always happens. Just when a body is finished eating and comfortable, just when a body has her feet up and a good magazine in hand, the phone always rings. Just as Miz Ida dragged a chair over in front of her and sat down on the couch, just as she got her feet and legs on the chair in just the right way, the pink princess started screaming.

"Hold on there, Princess, I'm coming." She scooted until she could reach her rose-colored antique. "Hello?"

It was Michelle on the other line.

"Guess what?" Michelle and Miz Ida spoke simultaneously.

"You go first, daughter."

"No, Miz Ida. You go, I can wait." They did the no-you-go-first dance a few more times and finally Miz Ida, the lovely vessel of winter grace, relented.

"I did it today, baby." Miz Ida was getting full just thinking about it. "We women—we mothers, grandmothers, cousins, and aunts—are going to have to take a stand. Our children are dying on the streets. No one else is going to rescue them. We're the ones that feel for them, who are we waiting on? We can't keep letting the enemy make us afraid of our babies. They may be in grown-up bodies and they may rage, but they are still our children. We have to take a stand for their lives. We can't let the enemy snatch them out of our arms. We have to take a stand for their very souls."

"Miz Ida, what are you talking about?"

"I'm talking about that young man who has been lying by the front door of this building. I guess I'm talking about all the men, women, and young people that are lying around or walking around dead all over this country. We women are going to have to take a stand."

"Miz Ida, what did you do? You don't have that man living with you do you? Miz Ida, you can't be taking everybody in off the streets."

Miz Ida rolled the magazine she was holding in her hands into a tube. "Well, Michelle, I can't tell you what I will or won't do. But, today, I did what has been in my spirit for months now. I stopped pretending that boy was invisible and I prayed. I'm sick and tired of the demon of drugs that has gripped this land. We got the authority and power, in Jesus' name, to bind that demon up and cast him out. Who knows what might happen if women all over this land got together and fasted and prayed? Who knows what would happen if all over this nation, for forty days, women fasted and prayed for our sons and daughters that are being held by the devil in the grip of drugs? We still got the same power, the same faith, that can move mountains. What if we got the courage to *use* it?"

Miz Ida was on a roll. "When the Lord was on earth with us, when He was moved with compassion, He moved in the lives of people to heal them. Jesus healed crowds of people of all sickness and diseases. When He was moved with compassion, He fed thousands. When Jesus was moved with compassion, he gave sight to the blind and he healed lepers. When the Lord was moved with compassion He taught and ushered multitudes into the Kingdom.”

“Miz Ida, you sound like you are fired up. What did you do?”

“I *am* fired up, baby. I’m stirred up because I’ve been thinking, and there’s no telling what a woman can do when she’s been thinking—even an old woman. I’ve been thinking about the compassion and mercy of God. The Father’s compassion will cause Him to accept His prodigal children back home.

“And I been thinking that if some women would pray, we could turn this whole thing around. No one has more compassion for our broken sons and daughters than we do. What if we stopped worrying about our own lives? What if we stopped worrying about being cute? What if we just let the tragedy of what we see well up on the inside of us? What if we let our compassion well up on the inside of us? What we need is some wailing women, some daughters who aren’t afraid to weep, to get ugly and cry out to the Lord. I just been thinking, Michelle. I been thinking.”

“What brought all this on, Miz Ida?”

Miz Ida had almost torn the magazine to shreds, she was so stirred up. “When I saw that young man, I knew today was the day. If God gives me the power to move a mountain, He sure gives me the power to get a young man to stand up, and that’s just what I told him. I felt like Peter and John on the steps of the Temple called Beautiful. I’m not a rich woman, but what I have is God’s treasure inside this old jar of clay—God’s spirit inside of my old body. So, I prayed in Jesus’ name and I believe that young man is going to get up.”

“Did he get mad, Miz Ida? Did he try to do or say anything to you?”

“Well, he tried to kick up a little bit. But, you know the old man always kicks up when the new man is about to kick him out and move in. He said a little something, but I forgive that, it’s just the price of a new life. And I’m a woman at war against the devil’s kingdom; I can’t fear the one who can kill the body, I just fear God—

He's the one that has power over my soul. I'm determined, Michelle. I've just been thinking that if we're determined, we can turn this thing around."

"You've been thinking, Miz Ida. I can hear that in your voice. And it's a dangerous thing when a woman starts thinking, because I have been thinking, too!"

Miz Ida began to fan herself with the tattered magazine. She had broken into a sweat. Right there, in her own living room, on her couch holding on to her own pink princess phone, Miz Ida had gotten worked up. "You have, baby? I just been going on and on—tell me what's been on your mind."

"Miz Ida, I been thinking that I want my husband back."

She began to fan faster with the tattered magazine. She was hot like she was sitting in a too tight pew in an un-air-conditioned church during a summer Holy Ghost revival. "Well, hallelujah anyhow!"

"I've been thinking it for a while, now, Miz Ida. Especially since me, Tonya, and Shad went out to lunch the other day at the train station. When Tonya started talking about why a woman should love a man, I thought, 'That's exactly why I love Todd.' Those things she said about loving a man have just stayed on my mind."

Tonya's words, as Michelle had recounted them, came to Ida's mind. *"What gives him value in her life is not the coins in his pocket, but the richness of his character."*

"I love Todd, Miz Ida, because he is a man full of love and peace. He is patient and kind. He is always good to me and I can count on him—even when I have mistreated him. On top of all that, Miz Ida, he is gentle—he wouldn't even think about hurting me or harming anybody else."

"He is her king, because of her admiration for the generosity of his wise and understanding heart."

"Miz Ida, I have never known a man like Todd in my life. The way he loves me is not human, it's supernatural. Todd is a gift from God—my gift from God."

"He is her lover because of his intelligence, which is spirit-led and without price."

"It took God to show me love and to show me the worth of a man who is filled with His spirit. There is no way to measure the worth of that. Women deciding which man they want by what kind of car he drives rather than looking at how big his heart is are just missing the boat. They're missing God's blessings."

"He is her husband because she has found him to be her match— both body and soul."

"Miz Ida, Todd is so much for me, he fits me so well in every way that it scared me. I ran from feeling the way Todd could make me feel. It has taken God teaching me and Tonya telling me, to get me to see what I was throwing away."

"Well, Michelle, it's never too late. It ain't over until God says so."

"That's what I know, Miz Ida. So, I have been praying."

Michelle's voice was full of passion and hope, a sound that Miz Ida hadn't heard from her in too long a time.

"Today the funniest thing happened at work. I was listening to the radio. This one song went off and this gospel song came on the radio saying a brighter day was coming."

"Do tell."

"And I don't know, something just went all through me."

"Sounds like the Holy Ghost to me."

"That was it, Miz Ida. A brighter day is coming and I realized that part of my brighter day is my Todd. I want my husband back. I love Todd, but I don't know how to fix it. I'm the one that made the decision to walk out. What am I gonna do, just show up and say, 'Honey, I'm home'?

"And I want to break it off with Trench. I'm through with that in my life. I told him not to come back after the last time I saw him. I know I let him back in after he hit me, but this time I told him that was it. Not that I haven't said that before. Somehow I feel I need to tell him that it's really over, so we can have closure. But if I call him—or leave a message with his momma—that's going to be just like sending him a greeting card. He'll come over and the whole cycle will just start over."

"You can break the cycle, though, baby. You don't want Trench—that was the old Michelle."

"I know, Miz Ida. That's why when I heard that song, I just starting singing in my heart. And I started praying right then. I did like you and Tonya do sometimes—I kept my eyes open and my mouth closed, but I started praying like crazy: *'God, I need a brighter day. Lord, give me a brighter day!'*" Michelle began to sing the chorus again.

Miz Ida's fanning arm went into second gear. "My goodness gracious! Things are turning around."

"Well, that ain't all, Miz Ida. When I got home this evening, I was flipping through that Bible Tonya gave me and I found something written in there called *Change Your Mind*. Wait a minute; let me read it to you." Miz Ida could hear Michelle rustling and moving about in the background. Soon she returned to the phone.

"Here it is, Miz Ida. Listen." Michelle began to read. " 'When I was a child, I was taught that it is a woman's prerogative to change her mind. If you have become accustomed to a thought or a habit you should get rid of, stop what you are doing and change your mind.'

"Miz Ida, there was the answer! I could just change my mind. I made the decision to leave my husband. I knew when I was leaving—I knew a long time ago—that I had made a mistake, that I shouldn't leave or that I needed to go home. I just didn't know I could change my mind. Here it was written down—God was using a man I didn't know to tell me it was my prerogative: I could change my mind.

"Then I started thinking, it's not as easy as all that. What if I'm too late? But, I kept reading. Listen to this! 'I know it isn't easy, but it is so necessary. It will help you immeasurably to speak to yourself and say, "I am better than this!" You don't have to change the other person's mind. You just need to change your own.'

"Miz Ida, it was like every thought I had, the Lord was speaking right back to me."

Miz Ida's fanning arm had shifted to third. "Well, do tell. God is just good like that. Yes, He is!"

"Then I thought about Trench, again, Miz Ida." The old woman's fanning arm slowed back to second while she listened. "I don't love him, Miz Ida, but I know him. He seems familiar to me. Why was I gonna risk losing Trench for a maybe with Todd?"

Michelle began to read again. " 'Be careful what you get used to. If you don't watch out, you can become accustomed to negative things, things the Father never wanted you to have, like pain or abuse. Some people have become used to poverty. Some have become used to fighting. They feel at home in pain. They cleave to it because they understand it.'

"Miz Ida, it gave me chills. God was using this man to tell me my own story."

Miz Ida's arm had shifted back up to third. "It never fails to amaze me, Michelle, that God who sits so high still looks low and is watching over every little thing we do."

"Then I thought, but what about Trench?"

Miz Ida's arm slowed again. All of this stopping and starting was going to wear out her gears!

"I need to come to closure. I need to make peace with Trench about this—even as I know every time I invite him back in, there will never be peace. So, I kept reading. 'Real victory occurs when you change your own mind. The power of choice is a great power. Be careful that you do not give that power away. It is your right to choose how you want to live. Even God respects that right.

'Instead of asking an abuser if he has had enough, you must ask yourself if you have had enough. This is always the greater question. Others may not ever get their fill of abusing you. If you have judged within yourself that abuse is not God's will for you, why are you asking someone else to choose? The greater question still is, "Do you, as a daughter of the King, want to live in this circumstance?"'

"What was written was right, Miz Ida. Trench was never going to get enough. What was going on was working for him. It was serving his purpose. God was trying to tell me He didn't want to talk to me about Trench. He was trying to talk to me about me.

"What I read told me that God wasn't a bully, that He didn't force His will on anyone. It told me that God has all power, but He loves me enough to give me free choice."

"Wonderful Savior!" Miz Ida's fan was back at third gear.

"I am a child of the King, Miz Ida."

"Yes, you are, Michelle."

"And my daddy loves me so much He wants to protect me. He doesn't want me hurt anymore, not on the inside or the outside. He loves me so much—even with all I've done—God wants me to come back home." Michelle began to cry.

"Don't you be ashamed to cry, baby. You give God thanks for those tears. They just show that God is giving you a new tender heart. And that's a good thing."

Michelle cleared her throat. "Then I thought, 'God, what if I do all this and it's too late? What if I do all this and Todd won't take me back? No man in his right mind would take me back after all I've done to him.' Then I read to the end, Miz Ida. 'By God's rich grace, you have the power to see a miracle. Don't forfeit it or forsake it. You can change your situation whenever you get ready.'[14]

"Miz Ida, I just started shouting like I used to see you do. I'm scared to hope, but I'm going to do it anyway—I'm not giving up my chance at a miracle! So ever since this afternoon, I been praying. And I just keep singing to myself. And I keep thinking, a brighter day is coming!"

---

[14]T.D. Jakes, "Change Your Mind—A Soul Secret," *Holy Bible: Woman, Thou Art Loosed* edition (Nashville, TN: Thomas Nelson Publishers, 1998).

Miz Ida's arm was moving so fast, the magazine was a blur. "Michelle, honey, I tell you something is about to turn around. Something happens when women start thinking and praying. Girl, you just hold on to your hat and get ready, get ready, get ready! It's going to be a brighter day indeed!"

Chapter Thirty-two

iz Ida had just settled herself down for the night. She had on her blue terry-cloth robe, her favorite yellow thread-bare cotton nightgown, her pink satin nightcap with the red lace hanging off of the rim, and a pair of white socks. For some reason, she just felt like sleeping on the couch, so she grabbed her pillow and threw a quilt over herself. Whatever came, she was ready. But she was counting on a good night's sleep.

Just when the lights were out, just when she got her head and neck adjusted right on her pillow, that's when the pink princess began to scream again.

"Hold on there, now." She and the pink princess were getting quite a workout lately. She peeked at the clock. It was almost twelve. Thank goodness for the glow from the telephone dial pad. She and the pink princess were very well-acquainted, but a body could break her neck feeling around for her phone in the dark.

Besides, who would be calling at such a crazy hour?

"Hello, Miz Ida." It was Michelle again. "I called him."

"You called who?"

"I called Todd and I had to call you back to tell you what was going on . . ."

⊖

Michelle felt so nervous and giddy, as though she were thirteen. At least she figured this was what most thirteen-year-old girls must feel like: tongue tied and embarrassed. She had rehearsed over and over again what she was going to say to Todd when she talked to him. But when he answered the phone, Michelle's planned speech left her. She should have known it wouldn't be as easy as she had imagined.

It had seemed like such a good idea. She had felt so confident before she called him. *It won't be a big deal. I'll just say something real smooth-like: "Daddy, order in, Mama's coming home."* She had imagined herself saying it so cavalierly, and with so much feminine confidence. Maybe she would say it like Angela Bassett—with mocha-colored sassiness, passion, and an overcoming attitude. Or maybe she would speak to Todd with the quirky, befuddled charm and ardor of some romantic klutz in a paperback novel.

But when she heard her husband's voice on the other end of the line, she did neither.

"Hello." Todd always sounded so calm and steady. Michelle missed that. She missed laying her head on his chest and listening to him breathe. She missed him, but for some reason—probably the thirteen-year-oldness of it all and the vulnerability of putting her heart into the hands of a man that she had wounded so deeply—Michelle just could not speak.

"Hello. Hello? Is somebody there?"

Click! She hung up!

⊖

"You did what, Michelle?"

"I just hung up on him, Miz Ida! What was on my mind? No, I know what was on my mind: nothing."

Miz Ida shook her head. "Oh, baby. Oh my, goodness. Well, baby, it's not the end of the world."

"I know it's not, Miz Ida."

"It could happen to anybody. You probably just got so nervous."

"That's what happened, Miz Ida."

"You've come so far. You know the Lord is with you. You can just get up your nerve and call him back."

"I already did, Miz Ida. That's why I had to call you."

⊖

Todd sounded a little more businesslike, like he had a little less patience to deal with foolishness, when he answered the second time. "Hello?"

Michelle still couldn't speak. She could hardly breathe.

Todd's voice took on that sound that men use when they've lost patience. It was the sound that said, *All right, don't mess with me now. I'm not your mother.* "Hello," he said again. Then, "Look, whoever this is, I don't have time for—"

"Todd, it's me. It's Michelle." She took a deep breath. "I'm sorry, you must think I'm crazy."

He was quiet on the other end.

"I know it's getting late. I don't mean to bother you. I just wanted to talk to you—I just needed to talk to you."

His voice sounded guarded. "It *is* a little late, Michelle." She could hear in his voice, though he tried to cover it, how deeply she had hurt him. "I guess I can talk a few minutes."

"I miss you, Todd."

He didn't say anything. He wasn't making it easy. Or maybe he was too vulnerable to respond.

"Todd, I was thinking . . ." What was she going to say? *I was thinking that even though I've batted your heart around like a hockey puck, I want to come back home.*

"I was thinking that I'd like to go to church with you on Sunday." Where had *that* come from? It hadn't been part of what she'd practiced saying, but it was something she had been thinking about. It was one of her new fantasies—to be sitting next to him again. She wanted to sit with him in joy now where she'd sat so many other times full of resentment. "I think I'd like to go to church."

He was quiet for a moment. When he spoke, his voice was subdued. "Michelle, what's going on? Do you need something? Because if you need something—you don't have to play games with me. You don't have to mess with my head to get me to help you."

It was like a knife in her chest, the knowledge of how badly she had hurt him. It was so clear, now, how deep she had cut him. The pain in his voice spoke volumes about the trust she had violated.

"Todd, I'm sorry. I don't need anything. I just . . . I just want to start over. I just want . . . I want to say I'm sorry."

"You don't have to feel sorry for me, Michelle. I'm a grown man. I can handle it."

"That's why I'm calling, Todd. You don't have to handle it anymore."

He cleared his throat. "Look, Michelle, do you get some kind of freaky kick out of being cruel? Why would you call me in the middle of the night to tell me that you're divorcing me? Why would you call me and tell me you want to go to church with me? Is that my consolation prize?"

Michelle thought of all the times that Todd had bared his soul to her. She thought of all the times he had stood before her emotionally and spiritually naked. It was time for her to get naked herself, to uncover the woman that she truly was.

☙

"When I heard Todd's voice, I knew that I had to stop hiding." Michelle's voice sounded so sad on the other end of the line.

Miz Ida wanted to just wrap her in her arms. She wanted to hold Michelle as she had held her when she was a child. "Oh, baby, I wish I could just hold you."

"You know what, Miz Ida? When I heard the pain in his voice, I remembered how I used to feel as a child. I remembered how unloved and rejected I felt. I remembered how I kept trying to offer my mother love, how I kept chasing after her affection. And I realized that I was doing the same thing to Todd that she had done to me.

"I always loved Todd. I was just too afraid to show it. I was too afraid to put my heart in his hands. I was too afraid to trust him with my love. When I heard Todd's voice, I realized that my mother was afraid to love me. She was afraid to show me that she loved me, to risk putting her heart on the line."

"Glory to God, baby. You finally see it."

"It's so sad, Miz Ida. Todd had to let his heart be broken in order to heal mine. When that thought came to me, I realized that all this time Todd has been giving me sacrificial love. Todd has been loving me all along—as the Bible says—like Christ loves the church.

"He took me with spots, wrinkles, and warts. Todd stood in front of me and covered my sins. What greater love is there than that, Miz Ida? He laid down his heart for me. He trusted his precious love in my hands, even though he knew—even if I recovered from my wounds—that I was most likely going to hurt him. Todd took me on and paid the price for things other people did to me, sins he didn't even commit. What greater romance is there than that?"

"My, my, my. Sweet Jesus."

"He loved me, Miz Ida, even when I was sleeping with another man." Michelle began to weep.

"You cry on, baby. Those are sweet healing tears. My, my, my. No greater love." Miz Ida began to hum "Oh, Mary, Don't You Weep" while Michelle cried on the other end of the line. When Michelle had quieted Miz Ida spoke.

"I know it's hard, baby. But don't you dare think it's over. Don't you dare."

Michelle sounded as though she was blowing her nose. "I didn't give up, Miz Ida. The story's not over . . ."

☙

Todd's voice fluctuated between pain and rage. "Haven't you had enough of hurting me, Michelle? Do you care that little about me?"

"I *do* care, Todd. That's why I called. I'm not calling to ask for a divorce. And no, going to church with you is not supposed to be your consolation prize." It was difficult for Michelle to keep her voice gentle. She had to work at it; she had been talking tough for so long. "I want to go with you—I'm asking to go with you because I love you."

Todd's breathing was his only response.

"I know it's been a long time coming, Todd. I'm praying that it's not too late." Michelle paused, but when he didn't say anything, she pressed forward. "It's pointless to make excuses. I did what I did. I have to live with that. That doesn't mean that I don't apologize. I do. I'm sorry from the bottom of my heart. But I can't change the past. What I want to do is to grab hold of the present. I don't want to let it slip through my fingers—I don't want to continue to throw it away. I want to do whatever I have to do to make sure that there is love in our future.

"Todd, there are no excuses. What I learned while I've been away—really just in the last few days—is that I didn't know anything about love. All I knew about love was what I saw other people do and what I saw on TV. The people that I saw were mean to each other and didn't trust each other. They talked bad to each other and used each other, and then they left—even my father. That was my image of love. Love was seeing someone across the room and liking his face, his body, or the jewelry he wore. That's all I knew about love—that's all I knew about love between a man and a woman."

She sighed. "Anything other than that I learned from Miz Ida, but in my mind that was 'grandmother love.' Grandmother love didn't have anything to do with men and women. What I had seen, what I thought was love, made me not trust anybody, especially not men. I think that's even why I had a hard time trusting and believing God. No man on earth had ever loved me or wanted to take care of me—before you. Why should I believe God was any different from men? They just wanted something from me—my body, my money. It seemed like that was all that God wanted—my money."

Michelle closed her eyes. *Please, God, please give me the words. Give me the strength I need to be soft and vulnerable. Soften and heal Todd's heart. Please . . . don't let me be too late.* "Then you came into my life. Here was this handsome, intelligent man who loved me and wanted to take care of me. Here was this man who could make me feel things that no other man had ever made me feel. It scared me, Todd. I didn't know whether you just knew the tricks better than all the other men. It scared me to think that you might be fooling me, making me think you loved me so that you could use me just like everyone else in my life. I had never met anyone like you. I did things to make you leave and you wouldn't go. Part of me thought, *He loves me and he's never going to leave.* The other part of me thought, *He's either trying to play me or he's just too stupid to get it.*

"So I just ran. I could feel myself falling in deeper. I could feel that I was getting in over my head and I ran. That's all I knew. That's all I had ever been taught."

Todd cleared his throat. "Michelle, you don't have to say all this. It's late and . . . you don't have to say all this."

"Yes, Todd, I do. Even if I'm too late, I still need to say it. I need to tell you that you are a good, decent, and honorable man. I need to tell you that you were the only man in my life that ever made me feel whole. Only I didn't know what wholeness was until God showed me—until I let God love me first.

"Todd, I have a friend at work—isn't that funny to think about me having a woman for a friend? Well, she's my friend and she's been helping me, Todd, for no other reason than she wants to be my friend. That's hard for me to believe. Your life has been different from mine and you may not understand it, but it amazes me that she wants to be my friend, and that she talks nice to me.

"And we have another friend, too. A man named Shadrach who has been helping us, kind of coaching us. It has been an amazing season in my life.

"Anyway, my friend—Tonya is her name—gave me this Bible, and I've been reading it. The other night I was reading it in bed and I turned to this chapter she had told me about. Well, she called this chapter the 'love chapter'—First Corinthians chapter thirteen. I started reading it and all I could see was you. I know you probably know the chapter already, Todd, but let me read it to you." She opened her Bible and began to read.

> Love is patient, love is kind.
> It does not envy,
> it does not boast,
> it is not proud.

"Todd, when I read it all I could see was your face. You weren't crazy, Todd. That's what I kept thinking. *Todd was right!* You were loving the way God says we're supposed to love. You were giving me real love. It was you—*patient and kind*. You stuck by me and were kind even when I was acting a fool. None of the people I had ever seen, not even on TV, were patient and kind to their lovers. It was *you—it does not boast, it does not envy, it is not proud*. Todd, you are a humble, selfless man. I never knew that humility was a part of love.

She continued reading.

> It is not rude,
> it is not self-seeking,
> it is not easily angered,
> it keeps no record of wrongs.

"Todd, this was saying that everything that I had learned about love wasn't true. The women and men I saw were always arguing, calling each other names, cutting each other down—I thought that was a part of love. The men and women I saw were always trying to get their own way, trying to use each other to pay bills, to buy cars, to get whatever they wanted—I thought manipulation was a part of love. The men and women I saw were always getting mad at each other. That was part of the love dance—or I thought it was, but God says that isn't love. The men and women I knew were always arguing and not forgiving. It was like they were keeping a scorecard. *Remember when you hurt me back in 1998, so you owe me*—I thought that was love."

Michelle fought to keep herself from crying. She had to get this all out. She had to tell Todd everything, she didn't know if she would ever have the courage to try again. She went on reading.

> Love does not delight in evil
> but rejoices with the truth.
> It always protects, always trusts,
> always hopes, always perseveres.
> Love never fails.

"Todd, in all the love I saw between men and women, one or the other was happy when something bad happened to the person they were supposed to love—because they were bearing a grudge. They wanted them to get payback. I even wanted my own mother to get payback. Everybody was that way except for you. And Miz Ida. But you were the only man I knew who was happy with the outcome as long as truth won. I never saw a love where the man and women were protecting each other, or covering each other. The people I saw were always looking out for Number One, except for you. You were loving like *God* loves. No matter what happened, even with Trench, you never gave up on me, you never lost faith in me.

You always hoped that things were going to get better, that I was going to get better.

"Todd, you have loved me no matter what. I needed God and the Bible to reassure me that what you were doing was real—that it was God's kind of love."

"Michelle, really. I wish you would stop." Todd's voice sounded like he was crying—or like he was trying to keep from crying. "It's enough."

"No, it's not enough, Todd. Because I never knew a love that didn't fail until I met you. Every other love in my life, until Miz Ida, failed me. You were the only man in my life that didn't fail me. It took God to show me that."

Todd cleared his throat. "What about Trench, Michelle? I love you, yes. But I can't take it anymore. I can't. I don't want to get back together—I don't even want to think about it until the Trench thing is over."

Michelle almost sang the next verses that she read.

When I was a child,
I talked like a child,
I thought like a child,
I reasoned like a child.
When I became a man,
I put childish ways behind me.[15]

"These last few weeks, Todd, I've grown up. All this time, I've been just a little scared, confused little girl in a woman's body. I've been talking to you like I was a child. I've thought like a child and tried to figure out what was going on in our lives with the ideas I learned as a child. I *just* grew up, Todd. You married a child, but now, I'm a woman. God has done more than save me, He has had compassion on me and taught me so that I could renew my mind.

---

[15] 1 Corinthians .13:4–8, 11–12 NIV

All the childishness, Trench included, is behind me. And I'm praying that what the Bible says is true—that true love, God's love, the kind you have for me—never fails."

There was no point in stopping now. She had to stand in front of him naked and unashamed. "Todd, I want to come home."

⊖

Miz Ida didn't know if she was going to get any more sleep that night. She sat up and turned the light on. "Honey, I prayed for it. You know I did. I prayed that someday this day would come. I just . . . as many times as it happens, it still overwhelms me to see answered prayers."

Michelle sounded very calm. "Miz Ida, he didn't say it was all over. We've still got a lot to talk about."

"I never thought I'd live to see the day—it just makes an old woman's heart feel good! My God! My God! People always talking about diabetes and blood pressure, but only God can heal a broken heart."

"We still have a ways to go."

"And God, my sweet baby Michelle—no, Michelle, you mighty woman of God—He's with you every step of the way."

Miz Ida hung up the phone and covered her eyes with one hand as she wept. God was good—even late at night.

"Thank you, Jesus." It made her heart happy to see God working, to see seeds that she had planted in Michelle's young life coming into full bloom. She waved her hands in the air. Her heart was full—just about full to busting—and there was no telling when she was going to be able to fall off to sleep.

Miz Ida had always dedicated herself to helping others. Their joy was her joy. Yes, it was going to be a while before sleep found her.

Chapter Thirty-three

iz Ida had had a quiet but full day. She had met with some of the other church ladies for lunch. Then she'd helped start dinner at the women's shelter. They'd sent her on home, after they had a handle on dinner, with a half of a baked chicken. They were good people there and they were always looking after her.

She'd heated up some string beans and cooked a little rice to go with her bird. Some music on the radio had caught her ear while she washed her few little dishes. Before she knew it, she was dancing, watering plants, and praising the Lord.

Now Miz Ida was pooped.

"Lord, thank You. Thank You for the place I live and the new home that's to come. Thank You for the people in my life and the new ones that are to come." She lay her head back on the couch and talked like she was talking to an old friend. "I see You moving, God. I see You doing things that none of us would have expected. We try to make our way and tell You which way we need to go. Thank You for not listening to us, thank You for being wise, omnipotent, and omniscient. Thank You, God, for making each day sweeter than the day before."

If she wasn't expecting Michelle to call, she would have gone back to her room and gotten in the bed. But, there was no point in stumbling through the house, trying to reach the pink princess in time.

Miz Ida didn't know she had dozed off until she heard the phone ring. The afternoon sun that had made a gentle slice across the room was gone. A sweet, peaceful darkness had surrounded her and lulled her to sleep. "Hold on, pink princess, I'm coming." She reached for the phone.

"Hello, Miz Ida?"

Just as she suspected, it was Michelle. "I'm sorry to call so late. I know I told you that I was going to call before Todd and I went on our date. But things just went a little crazy at the office and we never really got to go."

"You never got to go?"

"No, ma'am. You see, it was time for work to be out and me and Tonya were in the bathroom . . ."

⊖

Michelle stood at the sink checking her hair and makeup. There was no real reason she should be nervous about how she looked. It wasn't as though it had been years since she'd seen Todd. It wasn't even as though that was the main thing he focused on—Todd loved her for who she was.

Tonya was at the sink next to her redoing her own hair. It seemed that the hair song—the bun song—had been a great success.

"I guess it worked, huh?"

Tonya smiled, a lock of hair in her hands. "What worked?"

"Your song. You know, the one we sang at the restaurant."

"Like I could forget. I told Malik about it and my son just will not let the song go! He's very happy about my hair, but I think he likes the song even better."

Michelle began to sing.

"Hey yo! The bun is dead. Which old bun?"

They sang the next line together.

"Tonya's bun!"

They laughed.

"It's getting late, Michelle. I think we're getting punchy. We're laughing at anything."

"I think I'm laughing because I'm nervous."

Tonya stopped what she was doing and looked at Michelle's image in the mirror. "Nervous? What are you nervous about? If it's about Mrs. Judson, you don't have to worry." Tonya went back to arranging her hair. "The Lord has it all in His hands and all under His control. I've made peace about it. If she lets us go, then it's the Lord's will. He gave us this job and He can give us another one, too. I've never seen Him close one door and not open another one."

Michelle nodded. "I've been thinking the same thing. But that's not what I'm nervous about."

Tonya lowered her arms, leaned against the counter, and looked directly at Michelle. "So, what is it then?"

"I've got a date."

"Oh no, Michelle. Not Trench again."

Michelle shook her head. "Oh, no, girl. Trench is history. Thanks to you and the Lord, I have done some major growing up. I've stopped thinking like a child, and I've gotten rid of childish things."

Tonya waved her hand in the air like she was shouting at church. "Look at you, girl. You go on with your bad self."

"Oh, I finally got the email and saw the light." Michelle held out her arms and extended her two index fingers. She moved them in tandem from right to left. "Trench is out of here!"

"Girl, I can't believe this is the same woman from a few months ago."

"You mean the same woman who was giving you the blues and cussing you out?" Michelle stopped smiling. "When I think back on it, Tonya, and how I treated you—I'm embarrassed. I'm sorry." She touched Tonya on the shoulder. "You've been a real friend to me. Probably the first real friend I've ever had. I'm sorry."

"It wasn't all you, Michelle. I could have done better, too. And as for being a friend, I'm grateful for you. You hurt my feelings, but you changed my life. Sometimes it takes people out of our comfort circle to see what's not working and to help us change our lives." The two women hugged briefly. "Besides," Tonya smiled, "since you're out of bondage, don't you deserve a song?"

"What song?"

Tonya spent a minute or two trying to create lyrics to celebrate Michelle's deliverance. Finally, Michelle shook her head.

"You know what, Tonya? I think we need to leave that song alone. But I can tell you the song that got me through it all." Michelle began to sing.

"Oh, I know that song. It's Kirk Franklin and that's my jam." Tonya danced in a way that Michelle never would have expected.

"That new hair thing has set you free!"

Tonya laughed. "Yeah, I'm feeling like a new woman." Suddenly she stopped dancing. "So if Trench is out of the picture, then who . . ."

"It's Todd. We're going on a date—well, sort of a date. We're meeting after work to talk things over."

"Things like?"

"Things like maybe getting back together."

Tonya began to hum the song and dance again. "Girl, I tell you. The things you can learn from a woman in the bathroom! I am so happy for you, Michelle. I don't know what could make it any better." She danced a few more steps and then paused. "But, what about Shadrach? I thought you had plans for him? I thought you were attracted to him."

Michelle shook her head. "He never really liked me, Tonya.

Not that way. I knew it all along. He always talked about you like you were the best thing since sliced bread." Michelle laughed. "I sound like I spend too much time talking to Miz Ida." She laughed again. "But anyway, Shad has always been sweet on you. And, to be honest, Tonya, I was just being my old self. I didn't want Shad, I just had to have every man's attention, no matter how I had to get it. Shad was being a good friend to both of us. He helped—he coached—both of us. It was very easy to see, at the restaurant, that he just liked you a *tiny* bit more." They grinned at each other. "And I'm glad about it. I'm happy for both of you."

Tonya blushed. "Well, I've been kind of sidestepping him and trying to avoid him. I would never do something like that to a friend."

"Well, you stop stepping to the side, my *sistuh,* and you step right on up!" The two women giggled.

Tonya returned to arranging her hair. "So, how did all this happen with you and Todd?"

"I got up the nerve to call him." Michelle told Tonya about how what she'd said to Shadrach at lunch at the train station had touched her. "I've been thinking about what you said every since that day. You helped me to begin to understand love, and you helped me understand why I love my husband." She shared with her friend how she'd bared her soul to Todd and about the message she had read in the Bible. "When I talked to him, I just let the love chapter tell me what to say. I prayed and left the rest in the Lord's hands. I told him about you, about Shadrach, and how much you all helped me. I told Todd how I've been praying and reading my Bible and the other books you got me."

She shrugged. "I'm praying for a miracle. It might not come to pass. But I can't let it go without trying. I love him."

When they had finished, they walked back through the office. The other employees were gone and the office was empty. At least, they thought so until they saw Mrs. Judson standing by Tonya's desk.

"I had hoped that the two of you were still here. I know it's after hours, but this is urgent. We have a little matter that we need to get settled."

☙

"I tell you, Miz Ida, I thought hard about leaving, about telling Mrs. Judson I couldn't stay after hours. That I had a pressing engagement. But Mrs. Judson said the meeting would be brief. So I went along with it. I prefer not to go to dinner with an axe hanging over my head."

As Michelle spoke, Miz Ida prayed. God was faithful.

Lord, I know You're not going to bring this baby—my baby—this close and then leave her. I know You're not going to abandon her, Lord. But I have to tell the truth: my heart's just beating fast and a little sweat's breaking out on my forehead.

Lord, she's so close. Don't let things fall apart now.

Miz Ida gripped the phone, nodding as though Michelle could see her. "Mm-hmm. Then what happened?"

Chapter Thirty-four

iz Ida settled back against the cushions of the couch. God was at work in Michelle's life. She knew it. And the young woman's story only confirmed that fact. *You are so good to us, God!* She couldn't help but praise Him, even as Michelle began to talk again.

"You know, Miz Ida, it had been such a good day; it was hard for me to believe that it wasn't going to be capped off by something bad. Not to mention, that I was worried about being late or missing Todd. I was frazzled before I ever got into Mrs. Judson's office. It didn't help that she was acting agitated and strange. I thought—like Shad had said one day at lunch—the other shoe was about to fall."

⌒

Mrs. Judson paced back and forth across the office, until finally she paused and faced her window. Her silhouette was outlined by the rose of the afternoon sky that was fading into a dusky blue-brown. She jabbed her hands into the pocket of her suit jacket, then jerked them out again as she faced Michelle and Tonya. Though her movements were jerky, her expression was cool and unruffled.

"Tonya, you've functioned satisfactorily during your time at the firm. I appreciate your service. Michelle, I've noticed, since we last spoke, some improvement in your work performance—not your performance, really, but your professional deportment. And despite the fact, ladies, that I'm still not totally convinced about our *accidental* lunch meeting, I think it's only fair to give you both the benefit of the doubt."

Mrs. Judson shifted her weight from foot to foot, though her expression remained calm and almost disinterested. "I may feel it necessary to extend the time before both your promotions for one or more months. But, otherwise, everything is fine."

Michelle was about to stand up and voice her objection, but Tonya touched her arm. Mrs. Judson turned her back to them, facing her window. Her shoulders began to shake and then they heard her cry.

Still facing the window, she told them the story about her granddaughter's pregnancy.

"We didn't think it would be like this. We took Claudia in because she had no place to go. Now, it has backfired on us." Mrs. Judson slipped her cell phone from her pocket. "It's because of Claudia that I have this. She was constantly getting suspended or expelled from schools. The last time she was drunk and trying to force liquor on younger children."

Her husband, she said, just couldn't see Claudia's faults. He couldn't see that their granddaughter was pulling the wool over his eyes.

Mrs. Judson straightened her shoulders, adjusted her jacket, and then just as quickly seemed to surrender to defeat as her shoulders slumped. "My world . . . Everything is falling apart. All the things I counted on seem to be falling away. I don't know if I have the strength to put it all back together again." Her voice was choked with emotion. "I keep thinking that everything would be fine now if we'd never taken Claudia in. If we had kept to our own little world everything would be fine."

Mrs. Judson walked to her desk, sat in her chair, and laid her face in her hands. She looked tired and worn. "I don't know why I'm telling you all this. Perhaps because you two women love to pray."

She lifted her head. "My husband, Carl, and I have had some disagreements on how to handle this. He always wants to baby Claudia as though it were our fault that she got pregnant and that she's using drugs." She took a deep breath and straightened in her chair, putting her hands on the desk. "Carl and I never disagreed before Claudia came into our lives. I try to tell him that we're not responsible for the world. We can't change everyone. Claudia has to want to change if anything is to be done."

After some hesitation, Mrs. Judson told them about her son. "Carl Jr. has always been my pride. He was the model son. Not like his sister, who was on drugs, who probably taught Claudia all the bad habits she knows. I just can't believe . . . Claudia says Carl Jr. is the father of her baby."

She choked back new tears. "Of course it's a lie. It's all a lie. How could Carl Jr. appear to be one thing and then be something else entirely? That would make his whole life a lie, a masquerade. Where would he learn something like that?"

Her husband was taking his granddaughter's side. He had even called the police, who had picked up Carl Jr. for questioning early that morning.

Mrs. Judson looked from Michelle to Tonya. "If there really is a God, my family needs Him, now."

⊖

"Bless her heart. It makes me just want to hold her in my arms. When people that have been in control lose control, it's a sad state of affairs."

"You're right, Miz Ida. It was sad. When she fell apart, that's when her story began to crack. That's when she told us the whole story."

Miz Ida laid her hand on her heart and continued to pray. Could things get any worse?

iz Ida sighed. "She may not ever tell you, but you know it was a blessing that the two of you were there to be some comfort to her."

"Miz Ida, my heart just broke for Mrs. Judson. I never thought that I would be saying that. I have been in her granddaughter's place. I know how that feels. I know how it feels to live that way, in that kind of pain, day after day. I've been the child that got sacrificed so that people could pretend that everything was normal. I've been there.

"But when Mrs. Judson began to tell her story, I knew there were no easy choices for her, either. It made me so sad. And I kept thinking, how could anybody face something like that without God?"

Miz Ida shook her head. "She's relying on her self. It can be hard to make a change, to trust something other than yourself. I bet that woman is just doing what she's been doing all her life. It makes us feel better to think it's as easy as *do or don't do,* but there are no easy choices for a mother or a grandmother in that situation. There's no choice she can make that won't bring pain."

"That's exactly what Mrs. Judson said." She was quiet for a moment. "The room just got quiet, Miz Ida. Nobody knew what to say. What do you say when you hear something like that? I didn't know if I could or should talk. I didn't know which part of my heart or mind would talk. I guess that Tonya was thinking the same thing, because she was quiet, too."

"Michelle, bless your heart, it had to be hard for you."

"It was, Miz Ida. But when I was listening to Mrs. Judson and watching her, I guess I just didn't have time to think about me. She needed someone to help her—and as someone once said, you can be pitiful or powerful, but you can't be both. When she started talking, what I felt in my heart made the choice for me."

☙

Mrs. Judson smiled harshly. "So there you have it ladies. Sickness comes to suburbia. Or as you said at lunch, pain's not prejudiced. I would say my family and I are candidates for prayer if ever there were any."

Tonya's voice was still and small. "We'll pray for you and your family, Mrs. Judson. But you can pray for yourself, too." Her expression was so compassionate. "Why don't you come to church with me on Sunday?"

Mrs. Judson shook her head. "I would feel uncomfortable. I would feel out of place."

"Mrs. Judson, God doesn't care about color or class. He just wants to save you and mend your broken heart."

The gray-haired woman looked at Tonya. "I'm still not sure that I believe in God. I've been taking care of myself all my life. I don't know if I can trust anyone or anything else."

Tonya shook her head. "It doesn't make sense, Mrs. Judson. You want us to pray for you, but you're not sure that you believe?"

Mrs. Judson smiled as though she were trying to make a joke. "I haven't called on God before, so why should He hear me now? You pray for me. If there is a God, your prayers for me can't hurt. If there isn't a God, then . . . then at least all of us haven't wasted our time." She dropped her head. "My life is falling apart. I don't want to grab hold of something out of desperation."

Michelle slid forward on her chair and placed her hands on her knees. "Mrs. Judson, my life was falling apart too. It had been falling apart for years. I was in your granddaughter Claudia's place, only there was no one—no grandfather or grandmother to rescue me. I spent most of my life being hurt and angry. But I've found Someone Who is putting my life back together. I've found Someone Who loves me even though I felt like I was dirty and no good. I've found Someone Who can love the abused as well as the abuser. I have found Someone Who turned my life around. Mrs. Judson, I know that it's hard and maybe even frightening to believe in Him. But the Lord is only a prayer away."

ஒ

Miz Ida's heart almost burst with pride. "Glory to God, girl, you spoke truth to that woman!"

She could hear the smile in Michelle's voice. "We spent time talking to her, Miz Ida and praying for her. It just seemed that Mrs. Judson had a wall or a guard up that she would never let down."

"Give her time, Michelle. She needs time to explore, and she needs time to make her own choice. The Lord gives us all that freedom. We get freedom to make a choice."

"Well, by the time we got out of there, it was so late. I thought I had missed Todd and that it was over, Miz Ida. I kept thinking that he was never going to trust or forgive me again. But you know what?"

Miz Ida smiled now. "What?"

"When we came out of Mrs. Judson's office, there he was. With all that me, Tonya, and Mrs. Judson had just been through, Todd still made me feel safe, he made me smile. Todd and me were supposed to meet downstairs outside the building. When I didn't show, he said he thought I was standing him up. He thought about leaving, but instead he found someone who directed him upstairs. When we left Mrs. Judson, I found Todd sitting right there at my desk."

"Bless his sweet heart."

"Miz Ida, I don't think I was ever happier to see him. He put his arms around me, and I just felt like I was home. All the worries, cares, and heartaches just seemed to float away. We had a good talk on the way home—not as long as we would have liked, but I'm still grateful that he was there."

"God is good, child. God is good."

They went on for a few more minutes talking about the goodness of the Lord. They talked about His mercy and His compassion and His willingness to heal. They talked about how good it was to abide in the arms of the Lord. Miz Ida and Michelle talked until their eyelids got heavy and then they said goodnight.

Just before she closed her eyes, Miz Ida whispered to her old friend. "Lord, You are a miracle worker. Look what You have done for Michelle. Not only is she able to stand on her own, but now You've given her a heart to reach out and help somebody else. Nobody could do that but You, Lord."

Miz Ida switched off the lamp.

"Nobody but You."

Epilogue: More Seasons

n Monday morning at the office, Michelle turned on her radio and grabbed the first empty box off the stack near her desk. She looked around the pit, then at the elevators and saw Shadrach and Tonya talking. Michelle began to remove items from her desk and pack them in the box.

When Tonya arrived at her own desk, she looked at Michelle, and then at the clock. She waved at Michelle and pantomimed to her, *What are you doing here so early?* She dropped her things on her desk and crossed the room to see her friend.

"You're here awfully early. What's going on, Michelle?" Tonya pointed at the boxes. Then she smiled. "I'm sorry. Good morning."

Michelle smiled so big she thought her face might split. "It's moving day."

"Where are you moving? I mean, what's going on? Mrs. Judson said that everything is okay."

Michelle still couldn't stop smiling. "Mrs. Judson is wrong.

Everything is *better* than okay." As Michelle talked, she looked toward the doorway and saw Mrs. Judson coming in wearing dark shades. She looked at the two of them, started toward her office, and then turned back. When she got to Michelle's desk, she removed her glasses. She looked surprised.

"Michelle, what are you doing? Are you switching desks?"

"No, Mrs. Judson."

"I can see clearly that you're packing."

Now, Michelle was actually grinning. "Yes, Mrs. Judson."

"Where are you going?"

"I'm going home, Mrs. Judson. I'm moving back home with my husband."

Tonya laughed out loud. "Hallelujah! Mercy, mercy, me! You go on, girl. Work it, my sister!"

"Well, you don't need to take all these things to your home."

"I'm done here, Mrs. Judson. Last night could have been the last for me. So I decided for myself that today would be the day."

Mrs. Judson looked disturbed. "Are you quitting? Just like that? Don't you want the job or the promotion? You've been working all these months for a promotion."

Michelle continued smiling. "I changed my mind. This job never suited me, Mrs. Judson, and I never suited this job. I changed my mind."

Mrs. Judson's face looked drawn, but she regained her composure. "Well, certainly, it's your choice. Some women aren't meant to work."

It was all Michelle could do not to giggle. "Mrs. Judson, you're right. Some women aren't meant to work. But *this* woman is going back to school. I'm blessed with a husband who loves me and wants to provide for me." She dropped items into her box with a flourish. "I may have to tighten my belt a little, but I got all the stuff right now that I can use. Mrs. Judson, I'm going to take my time, enjoy my schooling and find the job I really want—*if* I decide I want a job. I'm a blessed woman to even have that choice."

"You're right, Michelle. It's your choice." Mrs. Judson walked away.

Michelle watched her until she entered her office. "I'm going to do the Miz Ida on Mrs. Judson. If I can pray to move a mountain, I can pray to heal her broken heart."

Tonya nodded. "Amen. Praise the Lord!"

Michelle nodded at her friend. "So, what about you, Tonya?"

"It won't be the same without you."

Michelle smiled mischievously. "You won't have any reason to watch the clock."

"Oh, girl."

"I'm just teasing you, Tonya."

"Who is going to watch *me,* Michelle, and make sure I keep up my hair and clothes?"

Michelle laughed out loud. "Shadrach!"

"Just rub it in, Michelle. Make me squirm. No matter what you say, I'm more than happy for you, but it won't be the same without you. But I plan to stay—*if,* that is, Mrs. Judson gives me the promotion that I'm due *now.* We can negotiate increments to get my back pay, but we will be negotiating!" Tonya's nod was firm and confident. "I have a son to send to college."

"Good for you. That promotion is long overdue." Michelle looked at her friend. "But what about Shad?"

Tonya blushed and smiled. "We still have a lot to learn about each other. He might be a little uncomfortable at first about a sister getting paid, but we're going to take our time and let the Holy Ghost work it out." Tonya touched the flap of the box that Michelle was packing. "I really am going to miss you."

"I don't think so. I plan on coming to see you, you coming to see me, and Todd and I meeting that son of yours. Maybe you and Shad and me and Todd can go out sometime." Michelle's grin was back. "Oh, no. It's going to be pretty hard for you to miss me."

Tonya looked across the room to Michelle's desk. Funny, but not long ago she could not have imagined being sorry to see Michelle go. She could not have imagined calling the woman "friend."

She opened her desk drawer, where there was a folded piece of paper—Malik's letter. He had been right, and so had Michelle: she had needed a life.

Tonya touched the note affectionately and then moved it to the side. She lifted out the folders she needed and laid them on the desktop as she glanced in the mirror in the drawer. She touched her hair. The bun was dead! No doubt about it, it was a new day!

Malik helped her on the journey, but as painful as the interactions had been, without Michelle, most likely she would still be a team leader instead of the supervisor she was about to become as soon as she had her meeting with Mrs. Judson.

Of course she had to give credit where credit was due. Tonya looked toward the bank of elevators. Shadrach had helped them pull it all together. He was a good man. Tonya giggled to herself. *He's my man!*

She opened the top folder to begin preparing for her meeting. *Thank You, God.*

No doubt about it—it was a brighter day!

⟲

Mrs. Judson stared out of the window of her office. Everything in her life seemed to be crashing in around her. Carl was gone and she could feel all that she had built slipping through her fingers. She recalled the night it all begin to slip away as though she was still living it . . .

There was no way Delores was going to let this happen. She ran from the small room where she and her husband usually sat—where they could just sit in peace before all the trouble. Delores ran to the stairs. She would block Claudia. She wouldn't let her granddaughter come down the stairs. She stood there, moving from side to side to block the stairway.

While she stood at the foot of the stairs, she could hear Carl in the bedroom packing. She left the stairs and ran to their bedroom. "Carl, what do you think you're doing? Stop it, Carl. I want you to stop it, now." Delores planted herself in front of the chifforobe to try and stop her husband's progress.

He began to grab things from the dresser drawers. "Delores, you're being ridiculous."

"Can't you see that this is all her fault? Everything that has happened to us was and is her fault."

Carl didn't answer, he simply continued packing.

"She had it planned all along to break us up. She doesn't have a family, so she wanted to break us up."

"Claudia is a child. She didn't break us up, Delores. We broke us up. I'm not leaving because I don't love you, Delores. I'm leaving because I have to save her."

"Can't you see that it's killing me?"

Carl stopped and held up his hands. They were full of socks and underwear from his wooden chest. "I don't know what else to do. I shouldn't have to choose between my wife and my grandchild. We both should be protecting her. You can't do it, so I have to." He resumed packing.

"You're choosing her over our son. You're choosing Claudia over Carl Jr. Who are you going to believe? If people find out, even if he's acquitted, his career is over. And what about us? What about the firm? Don't you see that this is going to tear us apart?"

Carl stood up and walked to her. He laid his hands on her shoulders. "Can't you see, Delores? If we have to lie to save who we are supposed to be, then the truth was never in us. If we have to sacrifice a child—or two children—to hold our nice little world together then it isn't a world worth saving."

"Who are you trying to fool, Carl? You're not strong enough to *survive on your own. You'll be crawling back. When you come back, don't bring that teenaged monster with you."*

"Don't make me lose respect for you before I go, Delores. I want to leave here feeling that there may be some slight chance that you may be right. Don't make me lose that hope before I go. Let me leave feeling that you didn't tell me and that you didn't do anything when you found out about Carl Jr. because you were just too weak—you just didn't have the heart. Leave me with something, Delores."

"Carl, you're ruining our lives. You said you loved me."

Carl looked very sad then. "I don't want to go, Delores. I don't know what else to do."

Within an hour Carl and Claudia were packed. It was raining outside. The asphalt on the drive was wet and almost shiny so that it softly reflected light from the lamps along the walk. Delores watched them leave through the raindrops on the upstairs front window. The two of them rolled six suitcases from the house and stuffed them in the trunk and back seat of a waiting car. Claudia looked even smaller in her dark coat; the rain plastered her hair against her head. Carl looked harried and beaten.

He would call her later, he said, when he and Claudia were settled.

Delores waited for the call to come. It came not long after midnight. It was the call she did not want to hear. She heard the sound that she had always feared she would hear in her son's voice. My uncle is the father. He was at the police station, Carl Jr. said. How could his niece make up a wild story like this? After all he had done for her.

Delores knew, when she heard his voice, that it was true—what Claudia said was true. Delores had been right about the sound in her son's voice all along. The sound gave it all away. It cut just as deeply as she knew it would . . .

Delores had not been right about other things. She still loved her son after she knew for certain what he had done. Delores still put her arms around her only son when he was released on bail to come home. It cut more deeply than she thought it would.

❧

Miz Ida watered her flowers and then headed out to visit baby José. It had been a good morning already. Michelle had called with good news: she and Todd were working things out. She was moving back home and applying to schools. Tonya had gotten her promotion and Shadrach, Tonya, and her son Malik were spending more time together. "Looks like it's getting deep," Michelle said. She really wasn't sure about Mrs. Judson. "She still has that wall up. No one can see in or see over."

Just before she hung up, Michelle's voice had turned shy. She sounded like a little girl.

"Miz Ida, thank you. Thank you for all the prayers and love you planted in me. You made the difference in my life, and in my mother's life. You loved me and you didn't judge me. No matter how ugly I acted you forgave me. It's been the same way with Todd. You're right, Miz Ida, God keeps showing me His love through all the people in my life. All of you have been loving and kind and forgiving. And I've been thinking, Miz Ida, much is required of those to whom much is given. I can't learn to love and forgive others and not let that blessing begin at home. If you pray for me, Miz Ida, I'm going to call Cassie—I'm going to call my momma."

The seasons were changing again. Miz Ida stood near a sign and next to a bench full of people waiting for the bus to come. A young man caught her attention and motioned to her, offering her his seat. Miz Ida sat down and smiled. It was so unusual to see a young man offer his seat. When people commented on how rude young people were, though, she always said the young just didn't know how to be good when no one took the time to teach them. It was good to see a young man so kind.

"Thank you, young man."

He nodded. "Do you recognize me?"

Miz Ida studied him. The young man was clean shaven and his

hair was newly cut. His clothes were not new, but they were washed and ironed. "No, son. I'm sorry to say it, but I don't."

The young man nodded. "It's probably best that way." He began to walk away, but stopped and turned back to Miz Ida. "But I said if I ever saw you again, I would thank you and tell you that I'm sorry."

"Sorry for what, honey?"

"Sorry for what I said to you and how mean I was to you. Don't you recognize me now? From the front doorway?"

Miz Ida laid her hand on her chest. "No, it ain't. Is that you?"

"Yes, ma'am."

She looked the young man up and down. "Well, what has come over you?"

"I don't know, ma'am. I guess you just spoke to me on the right day. Maybe I just needed somebody who cared enough to take the time to wake me up."

"My goodness, son. Praise the Lord! It's a new day!"

"Yes, ma'am. But I got a long way to go."

"Well, you be encouraged, young man. Don't give up." Miz Ida leaned back on the bench. The sun on her face felt good. It was indeed a new day. Miz Ida looked at the young man. "You go to church, baby?"

"No, ma'am."

She smiled at him. "Well, if you really want it to be a new day, we gone have to see what we can do about that. Son, every day with Jesus is sweeter than the day before."

No doubt about it, there was still a lot of work for her to do.

The Final Bow

I have enjoyed this journey, this time that I have spent with you. Like you, I thank the Cover Girls—Michelle, Tonya, Mrs. Judson, and Miz Ida—for sharing their lives and exposing their hearts to us.

No matter what your season, your condition, or your role in life, I want to remind you that your heavenly Father, your Daddy, loves you. His love transcends color, gender, socio-economic status, and gender. Don't try to hide your struggles or your pain from Him. You don't have to present a perfect picture to Him. You don't have to hide or cover your scars or your issues.

God wants to touch you where you hurt. He wants to heal that broken wounded place that you've been trying to conceal. The truth is, all of us have those things we cover. We cover our issues with clothes, money, jobs, relationships, and even addictions. God knows; He sees; and He cares. Run to His arms and let Him love away and heal those tender places.

Trust God to love you as only He can, and to prepare you for the wonderful and complete life He has always purposed for you. You are safe in His arms. Don't run from Him anymore, run to Him. You are Daddy's precious girl—it's time for you to take your place on stage.

Bishop T. D. Jakes